Scenes from Russian Life

VLADIMIR SOLOUKHIN

Scenes from Russian Life

TRANSLATED FROM THE RUSSIAN AND WITH AN INTRODUCTION BY
DAVID MARTIN

PETER OWEN · LONDON

ISBN 0 7206 0712 4

PETER OWEN PUBLISHERS
73 Kenway Road London SW5 0RE

First published in Great Britain 1988
© Vladimir Soloukhin, Moscow, 1987
English translation © David Martin 1988

Photoset, printed and bound in Great Britain by
WBC Bristol and Maesteg

CONTENTS

INTRODUCTION
The Prose Works of Vladimir Soloukhin

Vladimir Soloukhin was already a published journalist and poet by the time *Vladimir By-roads* appeared in 1957; yet it was this work which first caught the public's imagination, revealing the author's talent for portraying the simple scenes and characters of rural Russia in a way which made them new and fascinating even to Russians themselves, no matter how familiar they might be with the subject. Letters were written demanding a continuation, and in 1960 *A Drop of Dew* was published, in which the author describes his home village of Alepino near Vladimir (he was born there in 1924), showing a characteristic grasp of the individual human qualities of its inhabitants and an ability to appreciate the humour of a situation. There is the story of Norma, for example, who, deserted by her husband for another woman, takes him back as a paying lodger because she lives close to his work.

Soloukhin's concern for the future of rural communities, his love for his fellow villagers, for their humour, even for their quarrels, these things are all to be found in the present volume ('Tittle-tattle', 'The Fortieth Day'); and if one also bears in mind the enthusiasm with which Soloukhin has elsewhere treated such themes as wild flowers and mushrooms, it is easy to understand why his name his mentioned along with those 'village writers' who form an important trend in Soviet Russian writing today.

Yet it should not be supposed that his response to the countryside is limited to a picturesque presentation of the unsophisticated ways of the people or to a simple botanical interest in flora. In his novel *Coltsfoot* (1964), for example, Soloukhin emphasizes the ability of the natural world to impart an inner strength even to those jaded by life in the city; and elsewhere he asserts the superiority of old methods of harvesting, which bestowed a sense of spiritual harmony upon those who worked the land, over the mechanical processes of modern times. It is this appreciation of the less visible merits of traditional rural life that is most typical of the writer.

Soloukhin is an instinctive conservationist, as may be seen from his writings not only on the natural world but on the creations of man.

Whether he depicts a river so polluted by factories that its population
of frogs has jumped out on to the banks (in *Vladimir By-roads*), or the
careless destruction of icons and architectural treasures (in *Black
Boards*, an account of an expedition to the Russian countryside in
search of icons), the same warning is clearly sounded: no improvement
in present conditions, however correct or fundamentally desirable,
should make one indifferent to the loss of any part of the national
heritage.

Moreover, even in the area of architectural conservation, it is
characteristically the moral aspect of the situation that is of prime
interest to Soloukhin, rather than the physical surface. In *Black Boards*
he refers to his successful struggle to save his local church in Alepino
from destruction and relates to us the thoughts that occurred to him as
he walked about inside the empty building, its floor strewn with the
torn pages of ancient books:

> Here, within these walls, were married our fathers, grandfathers,
> great-grandfathers, mothers and many people who are alive
> today. Is the place where our parents were married really not
> worthy of better treatment?
>
> Within these walls our fathers, grandfathers and great-
> grandfathers lay in their coffins. Is the place that is ritually linked
> with the burial of our parents and ancestors really not worthy of
> better treatment? What is going on is only one step away from
> abuse of the graves themselves.

Soloukhin is known – and has been criticized – for his spirited
defence of specifically Russian values and traditions. The paean to
Russian-style hospitality which the reader will find in 'The Guests
Were Arriving at the Dacha' is in many ways characteristic; and
elsewhere, on a more elevated level, he sets out what he believes his
fellow Russians should hold dear. In this passage from *Black Boards* one
clearly feels an emotional preference for timeless spiritual values over
modern scientific necessities:

> You can study starfish, river molluscs, minerals in the Urals, the
> properties of rare metals, you can be an engineer, a party worker,
> a chemist, a combine operator, a footballer, writer, electrician,
> rocket technician, general, teacher, but if you are a Russian, you
> should know about Pushkin, about the *Lay of Igor's Campaign*,
> about Dostoevsky, the Field of Kulikovo, the church of Pokrov-

na-Nerli, the Tretyakov Gallery, Rublev's *Trinity*, the *Vladimir Mother of God*.

Black Boards as a whole is a work of extraordinary interest. In it Soloukhin explains his feeling for the vigour and emotional expressiveness of the Russian icon, sets out the various stages involved in restoring an icon to its original beauty, and describes with zeal the sort of people with whom his relentless search for icons in Russian villages has brought him into contact. Having arrived at a woman's house in pursuit of an ancient icon of the Resurrection and finding neither the icon nor any hope of eventually locating it, he remarks to the woman what a pity it is that such a thing should be lost, coming as it does from 'the darkness of centuries'. He is struck by her reply when she points out that, on the contrary, the icon had come from the 'light of centuries', but was now lost in the 'darkness of obscurity'.

It is indeed a paradox as well as a sign of the times that much of Soloukhin's unique appeal at home and abroad should have been earned for him by his consistent promotion in Russia itself of traditional Russian cultural values.

However, it should not be thought that the writer concentrates entirely on his country's past. In 'Sentenced', subtitled 'A Lyrical Documentary', the reader will find much of interest concerning the modern Soviet Union: the life of a writer and the structure of the health service being two prominent themes of the work.

Soloukhin's style is direct, frank, sometimes conversational. He generally writes in the first person, and this device adds further to a feeling of intimacy and openness that characterizes his writing. Yet this bluntness of style is at the same time the vehicle for an extremely sharp moral sensitivity; and the relatively narrow circle of friends and acquaintances who more often than not comprise his immediate frame of reference, particularly in the shorter works, opens the way to the discussion of problems to which we can all respond, no matter who we are or where we live. The unaffected, almost sentimental story, 'A Little Girl by the Edge of the Sea', for example, turns upon the question of abortion, the moral aspects of which have proved particularly vexing to Western societies over recent years. The subject is also topical in the Soviet Union, where the comparatively low birth rate amongst the Russian population is in part accounted for by the frequency of such operations: according to the magazine *Nedelya*, only one Russian woman in six will never undergo an abortion. It is the ethical and emotional side of the question, however, not statistics, with which Soloukhin deals in his story.

The author in fact combines two poles: a beguiling simplicity of setting and style with a lofty purpose, and alongside the colloquialisms of everyday conversation we find the language of a classical philosophic idealism: 'good', 'evil', 'truth', 'beauty', 'conscience'. He believes, too, that it is to the service of such universal values that art is called, and rejects utilitarian views of art, believing that if a thing is beautiful, however useless, it has every right to exist. In his long documentary work on Russian art and architecture, *Letters from the Russian Museum*, which he wrote after visiting the Russian Museum in Leningrad and published in the journal *Molodaya gvardiya* in 1966, he expresses a dislike for the genre painting of nineteenth-century Russia, with its emphatic criticism of social conditions. 'If they depicted a wedding,' he writes, 'they showed the arrival . . . of a sorcerer or an unequal marriage. You might think there never were any successful weddings or equal marriages.'

Criticizing genre painting for its *feuilleton*-like character, Soloukhin makes the general comment that it is better for an artist to produce a single, accomplished painting of a herring than to try to say something about a whole historical epoch – any epoch – if the artistic means that he uses in so doing are themselves of a poor standard: nothing is to be gained from 'art without art'. In *Coltsfoot* the hack contrivances of an artificial inspiration are likened to the forcing open of the leaves of a water-lily in contrast to their responding naturally to the light of the sun. Such force results in nothing but a torn bud. In the same novel the hero reflects that saccharin, artificial sugar, passes through the body without causing harm, and asks a question of direct relevance to so many works of literature produced in the Zhdanov era and beyond: 'Do artificial words and phrases pass through the human mind without trace in just the same way? Or can it be that from their multiplicity, from their abundance there gradually builds up in the mind a sort of poison, albeit weak, whose effect on the living soul remains uninvestigated and even unsuspected?'

In *Black Boards* we learn more of what Soloukhin expects of art when he describes pausing for a rest in a village café during his search for icons. A radio was playing and he happened to hear that the cosmonaut Titov was at that moment circling the earth in space. The occasion gives him the opportunity to compare what Titov is doing with his own activity as he searches for works of art:

On the one hand – accurate and cold calculations, cybernetics, mathematics, electricity; on the other – beauty, intuition, the soul and its flowering. Art *is* the flowering of the human soul. No, the flowering of the human soul is love. And art is the result of that flowering. . . .

Science is for the intellect, for the brain, for man's external welfare and physical comfort. Art is for the heart and for the soul. Science makes a man stronger mechanically, art makes him stronger in spirit, and it makes him a little better. And that is so necessary, especially in this age when the development of science and technology is going on unchecked.

Although the writer views icons – objects of spiritual contemplation – to a large degree as works of art, it must be added that, conversely, he sees secular art as first and foremost a product of the spirit, not as a means of expressing a point of view in the narrow sense. 'Russian art', he states, 'has always striven to be an art of the spirit', and in a general reflection to be found in a theoretical work, *From the Lyrical Point of View*, he returns to traditional religious terminology: 'The subject of art should not be positive and negative charges, not neutrons and protons, but the positive and negative in the human soul, that which is expressed by the age-old words Good and Evil.'

In *Letters from the Russian Museum* Soloukhin again refers to good and evil in the realm of art and names those Russian artists whom he considers outstanding in their depiction of the human spirit: Surikov, for his tragic-heroic portrayal of Russia's past; and Venetsianov, for his paintings of Russian peasants. Of the latter he asks, are these people really slaves? If so, he adds, they are slaves with the bearing and look of tsars.

The stark contrast between good and evil is a theme of Soloukhin's own literary work. He was amongst the first in the Soviet Union to write on the fate of conscience amidst the political pressures of the Stalin years, describing in *Coltsfoot* the awakening of conscience in the young hero Zolushkin, when he is forced by the secret police to level criticisms at two fellow students. He co-operates on this occasion but resolves not to do so in future. When asked to supply information on a third student, he refuses to do so, and the effort required for such an upward step in the direction of conscience is likened by the writer to that needed to lift virtually the whole world.

Later, in 'Under One Roof' (included in the present selection), Soloukhin was again to write of the difficulty and at the same time the necessity of opposing evil by means of a personal moral resolve, although this time not in a political context. Characteristically, the events of the story concern no more than a handful of ordinary people living in an out-of-the-way country cottage, yet they serve to introduce reflections on the escalation of evil throughout the entire world and on the need to adopt a morality that will disarm it and reverse the process. The action of the wife in the story in answering hate with love could well be called Christian; and Soloukhin himself refers to such actions as 'perhaps the deepest and most important side of human behaviour'. Certainly, when her husband first suggests to her that she take a present of yeast to a spiteful neighbour, she looks at him as if he were mad. Yet here we come close to what lies at the heart of Soloukhin's understanding of the moral dilemma faced by modern man: his behaviour might be rational, his world-view founded in science and therefore correct, but it is pursued at the cost of that psychological, spiritual and vital richness provided by the irrational and outmoded habits of an older morality which counters hate with love and prefers pity to ideology. Indeed, in *Coltsfoot* the hero comes to doubt the new morality as he had experienced it: 'Is a movement of the heart so insignificant? It is unthinking and even irrational, like a young child or . . . like song; but who says that one must resign oneself and stand on the throat of the song? More, if all that really had been the highest morality and the execution of duty, why had there been no deep sense of peace and satisfaction aftwerwards?'

Zolushkin feels pity for those who suffer in the name of progress as then understood: 'Perhaps when they were transporting people in their hundreds of thousands from the villages to the Solovets Islands or the Urals, someone also felt human pity for them, especially if they had small babies and were off to the northern frosts. . . .' It is the same pity for human life – expressed as it happens by the same Russian word, *zhalko* – that the narrator voices in a contemporary context on behalf of the as yet unborn child in 'A Little Girl by the Edge of the Sea', when he saves her from that more recent but equally 'rational' social ideology which has led to over-easy abortion.

In 1975 Soloukhin published, in a short work called 'A Visit to Zvanka', a critical analysis of the Ode to God by the eighteenth-century poet Derzhavin. In it he comments that if Derzhavin could have known about Darwin – had he had the correct scientific understanding of the world – he would not have written odes to God but shot himself instead. It is in the short story 'The Icy Heights of Humanity', however, that we find one of the author's most explicit statements concerning this paradox of modern times. The work describes a mother's visit to the grave of her son who has committed suicide. She partly prays to God and partly converses with her dead son. The writer, who is watching from a short distance, is amazed that her prayers should be so effective in calming her feelings:

> Does that mean, I thought, does that mean that her terrible inner wounds, which I would not have dared to touch upon, because I could not heal them or even hope to, that they calmed down by themselves? Does it mean that, where atomic physics, neuro-surgery and cybernetics would be useless, her blind, ignorant faith turned out to be more necessary than anything else? How absurd!
>
> We have all kinds of amazing specialists, but why on earth have we no specialists in the sorrows and joys of the heart, on a level with the technology of the twentieth century?

At the close of the story the narrator wonders what the iron robots of the future will make of feelings they may read about in books but will not possess themselves: 'They will doubtless first of all try to research into them, they will argue about them, deny or affirm them, write treatises about them, engage in disputes. Then they will calm down, having found some convenient term which explains all, such as our little word "supernatural".'

'Supernatural' – the word used by modern man of everything which does not appear to be scientifically verifiable and which, therefore, does not exist.

Despite the insistence of his moral inquiry, Soloukhin never engages in mere moralizing. Certainly he is fond, perhaps excessively so, of detail and fullness when chronicling aspects of Russian life – the list of dishes in 'The Guests Were Arriving at the Dacha' could hardly be extended – but when it comes to the deeper meaning of a work, he is quite able to speak in images alone. In the story just mentioned, the final picture of the young mother's embarrassment, given us without explanation, counterbalances the aimless moralistic banter of the guests which had occupied so many of the earlier paragraphs. We are left to draw our own conclusions. Similarly, in 'A Winter's Day' one only has to place the final image of the sick huntsmen alongside the opening description of the lilac dawn for the central idea of the work to become clear: the idea that – to quote the thought ascribed to Gurov in Chekhov's story 'The Lady with the Little Dog' – 'Everything is beautiful in this world, everything, apart from what we ourselves think

and do when we forget the higher aims of existence and our human
dignity.'

Soloukhin deserves to be better known in the West. He has been
recognized and popular for over two decades now in his own country,
where he seems to have enjoyed a degree of *glasnost* all his own. He was
awarded the Gorky Prize for his prose works in 1979. Certainly, under
the present policy of greater openness we can expect the sort of ethical
and aesthetic problems raised by him to receive much more
prominence in Soviet literature and art, a development which can
only be welcomed. In a collection of philosophical reflections
published in 1968 under the title of *Autumn Leaves*, the writer includes
an anecdote which it is perhaps apposite to recall today: 'They say that
when Ferdinand the Great was dying, he summed up his activities in
various spheres of life. Having spoken about military, economic and
political matters, he said, "Now, as far as art is concerned, as Emperor I
did everything I could for it: I did not interfere." '

In an interview with the BBC, broadcast in October 1978,
Soloukhin expressed a wish that there should be as few obstacles as
possible standing between readers in Great Britain and Soviet books,
as also between Soviet readers and British books. The same could
equally be said of removing obstacles between the Soviet Union and
other countries. The present volume is offered as a small contribution
towards the fulfilment of that wish.

D.W. MARTIN

SENTENCED
A Lyrical Documentary

Not loss of life I fear, not breath's cessation –
What's life and death? – but loss of that great light
Which shines above the fullness of creation
Then, weeping, goes for ever into night.

A. Fet

1

At his personal request and at the request of the Foreign Commission I
was showing a foreigner around the Troitse-Sergieva Lavra. The
foreigner was a well-known person of high rank and he was received in
the monastery by the Patriarch of All Russia, Alexis. Naturally, I too
found myself in the Patriarch's chambers: caviare on bread, little cups
of coffee. A glass of cognac should anyone so desire. Usually they do not
pay any attention to the person accompanying the guest, if he is simply
an interpreter, a guide, efficient but nameless. But this was a special
case; the sound of my name is not unknown to the Russian ear.
Although the Patriarch simply looked at me with interest and nodded
benevolently and approvingly, as a sign that that sound was indeed not
unknown, one of the guests, who had come to the chambers before us
and now happened to be on my right at the table, began to express the
most enthusiastic feelings, having for the time being forgotten about
the foreigner and, seemingly, even about the Patriarch.

'Ah, what you wrote on the power of the milieu!' (He said 'milieu'
rather than stressing the final syllable.) 'I just shouted out to Tatyana
Sergeevna in the middle of reading: "Tatyana Sergeevna, Tatyana
Sergeevna! Come and see what he has written here on the power of the
milieu!"'

The speaker was a man of about seventy, but he certainly did not
look it. Lean, athletic, agile, lively in conversation and manner, he
immediately won me over and I felt at ease with him as with a friend, in

spite of the difference in our ages. At the same time he gave the impression of being a highly educated person, as indeed he was. He had studied medicine at Moscow University before the Revolution, completing the course, as it happens, in 1917. This was the eminent surgeon and academician Boris Aleksandrovich Petrov, an honorary doctor of many foreign universities and societies and, as regards his immediate position, head of Surgery at the Sklifosovsky Institute. The question arises, however, as to how he came to be in the Patriarch's rooms.

The Ostapov family, Aleksey Danilovich, Lyudmila Vladimirovna and little Serezha, had been very close to the Patriarch before his death. Professor Petrov received a telephone call from the Patriarch's office. The Patriarch of All Russia requested him to make haste to Odessa (the Patriarch's summer residence is there) and save a woman whom only an immediate operation could snatch from the jaws of death. A Chayka limousine sped Professor Petrov and his assistant off to the airport, where an aeroplane stood waiting with its engine running. In less than two hours they were in Odessa, where once more a fast Chayka awaited them. The operation was a success, and Boris Aleksandrovich was hailed as Lyudmila Vladimirovna's saviour. Every year after that he received an invitation to a family celebration at the Ostapov house and, as a rule, was granted along with it an audience with the Patriarch, in whose rooms, as has been explained, we made each other's acquaintance, an acquaintanceship both interesting and close from the start.

The Petrovs have their own car. The monastery has been shown to the foreigner and he has been dispatched to Moscow. Tatyana Sergeevna is driving and Boris Aleksandrovich with characteristic liveliness and a certain equally characteristic eccentricity exclaims: 'The chief thing is movement. And most important in movement is speed. Speed, speed, speed. The Sadovoe Ring Road in an hour and forty minutes – that's speed for you! And at home a shower and a fleecy towel. When I was younger I used to take the electric train out to Pushkino and trudge back on foot at a good sporting pace.'

'To the outskirts of Moscow?'

'What? All the way home, right to my apartment. Movement is the foundation of life. The wind shakes the trees. For them that represents the only possibility of movement. Do you think that it harms the trees, that the wind loosens them and breaks their boughs? Like hell it does! The shaking strengthens their root system, extra roots grow. Their life becomes the richer for it.'

'Boris Aleksandrovich,' I suddenly found myself saying, 'it's so annoying!'

'Oh, what?'

'Here I am in the same car with a surgeon such as you. You could say we have made friends and – I have nothing that needs cutting out! But then, when the need arises, a person of your stature will be way out of reach!'

'Vladimir Alekseevich,' Petrov answered seriously, 'if the need arises, come straight to us. We'll cut it out in the best of style. First-class service. Tip-top. Only ask in good time. I don't like terminal patients. I like to restore people to health, not prolong the agony for a few months. . . . Oh, do overtake that murder machine, hell!'

Tatyana Sergeevna switched on the left indicator and began to overtake a heavy lorry which was moving quickly and enveloping us in clouds of exhaust-fumes. Ask in good time, I thought. I could ask now if you like, only nothing hurts.

Yet at the same time, as I now recall, I could even then have shown the surgeon a certain place on my body and, perhaps, it would have been 'in good time'. But if you run off to a professor with every little mark and bump. . . .

'Yes, it's very annoying,' I repeated. 'I'm travelling with you in the same car, and there's nothing to cut out.'

'I hope to God there never will be. But if the need arises, there'll be first-class service.'

'But could I see perhaps just one of your operations? As a writer, I am interested.'

'With pleasure. I have an interesting operation on Thursday. A silly girl of nineteen. She gulped down some concentrated vinegar, out of love. They're beyond me, today's youth. They're all brought to us at the Sklifosovsky, you know, when anything happens.'

'They poison themselves?'

'In Moscow they prefer to jump.'

'What do you mean?'

'Modern buildings are high. Take the University. Wonderful possibilities for jumping. The fifteenth floor, the twentieth – superb! But, you know, some of them don't smash themselves up, not to death. They're brought to us. After all, we have people specializing in resuscitation. They bring people who have tried to hang themselves, too. Well, when you come, I'll show them to you.'

'And this nineteen-year-old girl? Did she decide that concentrated vinegar was better?'

'She's from Syktykvar. She downed the concentrated vinegar and burned the hell out of her oesophagus. It healed, but closed up. She can't swallow. They made a hole in her side and put a rubber tube into her stomach with a funnel on the end. Very unaesthetic. She had to chew up the food herself and spit it into the funnel. Terrible! the torment has gone on for over a year now. On Thursday we'll make her a new oesophagus out of her own large intestine.'

. . . Stepanida Ivanovna impressed upon me from childhood the notion that there are on earth two most sorrowful places: prison and hospital. However strange it may be, considering the neurotic and generally unquiet times in which we exist, I lived, as one may say, to have grey hairs without coming to be in either the one place or the other. And there used to glimmer within me the hope that, perhaps, I would go on to live out my time without tasting the great sorrow of the prison or the hospital. There are, of course, people who die suddenly, if they are lucky. Like, for example, a well-known critic died not long ago in the House of Writers whilst playing chess. 'Your move,' his opponent says, but he does not seem to hear. Well, in chess one is supposed to spend time thinking and it is not done to hurry one's partner. Nevertheless, five minutes later Fedor Markovich was once more told that it was his move. When he showed no reaction this time, too, they thought of jogging him to see if he had not dropped off. They jogged him and, as it turned out, he was no more. He was far away, away from chess, from the Central House of Writers and, generally speaking, you cannot say where he was. But, as the Russian people say, you won't buy an end like that for money.

Yet, just in case, when I am at a dinner (on New Year's Eve, perhaps, or at a celebration or banquet), I like to propose somewhere at the end of the evening: 'And now, friends, let us drink to heart failure! Although she already occupies first place amongst us on this earth, still let us drink to her in any case, because if the one that occupies second place. . . .'

At this point my tipsy friends interrupt me noisily, crying out in unison that I have picked the wrong time to come up with such a topic (say it is a wedding or birthday celebration); but they are wrong. For even the ancient Greeks whilst feasting would set up a burial urn for everyone to see, so that in their enjoyment of the most sweet intoxication of life they would remember that moment which is unavoidable for all without exception, although some people have the impression that all conversations on the subject do not concern them, but someone else.

'To heart failure!' I insist. 'To her, the dear one, sudden and quick and – even better – during sleep!'

But, generally speaking, I have managed to live half a century without even seeing people die – that is, without seeing precisely that moment when, together with the last breath, life itself flies away. My grandfather, Aleksey Dmitrievich, died easily and without fuss at the age of eighty-five. In the morning he had been to church (it was an early Easter with snow, but the snow was thawing). He sat down to drink tea and started to pour it out of the glass, missing the saucer. They put him to bed, and at night, when I was asleep, Aleksey Dmitrievich was no more.

My father, Aleksey Alekseevich, died in our house at Alepino when I was in Moscow. He got up one night to visit the yard, went dizzy, staggered and fell – and that was that. He was also over eighty. Stepanida Ivanovna died at that age, too, but I did not watch it happen.

I have chanced to see not a few corpses in my lifetime, if only while standing in guards of honour, but I have never got to see the very moment of death.

So, I came to be in a hospital for the first time in my life not as a patient, but as a sightseer, a writer indulging his curiosity. In a white coat I immediately resembled (in age and general appearance) a professor (hardly a probationer student). That, in all probability, was what the patients took me for alongside the genuine professor, Boris Aleksandrovich, as he conducted me around the Sklifosovsky Institute, through its narrow corridors, from ward to ward, upstairs and down. 'The professors are coming round!' And from every hospital bed were directed towards us imploring looks full, apart from entreaty, of a secret hope waivering, like a red needle, on the edge of total hopelessness. But still – professors! Boris Aleksandrovich, going up to a bed, would manage in two or three phrases to say what was most important – that is, what the patient wanted to hear from him.

'Well, how is your bladder?'

'It hurts, sir.'

'On Monday we'll operate.'

The patient wanted to say something, and Boris Aleksandrovich noticed it.

'What else is the matter?'

'I don't really want it on Monday. Perhaps on Tuesday or Thursday.'

'Are you superstitious? All right, we'll change the operation to

Tuesday. Sleep soundly, get your strength up.'

'Thank you, sir. I'll be praying to God.'

'Pray. No harm will come of it. Well now, how about you?'

'I find it difficult to swallow. It is as if something is stuck there.'

This woman, worn out, with huge yellow blotches under her eyes, has a look which no longer asks for help but shows indifference touched with an inner cynical bitterness. But no, in the depths of her eyes, too, there is still the faint light of hope.

'It will go. At this stage of the illness it's always like that. That's normal. Later on it will be better, completely all right.'

When we left the patient and went out of the ward into the corridor, Boris Aleksandrovich remarked without turning round, so that I would hear as I hurried along behind: 'A huge cancer of the oesophagus in the final stages. A monstrous tumour. Inoperable.'

'But then why say it will be better – completely all right?'

'In the first place, as a doctor, in no circumstances do I have the moral right to tell a patient that he will get worse and die soon. And, in the second place, she cannot get any worse. Anything now is better for her, including death. . . . Well now, here we keep supplies of blood for transfusions. In our Institute, seeing as they bring us badly injured people from all over Moscow, beginning with car accident cases right through to the victims of muggers, blood is a prime necessity. Now we have started to use blood from corpses, but at first it was considered unethical.'

'What do you mean, blood from corpses?'

'What I say. We prefer it to fresh blood.'

'What was it you prefer?'

'Blood from corpses.'

What a nice conversation. But I try not to change the tone (perhaps he is having a friendly joke at my expense).

'And why do you prefer a corpse's blood to living, fresh blood?'

'It contains a great deal of immunitive matter. You see, if a man is dying of an infarction or thrombosis, for example, then his body defends itself by releasing various substances into the blood. Alarm! Catastrophe! Fire! Throw everything into the blood! Anything to make it more fluid and efficient! But the man dies just the same, and then one may take the blood which has been enriched by these substances. It was considered unethical for a long time. Cadaveric blood – the name alone is enough. . . . I remember at first I used to take it in secret in the garret. To get the blood to pour out well, you have to tip the corpse up together with the table, head downwards.

One of them went and slipped.'

'The corpse?'

'Of course. I grabbed him and we embraced. God knows what it must have looked like. . . . And this is where we keep the spare parts.'

Boris Aleksandrovich opened a large refrigerator: it opened at the top like a trunk. There I saw a large number of fresh bones. I think they were for the most part joints and kneecaps.

'Instant freezing at seventy degrees below and you have superb spare parts. Now, keep calm. We are going into the resuscitation section.'

'Bringing corpses back to life?'

'If one is to be accurate – yes. But, of course, not exactly corpses. There must be a glimmer of life. If you take someone down out of a noose within three minutes, there is hope of getting life back into them. But any later, and irreversible changes take place in the brain.'

On a high, narrow table there lay a small, plump or, rather, solid-looking woman. A shorty, one might have said of her when alive. From the instruments which stood at the head of the table there stretched out to the woman – to her nostrils, mouth, the veins on her hands – slender rubber tubes, and on the woman's short neck I made out a violet weal, the mark left by the noose they had taken her down from a few hours earlier.

One could not say that the resuscitation team was fussing over the woman. They were making observations, of course, looking at her from time to time, checking her pulse, blood pressure, temperature. But there was no fuss, and no need for any further visible action. A piece of apparatus fed air into the lungs and sucked it out again. This was done to the rhythm of normal human breathing. Breath had been forced into the body for a few hours already now in the hope that the brain would start working, as well as the patient's own breathing, instead of artificial respiration, and that consciousness would then return. After all, the heart had started up. As I understood it, the difficulty of this case (and such a case was by no means an exception or rarity there) was that the brain would not start to function, and there was practically no hope that it would. But, on the other hand, how could one simply switch off the breathing apparatus? How could one pull out all those little tubes which sustained her and supplied drugs, if the heart was still beating? True, she put the noose on herself. True, she was already dead in reality and by this time would have been long since rigid, were it not for this attempt to bring the corpse back to life. Nevertheless, to switch off the instruments and pull out the tubes whilst the heart was still contracting – it would be just the same as killing her a second time.

Here, with my writer's meticulous nature, I should have asked about everything: how many hours do they intend to keep her on the table? In what percentage of cases are they successful? How many people are brought to them every twenty-four hours? Is there a regular pattern? Which are the more common – young people or old? Men or women? When do most cases occur? On weekdays, holidays, before holidays, after them? What percentage of those revived regret they were revived, and how many are glad?

But I did not go into such details and nuances because I had had an idea. What, I thought, if I were to write a small book on this Institute? I had already produced *Letters from the Russian Museum*; now there would be *Letters from the Sklifosovsky Institute*. There, it was art and the human spirit; here, flesh and suffering. And, anyway, the human spirit too. And social elements. Statistics, conclusions. It is not as if there were only a few topics for reflection. The history of this Sheremetev Hospital. Its pattern of growth. Their attitude towards life and understanding of death. Oh yes, there will be something to talk about here! Of course, only with Boris Aleksandrovich's help. Now, it is true, in the coming year I have no time to concern myself with the Institute, I have to finish what I have already begun. Let the idea mature. But afterwards – without fail, absolutely without fail. In a year or as soon as there is any free time. I shall have to set aside at least a year for it. And the personality of a surgeon such as Petrov will be the centre of the composition. His presence will ensure the correct balance of the different parts. . . .

'Boris Aleksandrovich, if I should ask, would you give me permission to visit your Institute and be present at a resuscitation?'

'What, have you felt the urge to write something? By all means! You can have access to all the stages of resuscitation: my operating-theatre, the morgue, a place in our ambulances when they go out to the scenes of accidents and what have you. Superb!'

There the woman lay. The breathing apparatus was switched on. Consciousness was not returning to her. We went out into the corridor. I saw with some surprise that there were three chairs in the corridor occupied by people in overcoats. Just as if they were waiting for a train at a station. What are they waiting for? Hardly for a turn at being resuscitated! Oh yes, they are probably awaiting the results of the resuscitation. Will she live or not? The patient is a relative of theirs. I know already: no hope; but they do not know that yet. I am this side of the dividing line. On the one side there are all the patients and in general those people who are to become patients, and on the other – all the doctors. Not only on account of the white coat – things had happened which meant that by now I was psychologically on the other side of the dividing line. I was behind the scenes and not in the auditorium, that was it. All right, I was not on the stage, I was there only as a guest, but it makes no difference. Here is the gridiron. Here are the dressing-rooms; here are the artists with their little suitcases. Here is the scenery, knocked together out of cardboard, plywood and rags. Ropes. Backdrops. A switchboard with levers and buttons. I am behind the scenes. Whilst the people in the audience take up their places and the circle of their impressions consists of the cloakroom, its attendant proffering opera-glasses, the brightly lit foyer, the bar, the seats, my circle of impressions is made up of businesslike bustle, creams and ointments, stage clothes, gargling, nerves and the distant rumble of the auditorium as it fills up on the other side of the curtain.

'Now then, when will you need permission for unrestricted entry into the Institute?'

'I have to finish writing a book. In not less than a year, I should think.'

'Fine. As you wish. Everything here will be at your service.'

Who could have known that in a year's time I should myself have to submit to the surgeon's knife and that there would be no possibility of that knife being Boris Aleksandrovich's, because in sixteen days and nights (!) the resuscitation team (a monstrous thrombus in the main *truncus cerebri*) would not achieve any results, and that during the funeral at the German Cemetery one of the professors would come up to me from behind and say in my ear: 'In actual fact we are burying the Sklifosovsky Institute.' And upon my look of bewilderment would explain: 'The institution, of course, will remain. I am talking about its tradition, style and spirit.'

2

These thoughts could have occurred even without my visiting the Sklifosovsky Institute. Nevertheless, the Institute directed and encouraged them. It is not difficult to see that all the diverse causes of death in human beings may be divided into four basic categories:

(1) People do not want to die, but various diseases attack and kill them, either slowly or quickly.

(2) Healthy people, free of illness, who should have lived on and on, kill themselves.

(3) People who are neither ill nor desirous of a voluntary death perish in an accident: car and aeroplane crashes, train and boat catastrophes, earthquakes, floods, fires, explosions and the whole register of human disasters from war to the three-litre jar of preserved fruit which a careless window cleaner recently knocked down from a height of four storeys, straight on to the head of a girl of five who had been left by her father outside the door of a shop whilst he joined the crowd inside to buy a bottle of wine for himself and fruit-drops for the little girl.

What, then, is the fourth category? Apparently, a man may live to such an age when dying for him is just as natural as living. The thread of life becomes so thin that it falls apart by itself, without the presence of any further external force, be it an illness, a noose on a rope, a lorry running over a pedestrian. . . . The possibility of people's reaction to death being identical arises only in the case of a natural and painless falling asleep: dying is like going to sleep and there is nothing really to talk about. There are no problems, just as there are no problems, well, say, when the sun goes down or the yellow leaves fall from the trees.

But instances of death such as that (when the passions cease totally to war within a man) are exceptionally rare: that is, when those around him accept the man's death as tranquilly as he does himself. We more often see innumerable shades in between.

But two extreme cases first of all.

That spring, in editorial offices, publishing houses, the House of Writers (amid the crowded bustle of the foyer and the tables in the restaurant), simply in writers' own apartments, in Lavrushinsky Alley, Lomonosov Avenue, near the airport metro station, was heard, like the whisper of an ill-omened wind: Yashin, Yashin, Yashin. . . .

It caused no one, I think, to put down his pen in shock, nor did it interrupt the tapping of the typewriter but, just the same, people knew. Yashin is ill. Not in any ordinary way. After all, there are plenty of people with everyday illnesses. He has got *that* disease and, it seems, has already had an operation. At the Kashirka. Blokhin himself performed it. And straight away those who heard the news began silently to reckon up how old Yashin was and then, with anguish gripping their hearts, to realize that Yashin was only fifty-four.

I had met Yashin over the years in one way or another before then. For example, I would invite him to Karacharovo or the Grigorov Islands to go fishing through the winter ice. Or he would read his latest verse at his place in the country. Or I would break off for quarter of an hour to chat at his table. Or at some big literary evening I would be on the same bill by coincidence and, therefore, at the same table on the stage before a large auditorium. And everything was going along fine. But the clock of his illness, as it turned out, was already ticking away, and nobody heard its hasty, irreversible ticking in time.

But did he really not hear anything himself? Was he not tormented by foreboding? Were there no aches, no pains? Did it not envelop him, as he slept, in turgid nightmares or prophetic dreams, as when a near one who has died appears and summons one, or even tugs at one's arm?

But then, we each of us have our share of aches and pains! And anyway it is known for sure that Yashin had been to see doctors from time to time over the previous two years. They treated him for colitis and gastritis, and for some other nonsense. And apparently he told the doctors more than once: 'Look for something seriously wrong with me. You've treated me enough for piles. I can sense that I am really ill.' But the doctors missed the serious illness. In Vilnius, where Yashin happened to go on literary business, he got talking to a friend. The friend suggested a particular doctor. The doctor finally got to the bottom of things and made the correct diagnosis. And sent him straight off to the Kashirka.

Before entering the cancer hospital – that is to say, the Oncological Institute – Sasha made a tour of all the places in Moscow that were dear to him. He visited the Pushkin monument, walked the length of the Arbat, stood a while at the Kremlin, sat some time in The Aragvi. So one can see that he understood the seriousness of the situation. In a letter to Vasiliy Belov he wrote as much (here I am quoting from memory, because the letter is with the addressee): 'They have found that the disease is already well advanced. Now I am not after buckets of tears. Do you remember the birch I showed you on Bobrishny Hill? Well, I want to lie there. Only there. . . .'

Whilst he was making his tour of Moscow, perhaps Yashin met people he knew, perhaps he even said farewell to some before entering the hospital, but they still did not understand the reality of the situation: 'Well, never mind, they'll cut it out and you'll get better. Plenty of people go to hospital and then live to be a hundred. All the best. Don't let it upset you.'

But soon in editorial offices, publishing houses, the House of Writers, simply in writers' own homes, the whisper went round: Yashin, Yashin, Yashin. And if the whisper is in the air then that, you may be sure, is the way things really are.

The tragedy was made worse by the fact that Yashin as a writer, in spite of his age, had still not produced his best work. He was gaining in strength but was still just beginning to attain his full stature. It only rarely happens that a writer's importance should not fully reveal itself by fifty, and his potential remain undiscovered. Usually by that time a writer's artistic personality is fixed, as well as his place in art. Some growth may continue but only, so to speak, horizontally. One can produce a great deal even after fifty, but it is a matter of quantity. To come up with something qualitatively new in the second half of one's life is no longer so easy.

Aleksandr Yashin was one of those rarest of cases in art when everybody felt that, given the swiftness of his development, his main work was still ahead. He even felt it himself and for this reason was anxious not to die. He kept asking Professor Blokhin after the operation, when he had begun to grow weaker every day: 'Do something! Give me three months. I must finish writing a story. Then I'll die. Keep me going somehow. Use any injections. After all, you represent twentieth-century medicine! I'm not asking for life, but for three months. Do anything you like. But do something!'

Mitya Vorobyev had more than three months that he could have shared with Yashin. Who knows how long he had been allotted to live on earth. He was forty-two, tall, robust, handsome, would bathe in the river up to November – until the ice came – and then continue by diving through a hole in the ice. But all his future life suddenly ceased to be necessary to Mitya Vorobyev, and he could have offered any number of years to one in sore need. It would be as if someone were standing at a crossroads asking for twenty copecks for a loaf of black bread, and a chance passer-by suddenly threw into his hat a tightly bound bundle of banknotes worth several thousand.

A painter (and collector of paintings), a music lover (and collector of old gramophone records), a hunter, writer of poetry and prose, the author of many good books, that is to say, a man who lived life actively and richly in many spheres, Mitya Vorobyev calmly went off to his cottage in the country, calmly emptied the water out of the central heating and, in the garden (so that the cottage itself would not be associated with death), shot the back of his head into smithereens with a rifle.

What comparison can there be between these two monstrous events? A man who craves a mere three months of life is not given a single extra day, whilst one who has decades at his disposal himself refuses those decades, and does not want a single hour? The two extremities in our attitude towards death. Or, rather, life. An entire, huge and varied scale of feeling lies between them.

There is old Ogasha, a ninety-year-old woman in our village, who sits out in the porch in the sun and mutters: 'I'm always praying, Lord, won't you come for me soon? Who on earth needs me? I am no good to anyone – Lord, forgive me – I'm just a heap of rubbish.'

There was the writer N. who, in a fit of helpless temper (in which he had lived his whole life anyway), shouted at the doctors: 'You bastards, kill me! You pigs, give me an injection! . . .'

There was the well-known actor, Vsevolod Aksenov, who, when he realized that he was dying, calmly staged his own funeral by writing down where the coffin should stand, who should lead the funeral gathering and what music should be played there.

There was the great physiologist who, when he was dying, observed the changes that were taking place in him during his final hours and dictated them to his secretary, and answered telephone calls, also through his secretary: 'Say that Pavlov is busy, he's dying.'

There was Louis XVI who mounted the scaffold and, upon seeing for the first time since leaving his dungeon a living person with whom he could exchange a few words, asked the executioner who had the axe in his hands: 'My dear man, what news is there of La Pérouse's expedition?'

Not long ago we were sitting drinking tea, and amongst us forty- and fifty-year-olds there was a man who had already lived for eighty-four years. He was cheerful and active. To this day he has not given up his profession (music lessons). Over tea he was full of jokes and tales about his stormy life as a performer. As it happens, it was just about the time that Marshal S.M. Budenny died. Naturally we started to talk about his death.

'All he needed was to live,' the old man said with some distress. 'He had everything – honour, time on his hands, peace, material comfort. He could go fishing, mushrooming, travelling. Or simply look at the flowers, the sun, the open spaces.'

'But he lived a good long time,' I objected timidly. 'Ninety-two years.'

'So what, ninety-two! With his good fortune all he needed was the life to enjoy it.'

At first we thought that Leonid Fedoseevich was joking. Then I remembered that he was eighty-four years old himself and that, although 'ninety-two' was for me an abstract, almost astronomical figure, not a bit different from two hundred and fifty or two hundred and twenty, for him on the contrary it was imminent and real, like fifty-five was for me, a forty-nine-year-old.

3

Above Kobulety there shone a clear, blindingly blue sky, a rarity for those parts in September, usually a time of noisy, subtropical cloudbursts, beautiful in their own way and sometimes lasting without a pause for two weeks on end. And – what was really a great rarity, even a luxury – in the distance to right and left as one faced the horseshoe-shaped sea, on the far tips of the horseshoe, the mountains seemed in the mornings to hang amid the transparent blue, outlined in broken lines of pinkish white. Usually in Kobulety they are hidden in clouds or mist, so that you can see only the nearer hills, which are not at all pink and ethereal, but dark green, sombre and weighted down from above by grey bales of wadding-like cloud.

But the sky shone with a blinding light for the whole month, making the sea which stretched out beneath it no less blue and no less blinding in its turn. In the distance, where one would suppose the shores of Turkey to be – they are not so very far away at that point – both blues joined together in a line which was scarcely discernible amidst the dark blue haze. Only whilst the sun was setting did it become apparent that here were two blues, for one of them did not prevent you from seeing half of the sun, red and swollen, whilst the other hid its lower half, gradually sucking in its entire sphere, as if the sun were not heavy enough to sink and disappear in a single moment.

The two blue elements differed also with regard to the sharpness of the human sensations they caused. The upper one never ceased to bring joy to the eye and, therefore, to the soul, but, although you admired it, you did not know what to do with it next. Well, you could feel the breeze on your skin and breathe (the air along the shore was infused with the smell of the sea and pines), but what else? On the other hand, it was possible to enter into the lower element, to plunge into it, to immerse yourself head and all, so that it gripped, enveloped, embraced and squeezed you.

Just two weeks earlier I had for the one and only time in my life climbed a real peak in the Tien Shan Mountains. This modest victory, yet, to give it the correct word, quite severe test of physical and psychological strength that I had come through, filled me with a particular sense of joy in life. Apart from that, it so happened that a young and beautiful woman came to the sea every day and sat next to me.

That is a very lucky coincidence, because I have now, for the sake of artistic expressiveness and the plot, to place my hero in conditions of the greatest *joie de vivre*, to submerge him in the fullness of life, to put him in paradise with all its heavenly attributes. Where, then, could I find a place for this paradise if not Georgia, if not on the shore of the warm sea? What time of year could I take for this paradise if not September by the sea? And can I, after placing my hero in paradise, leave him without an Eve?

Eve was twenty-four years old. She had just completed her course at Moscow University (studying Russian), and this weight off her shoulders must also have added (amongst other things) to her joyousness, carefree air and, to be exact, happiness.

She was a tall, faultlessly built woman with fair hair which fell on to her shoulders. She had grey, slightly sullen eyes, an aquiline ('Polish') nose, though not very noticeably so, a large, beautiful mouth with a widish gap between two of her upper teeth, which were as white as porcelain.

Apart from all her permanent qualities, that autumn there was one further thing about Eve which seemed to be meant just for me. She had never seen the sea. She had never swum in the sea. Never felt the sweeping caress of the blue sea at twenty-two degrees. Never rolled in the foaming surf with its sharp smell of seaweed. Never started on sudden contact with the lilac-tinted balls of jellyfish. Never hunted for brightly coloured pebbles amongst the shingle on the shoreline, nor looked into the dark-blue distance, where toylike white ships float by from time to time.

What is more, she had never been to Georgia, did not know the Georgian bazaars or Georgian hospitality. She had not seen the mountains or the mountain rivers, or the tea plantations, the orchards of tangerines and oranges, the bamboo groves, the Adzhar villages. She had never drunk Madzhari, nor eaten *khasha*, nor tried 'Isabella', nor held in her hands and smelled the magnolia flower, nor sat on the terrace of a small restaurant on the sea-shore, nor collected chestnuts, nor bitten into boiled corn-cobs, smearing them with a pinch of coarse, sharp-tasting salt whilst they were still hot.

There lives in man one age-long need – to share joy. Or, perhaps, to be more precise, to involve someone else in one's joy, especially someone close. A man enthusiastically shows another his town, his books, his piece of land and cottage out of town, the place where he was born and grew up. But what is a piece of land or even a town in comparison with the Black Sea? To show it to someone who has never seen it, to relive all the intensity of feeling and joy at first knowing it, at being astonished by it, at feeling love for it for the first time – that alone is a source of genuine and deep happiness.

Added to everything else, Eve could not swim, and I was to spend the month teaching her to float and move about in the water, if only a little.

'Aren't you afraid?' I asked Eve. 'Now we shall have the sea in common. And that's not like going to the cinema. It's something mighty and long-lasting. You'll become enveloped in memories of the sea. Those memories will bind us together. You're not afraid?'

'I'm happy,' answered Eve. 'This is the happiest month of my life, and it's not only because of the sea.'

'Why, then?'

'No one has ever treated me like this before.'

'How did they treat you?'

'Badly. Cruelly. They used me. I behaved the same way back. But now – the sea. Heavens! My life – and the Black Sea!'

I do not know what she meant when she said that, but whatever it was, her exclamation was to the benefit of the Black Sea.

The first morning could not have been better. There might have been a breeze. The sea might have been wrinkled or rippled, and I wanted either huge breakers rolling on to the shore, or a mirror-like stillness, with the sea-bed shimmering through it as if there were no water at all.

It was just such a quiet morning. Of course the sea cannot become completely calm and motionless, showing no signs of life. The water at our feet was living, not a glassy, faceless mass. But what kind of movement was it making? If I placed my foot exactly on the boundary between black and blue (that is, between the shingle and the water), the water with its rhythmic rippling would occasionally reach my ankle. It was just strong enough to lap over a strip of shore about thirty centimetres wide, but to lap over it so quietly and gently that not a single pebble moved.

Eve threw off her cotton robe and carefully went up to the blue. Oh, that womanly gracefulness, its almost feline elegance when, standing on one foot, she touched the surface of the sea with the other and drew it away quickly as if burnt, although the shingle here was noticeably colder than the water.

'When Neptune saw you, he was struck dumb at first, but now he will pull himself together and send fish to your feet so that they can bring you his greetings.'

'What must I do for that?'

'Go at least knee-deep into the sea.'

At decisive moments a woman's curiosity will always triumph over her fear, and Eve waded into the sea.

'Well, where are the fish?'

'Show them that you are ready to receive them. Wiggle your toes.'

Eve wiggled her toes and saw the black backs of the fish swim towards them out of the deep water on all sides. They appeared suddenly, as if they had not swum up but had been created at that very spot out of the undulating patches of light and shadow on the sea-bed.

'How interesting! And where is Neptune himself? I want to visit Neptune!'

The shore receded beneath the water quite sharply. Every step would have to be made not so much out to sea as downwards. So I took Eve firmly by the hand and led her – she had found sufficient strength not to resist or squeal – until the blue water touched her shoulders, which, possibly, had still not completely lost the nocturnal warmth of her bed.

'My life – and the Black Sea!'

'Your life flows into the Black Sea.'

. . . About eight kilometres from Kobulety in the direction of Batumi there is a little place called Tsikhisdziri. The sea-shore here is high and steep, unlike at Kobulety; to be more precise, the ridge of foothills, which is set back a few hundred metres from the shore at Kobulety, comes right up to it here. On a high cliff overlooking the sea, some three hundred metres up, there are the remains of an ancient fortress, some fragments of a wall which look like a decayed tooth. Next to them they have put up a small restaurant with a terrace suspended above the sea (at a height of three hundred metres), and deep in foliage. Everything here is enveloped in round masses of greenery. When you stand next to the small building that houses the restaurant, you cannot see the sea at all because of it. But when you go out on to the terrace, you would think you were flying, soaring above a blue abyss, in places darkened by the shadows of cumuli, in others covered by golden scales of reflected sunlight.

We came here for the first time with Fridon Khalvashi, a writer from Batumi, and so whenever we came again they met us not simply like ordinary, nondescript tourists or holiday-makers who had dropped in by chance, but obligingly, courteously, as one would guests. We would soar above the sea together with our little table, upon which a Georgian by the name of Givi would artfully set out various things to eat and a couple of bottles of Saero, a light white wine, the wine most frequently drunk here in Adzharia.

After only half an hour's soaring, however, Givi would come and put three more bottles on the table, and then another five, answering our bewildered looks with: 'They've sent you this from another table.'

It would be nice to think that, perhaps, the wine was sent to me, a writer associated with Georgia by long friendship. But it would be nearer the mark to suppose that the wine was sent because of Eve, even though she always sat facing the sea, with her back to the restaurant.

If we had taken and stored up all those bottles, we could in no time have opened our own tavern like the one in Tsikhisdziri. But we had to leave the wine on and around the table, perhaps in doing so offending the Georgians who from afar would zealously watch how we reacted to their gifts.

The best thing in the Kobulety bazaar, in the whole, as I would say, aromatic bazaar, was for us a type of grape called 'Isabella'. They say it received its name from Spanish (if not Portuguese) sailors, who found it in South America and got it to grow in their own country. Abkhazia is undoubtedly the chief area in which 'Isabella' is grown in our country. Yet the vine grows in other places along the Black Sea coast, including Adzharia.

There are a thousand different sorts of grape, varying in colour, size and shape, time of ripening, degree of sweetness, of astringency, in smell and even nuances of smell. But the taste and smell of 'Isabella' are so distinctive and different from other kinds of grape that someone not used to it will even dislike it. It seems sharp. Because taste is one thing and after-taste another. 'Isabella' has an exceptional after-taste, found only in that type of grape. More, the grapes of the 'Isabella' variety are distinctive also in the way they feel. You squash the grape in your mouth and expect the juice to run out of it straight away, pouring over your tongue, lips, palate, your whole mouth and even the back of your throat. Especially if you squash two or three at once, or even four. But nothing of the sort happens when you eat 'Isabella'. The skin bursts and the inside of the grape slides out of it in a firm, slippery ball, which in turn has to be squashed with some small degree of effort. Although one can swallow it whole: the thick mass inside the grape manages just the same to impart to your mouth all its sweetness and all its, as I put it earlier, after-taste.

You might take some time to get used to 'Isabella', or you might take to her immediately, or you might go away thinking that you never did get used to her but, when you pick up another type of grape and start to eat it, you suddenly feel that, alas, it is somehow lacking. It seems empty, uninteresting, like sugared water. Then you will recall 'Isabella' and decide to try and return to her, to renew her taste in your mouth. But, for that, one has to go to Abkhazia, or anywhere on the Black Sea, because for some reason they do not bring 'Isabella' as far as Moscow, or the wine that bears her name.

Yes, you have before you a man who has drunk genuine 'Isabella'. At least he thinks it was genuine. Because one really cannot be certain. It was not for nothing that, when I asked Darya Ignatevna Sokolova (who has a fine house in Lidzava): 'Where, at which of your neighbours' houses, can I get some real "Isabella"?' – not for nothing did Darya Ignatevna answer: 'Vladimir Alekseich, one really cannot be certain.'

'But your neighbours, people you know well. . . . If you ask them, will they really not let you know if theirs is genuine "Isabella" or not?'

'Vladimir Alekseevich, I could be certain only if I made it myself. And even then. . . .'

There is, indeed, a secondary type of 'Isabella'. They crush the grapes and pour off the juice, add water to the remains of the grapes and put in some sugar. The result is a liquid of just the same dark-red colour as the real thing, just as sweet and with the same unique aroma. And the same wine is made from this liquid. Almost the same. If they tell you it is the real 'Isabella', you will drink it as if it were. You'll smack your lips, savour it, close your eyes, praise it and feel glad that such a rare opportunity has befallen you, too, and no one will ever tell you that you drank the secondary, not the genuine 'Isabella'. One wine-maker admitted to me that nowadays the real 'Isabella' no longer exists – and why should you bother about it, if just the same wine, such that you cannot tell the difference, can be produced from grapes watered down and sweetened with sugar? And, in the opinion of the wine-maker, the genuine thing made from pure juice would be an incomprehensible and impermissible luxury, an extravagance and complete over-indulgence. But that is not true, it cannot be! Is there really no wine-maker who makes for himself just a little genuine 'Isabella'? Fridon was going to take us to Upper Adzharia, to a remote place in the country, where there lives a wine-maker whom, they say, you can trust as you would trust yourself.

These, then, were the sensations and feelings of anticipation with which my life was filled during that September. In the morning I

would work (without which some of the fullness of life is lost for me),
and the rest of the day would be taken up by the noises of the bazaar,
swimming, a late afternoon walk along the front, sometimes a film; but
all the time I caught myself enjoying one further sensation, one that I
valued highly. Whether I sat at the little table in Tsikhisdziri looking at
Eve, or watched her cross the road, or ate 'Isabella', or entered the sea,
I could not believe that it was she, she and no one else, who remained
with me in the evenings.

But there were dark sides to that. News of this fair-haired, slim and
beautiful woman soon spread through the resort. Kolya Makarov, a
Moscow acquaintance of Eve's, ran into her at the post office and
exclaimed happily: 'Oh, so it's you they mean when they talk about the
beautiful Moscow woman. And I've been wondering who on earth it
could be.'

She could not go out into the street alone, or to the beach, without
men trying to push themselves upon her, offering to take her
straight away on a trip to Batumi or even Tbilisi.

'Listen, Miss, I have a car, I have money – tell me what you want.'

Once I saw (I was watching on purpose from the other side of the
street) Eve walking along the pavement from the bazaar, and next to
the pavement for the entire three kilometres a Volga followed her at
walking speed and with an invitingly open door. Finally I crossed the
street and, before the driver of the Volga realized what was happening,
we were both – Eve and I – sitting in his car.

'Am I right in thinking that you are offering us your services? Take
us to Tsikhisdziri, please.'

The Georgian, lost for words but maintaining the politeness that is
second nature to his countrymen, turned the car around without
speaking and took us where we wanted. He would not accept the three
roubles I tried to press upon him.

Eve had to put up with even more trouble on the beach, especially
during the hours when I was working. And so once (the story, having
turned off to one side, and seemingly for no reason, is now emerging on
to a straight road and heading in the right direction) I even had to
exchange angry words with a distinguished-looking and to all
appearance well-bred man, a holiday-maker from our sanatorium.

'We've come from Moscow and are, when it comes to it, guests in
these parts. Where is your nobility, your chivalry? And why do you all
pounce on her like savages? If it were just compliments and a bit of
attention, that would be fine, but instead it's a car, oranges and money
all at once. What's the matter, have you never seen a beautiful woman

before? Or do you think she has never seen your oranges?' All my pent-up irritation broke loose: 'Move ten paces away right now and don't dare ever to come nearer to her than that!'

The Georgian, who did indeed turn out to be a man of upbringing (unless he took fright), went away and spent the day lying on his sunbathing-board, not turning his head towards us but, evidently, still harbouring a feeling of malice towards me. The next day, when Eve and I had come out of the water and were rubbing ourselves down with thick towels, he came up to me and, cleverly hiding his real feelings, said: 'Listen here. I don't want to fall out with you, because you'll soon be dead. You see that little black lump on your skin? Do you know what it means? It's a melanoma, my dear chap. The fastest developing form of cancer. I am a surgeon. I cut out tumours like that myself. If I were you, I'd return to Moscow right away.'

'Yes, what have you got there?' joined in Eve.

'What rubbish. He was simply taking a very sophisticated form of revenge. We had a writer in Moscow – he died quite recently – who liked to say nasty things to people. He'd go up to someone and say: "You don't look too good. And your face is a bit grey. My dear fellow, it's not cancer, is it?" "What are you saying?" The victim gestures with his hands. "I feel well." "They all feel well at first. You can believe me. I've seen a few things in my time. You've got cancer for sure." "But I'm still young." "Doesn't mean a thing. Cancer likes young flesh even more. It'll eat you up in no time."'

'What a dreadful man. But, really what have you got? Has it been there long?' Eve would not give up.

'Two years already. But do forget about it. Must some silly wart on my thigh cast a shadow over our life here? The sea, the sky, the trees, "Isabella", to top it all – you. Paradise, and suddenly – a wart. In all probability it's a little knot in the blood-vessel. The only unpleasant thing about it is that it hurts if you knock it. Yesterday, for example, when the surf was dragging me across the shingle.'

At this point Fridon appeared on the beach in his grey suit and tie, and we went off to dress in order to go to Upper Adzharia and drink real 'Isabella' there. Life is wonderful!

4

These lines, well known yet ever merciless,
As in the past, so now resound:

'Your radiance, its gentle forcefulness,
Has ringed my life with light around.'

With light, as when the crimson morning breaks,
My life is filled, filled like the night
When over deep and peaceful lakes
There climbs the moon in majesty and might.

Just so the empty garden in the spring
Is lit with apple trees in bloom
And shines, within the candle's golden ring,
An ancient icon in a room.

Just so the sun with morning brightness
Pervades the valley's misty grey –
As is the snow-clad mountain's whiteness
Illumined by its dying ray.

In thankfulness and loving homage
I breathe those calm, ethereal beams.
Like snow, a lake, an icon's image,
So, too, my soul in answer gleams.

5

If I had taken the Georgian surgeon's words seriously, it would really
have been a case of a bolt from the blue. One could not have
purposefully thought up circumstances rosier or more idyllic for
announcing to me such an unexpected and fearful piece of news.
Pushkin's tale, 'The Shot', is founded entirely upon just such a
contrast. Why should I kill you when you do not fear death, are
indifferent to it and, perhaps, are even tired of living? No, I will kill you
when you are happy, when you want to live. My arrow will reach you
amidst the plentiful feast of life.

However, I did not rush to the airport or even to some clinic in
Batumi, nor even to the doctor in the sanatorium, but instead we went
off to Upper Adzharia in search of 'Isabella'. After that we spent a
whole two weeks bathing, then I flew to Tbilisi for the Ten Day
Festival of Russian Poetry and was back in Moscow only by 10th
October. And after returning I was soon off again, this time to
delightful Karacharovo on the Volga, to the good offices of Boris
Petrovich Rozanov (about which later).

Can such a lack of concern be explained? In the first place, it was easy to take the Georgian's words as a malicious joke. Secondly, I had been going around with this thing on my thigh for two or three years. It did not cause me any trouble, I had grown used to it and paid no attention to it at all. Thirdly. . . . Thirdly, every year in our (i.e. official, union-financed) clinic, they carry out the so-called 'dispensary procedure'. This is something I now think of as a first-rate undertaking. Once a year every writer must visit all the medical departments (ear, nose and throat, the surgeon, the oculist, radiography, ECG, skin specialist, a general medical and tests) and make sure he is healthy – or find out if he is not quite so healthy and begin treatment. It is a boring business, sitting in a queue outside the door of each department. You usually lose a whole day over it. So the writers do all they can to get out of it. The clinic employs force, and there is only one way it can force you: should a writer need a medical certificate from them for the House of Arts or a sanatorium, such a certificate is not to be issued until he has passed through the dispensary procedure. A large number of such negligent writers build up towards the end of the year, and off they go in groups, if not in crowds – in long lines, certainly – wandering from department to department, as listed on the form, doing their duty towards their home clinic. I, too, do my wandering every year, there is nothing you can do about it. And now the time has come to testify. One year (the first year of Its appearance) I said nothing about It and when the surgeon asked me if anything bothered me, I answered that all was in order. And, feeling pleased that I had got away from the surgeon so quickly, I hastened on to the next doctor. The following year I showed It to the doctor, giving him to understand that I myself thought it of little importance, and this was indeed confirmed by the doctor's casual glance and remark: 'It's nothing. I'd say it's a small nodule on a blood-vessel.'

'I think so, too. Nowadays, you know, we all know a thing or two.'

'Unfortunately. Look after yourself. Goodbye.'

The third year I again showed it and again met with no alarm on the doctor's part. True, I was given advice, but quite calmly and quietly: 'It's nothing. Show it to the oncologist anyway.'

Perhaps there was a large queue for the oncologist and I was in a hurry, or he had gone out of his room and I did not want to wait – anyway, that year I did not get to see him. I was put down as completing the dispensary procedure as things were: they probably did not stand up to my earnest entreaty. As if it mattered, to miss one department out of ten; and such an unpleasant one at that. And, anyhow, what business had I at the cancer specialist's? I just do not have cancer! And if there were a cancer hiding away somewhere, it would not be found out in three minutes. And if it makes itself known, then any writer would come running without any dispensary procedure – and not at an appointed time – complaining of pains, nausea, a cough, ominous forebodings and general weakness. To put it bluntly, the third year I was clever and missed out the oncological department. That was at the end of December, and in the September of the following year the Georgian surgeon on the beach at Kobulety made, as you will recall, his diagnosis.

I could not say that the Georgian's words left me entirely unaffected. First of all, I began involuntarily to remember how and in what circumstances It had appeared. But that was just the point; It had appeared from nowhere, in no circumstances in particular. Simply I once felt on my left thigh, on the smooth and even skin about ten centimetres below the groin, a small though rather sharp, pinching sensation. I lifted the edge of my underpants, had a look and saw a little black bubble endeavouring to surface from the depths. For some reason it occurred to me that a blood-vessel had become enlarged just there, forming a sort of tiny hernia, like the knotted veins that form on people's calves, and huge ones at that. My little bump, when it finally clambered out of the slot it had made for itself, turned out to be the size of a pea. It pricked and pinched a little whilst it was parting the muscle fibres. and for the first few days after establishing itself on its new site, but then everything settled down and I started to live with this little bubble without considering it at all significant.

I remember now that, apart from my own clinic, I showed it to the doctor whom I saw in the sanatorium at Kislovodsk, and there, too, I was put at ease and told it was nothing, and that there was certainly no need to cut it out.

I cannot help feeling surprise as I look back on things now, not at the fact that none of the three or four doctors who saw my bubble made the correct diagnosis (which later on required complex examinations and tests), but that not one of them was even put on his guard, although it had the undoubted appearance, as I now know, of a typical tumour.

So, then, I could not say that the Georgian's words on the beach left me entirely unaffected. I recalled how It had appeared, and I started to think of showing it to an oncologist after all. I even made two appointments to see the doctor (which we do by telephone), but matters of no great importance prevented me from going to the clinic on both occasions.

The first time, I remember, the appointment was for three in the afternoon. But on that day, at three o'clock as it happened, there was by coincidence a meeting of the presidium of the Literary Fund, and seeing as I had already missed a few of its meetings, it would have been extremely embarrassing to miss another, so I chose the meeting instead of the clinic and spent a few hours there. We went through applications from members of the Literary Fund concerning travel expenses, grants, memorials for graves, heard the report of the commission of inquiry on the House of Arts at Peredelkino, and all this was fine and wonderful, but on that day I did not get to see the doctor.

The next week I again made an appointment for three o'clock. Before then I had to see to a few small matters. I had to call in at the Young Guard Publishers and have a word there in the design department so that they would find me a good engraver for my coming book, then stop by the Soviet Writer Publishers and hand them back four poetry manuscripts which had been given to me for reading and evaluation, then call at the typist's and get from her the typed copy of the manuscript for a future volume of poems, then drop in on an old woman whom I did not know, to look at a supposedly old icon of hers, then stop by the Savings Bank and take out a little money, because I had no money left on me. Whilst all this was going on I had to ring up six other places and take similar decisions concerning books, journals, articles, poems and translations, decisions which could be made over the telephone. I thought I had timed it all exactly. But when it comes to it, you always finish by spending on any given matter twenty-five minutes instead of fifteen and fifteen instead of five. It's quite enough to meet a friend on the stairs, say hello, ask a question, answer one, tell him about something and listen to what he has to say – and there's twenty minutes gone. The telephone numbers I needed on that day, as luck would have it, were all engaged, so that the sharp, frequent pips echoed painfully in my ears. Instead of at three I was free of engagements only at a quarter past four. I could still have gone to the doctor, but by then I was feeling so hungry that I set off to the House of Writers instead of the clinic, and instead of an oncological department turned up at the restaurant, where I fed until six in the evening. And the next day I went to Karacharovo, intending to spend a projected one and a half months there, to write down three short stories I had long since had in my mind, and to complete a short piece on Derzhavin which I had begun much earlier. And there were a few other trifles. In particular, I had to free myself as soon as possible of a translation of works by Abutalib Gafurov, national poet of Daghestan, which I had first started work on as early as the spring. Actually it was not a book but a heap of literal translations of his verses, long poems and prose – everything that Abutalib had written in this life – for me to render into good Russian. I had to use my own judgement in choosing from it all pieces to make up perhaps just a small book so that (as the Contemporary Publishers wanted), the Russian reader would acquire some idea of this ninety-year-old poet who was known more than anything else because of Rasul Gamzatov's *My Daghestan*, with its frequent parables beginning: 'Quoth Abutalib'.

I had no feeling of alarm at all, otherwise I should not have changed a visit to the doctor for a meeting and a meal; and I still found that in spite of myself I could not wait to return to unfinished work, to get down as soon as possible to things already planned and in general to put my literary house in order.

But why Karacharovo and why the necessity to leave Moscow? I shall begin with the second half of the question. By the time one is fifty certain habits form which are difficult to break. Moreover, it is well known that every writer has habits of his own which from the outside seem sometimes to border on eccentricity and caprice. Chekhov sat down to work only in his best 'going out' clothes. Kuprin, by contrast, liked to write (at least before his period in emigration) completely undressed. Balzac created artificial light by closing the curtains and lighting the candles. Schiller put his feet in a basin of cold water. One might write only in pencil, another only in school exercise books, a third only whilst listening to music. The list of such habits is long. I, too, have formed a habit of my own: I can work at full strength only outside Moscow. I have a flat in Moscow and a good writing-desk; but you sit down in the morning and realize that all your thoughts are going off in different directions and not focusing, as they are supposed to, on the sheet of paper. But, on the other hand, be it just a shabby hotel in a shabby little town, a tiny room with a miserable view on to the back yard, you sit down at the table and production gets under way before your eyes and sheets covered over with writing pile up.

Things go better than ever, of course, in my native Alepino. But we do not live in our house in winter, only from May onwards when the spring warms the earth through. And so you bob backwards and forwards all winter between Houses of Arts and various 'dens'. One such superb den is the 'second' block at the Karacharovo Rest Centre. Sometimes you work it out and find that over the year you have had about 230 non-Moscow working days and correspondingly 130 non-working days in Moscow.

Even in Moscow I can write anything that requires just one sitting, one working morning: a small article, a review, something for the radio. But as for writing a long piece from day to day, living in its sphere of reference, it cannot be done. In Karacharovo, too, I do not sit working all the time. I go for walks, eat, even watch a film. Yet Karacharovo does not pull me out of the sphere of the piece I am working on.

I started to go to Karacharovo on the Volga about fifteen years ago, first of all simply to fish through the ice. The manager of the Karacharovo Rest Centre, Boris Petrovich Rozanov (a nephew of the remarkable Russian writer, Sokolov-Mikitov), is a man with a cultured mind and a fine heart. He made us (me and my fishing companions) comfortable in every way, and the fish we caught there, especially near the Grigorov Islands, on the Babnya near Korchevaya, was excellent.

My enthusiasm for fishing gradually waned, but instead I suddenly had the happy idea of asking Boris Petrovich if I could come, not to fish for two days, but to work for a month. Doubtless he would find a single room and set it apart for me, and I am not fussy as far as food is concerned. That is, of course, I like to eat well, but I can be satisfied with much less.

During my first working season at Karacharovo, Boris Petrovich put me in a separate room, but in the communal block. Life was possible there (and even work), but still the babble of holiday-makers in the corridor, the radio playing loudly in other rooms, and even singing to an accordion made things none too pleasant. But all the while in the grounds of the Rest Centre there stood what was for me a virtually legendary, so-called 'second' block, a separate little house. I put in a request to go there and after some time they gave me permission.

Every winter from that time on I aimed to come to that remarkable, wooden, cosy, one-storey house. All I had to do was co-ordinate my plans beforehand in case anyone was living there at the time.

Earlier it had been the estate manager's house. When they turned the estate (which had belonged to the Russian painter, Prince G.G. Gagarin) into a trade-union rest centre, they kept this house for visitors. A small foreign delegation, perhaps, or a trade-union employee with his family. Once the Grand Master Petrosyan lived and trained in the house for two weeks, in preparation for an important tournament. For many years Konstantin Aleksandrovich Fedin liked to come here. Then they built for the guests a modern, detached house of a quite different order (glass, concrete and blue-tinted baths), and the old-fashioned, wooden second block with its small windows suddenly seemed provincial and parochial, rather like the Arbat in Moscow did when they built alongside it the wide, modern Kalinin Avenue, also known as 'New Arbat'.

But the parochial atmosphere of the house, in the shade of Gagarin's age-old limes, actually made it particularly appealing. Plenty of room, so silent you could hear your ears ringing, and complete solitude. Roominess is not the least important thing. There is a reason why fish kept in a small reservoir stop growing and you finish up with old and tiny little carp.

How much of my best writing was done in that little house, and how many quiet, blissful days spent there! And more, right next to it there is the broad mirror of the Volga with its wooded far bank. And all around there are, furthermore, the straight, criss-crossing paths of the old park with its rustling yellow leaves in September and snowdrops in April. And now, feeling the need to stop, look about me and, as they say, tie up a few loose ends, I felt myself irresistibly drawn to Karacharovo, to my, as I dare call it, abode.

I settled in there as usual, set out all my papers and books, sharpened my pencil and quickly got into good working form, but suddenly I felt I had to make the trip back to Moscow.

A subconscious idea must still have been gnawing at me, since I attacked it anew, and this time nothing prevented me from going to the clinic. The oncologist, a lady in late middle age with, doubtless, a good deal of experience, sat me down on the chair which stood, as always, next to the desk, and began to thumb through my medical records in which, despite their thickness resulting from a plentiful variety of entries over many years, there was still nothing about any disease. Well, there was a cold in the nose, posterior vasomotor rhinitis. There was the tonsilitis and influenza which got me in their grip every year, shaking me up for ten days at a time, together with a high temperature. From her point of view, all that did not constitute a disease.

'Well, then, what is it you want to tell me?' asked the specialist when she finally tore herself away from the mass of writing.

'It's like this. For three years now a sort of black thing has been sitting on my thigh. Earlier I did not take any notice of it.'

'Show it to me.'

'Here it is. It's been there three years now.'

The woman touched it with two fingers straight out, moved it from side to side, tried it from above to see if it was hard.

'Get dressed. I do not think it is anything VERY terrible. But anyway it must be examined. And now we've decided to examine it, we go straight to the top, that is, THERE.'

'Where, there?' I had not understood.

'To the Oncological Institute. I'll write you a letter of introduction straight away.'

'When must I go there? You see, I live and work in Karacharovo and I've got three stories . . .'

'You've walked around with it for three years, carry on doing so a bit more. But I should not put it off. My advice to you is to go tomorrow.'

I suddenly felt a light, cold sensation inside my breast, tugging slightly around the heart. They do not send you to the Oncological Institute for nothing. But I immediately began to think defensively: So what? Of course an investigation is necessary. They'll investigate it, and I'll know that IT is really nothing. But do I really have to go tomorrow? What about Karacharovo, my papers all set out, my unfinished stories?

I suddenly, distinctly and with merciless clarity understood, in the time it took me to walk from the doctor's surgery to the cloakroom, that my life before visiting the doctor and my life after the visit were already two separate lives, with separate laws, time-scales and notions of what is important and unimportant; as, for instance, what happens in the life of a state before and after the declaration of war. Holidays are cut short, meetings postponed, all sorts of trips, purchases, interior decorating, plans for the summer are called off – everything proceeds differently from the way it did an hour earlier, that very morning. But the mind does not renounce the uneventful, everyday course of life immediately, it still needs to switch over to the new ways, but then in time it actually becomes accustomed to them.

6

The letter of introduction was to the Kashirka, the Blokhin Institute – that is, of all the possible places specializing in cancer, to the most cancerous. I had to go with my piece of paper to the Registration Desk (the first cog of the machine to hold you fast) and, gripped by this first cog, I would begin to move and turn around and about the corridors until the machine finally either loosened the grip of its strong levers or got hold of me with even more relentless ones to drop me face upwards on the narrow operating-table.

Our senior doctor, adding his signature to the introductory letter, gave me this advice: 'The Kashirka is purgatory and hell at the same time. For God's sake don't get swept up in the general flood. They come from all over the country with their various forms. . . . There's hardly time to operate. But you go straight to the head of the clinic personally. Her name is Chebotareva. Telephone beforehand. Tell them who you are. . . .'

The head of the clinic, after looking at my papers, wrote something on the letter of introduction and sent me to the Registration Desk. At the Registration Desk they unemotionally filled in a card and gave me a number.

'Remember your number. When you come here to us, say it straight away. Right now, go to the doctor in Room 206.'

So my movement along the corridors had begun. And where? At the Kashirka, Blokhin's place. In the past, the combination of the sounds 'Kashirka' and 'Blokhin' alone had made me feel anxious. I came here to visit Yashin when he was dying. You pass it on the way to the village of Kolomenskoe or Tsaritsyno, and when you glance over to the right at the low buildings of glass and concrete, and at the cranes all about, you increase your speed. You think to yourself: They are expanding, extending. But as for getting caught inside – God forbid! But have not I done just that? But what does 'caught inside' mean? I'm not here for anything special. An examination. They will feel it and make sure it is nothing. It is other people who are caught here. The ones who are kept in bed, operated on, irradiated. Now, Vasiliy Leonidovich last year – he really got caught. He was intending to go to the sanatorium at Kislovodsk and set about obtaining a holiday resort card in the regional clinic. But the doctor who was X-raying him said: 'Is that an ulcer you have there in your stomach? Have a good check-up.' A few days later he was already laid up here, at the Kashirka, at Blokhin's (instead of the Kislovodsk sanatorium!), and after the operation, as often happens, he never perked up. He went about for a few months, moaning and groaning, and then quietened down for ever. Yes, he really got caught in the Kashirka. But me? This Kashirka has nothing to do with me. Just a moment. Where, then, have you come to, if it is not the Kashirka? Perhaps you are now walking in the foyer of the Bolshoi Theatre, along the beach at Kobulety, or you are on the way to Zhuravlikha after mushrooms? Is this really happening? Once more a gripping feeling about the heart. After all, everyone is under the impression that they are here for investigation or prophylaxis. Even if they operate, they tell one person it is an ulcer, someone else polyps, a third a wart. But then they have a different set speech, too: 'Well, we've had a look at you. You are not our patient. Go for treatment to your own clinic.' That's what they say in some cases. But if they keep you in here. . . . Let's get to Room 206 as quickly as possible.

Before each door in the corridor the patients sat on chairs, or simply stood close to the wall, with forbearance and resignation. I peer into their faces. They do not seem to have the look of cancer patients. There are, of course, those who are weary, wilting and faded, grey looking, but all in all they are the ordinary faces of today, as if they were not in the corridor of an oncological institute but in a queue at a shop, or in the tram, or in an ordinary hospital outside a similar-looking doctor's surgery. I, too, joined the mournful queue. I impatiently started to pace backward and forward along the narrow (made yet more narrow by the people sitting in it) corridor. Inadvertently I muttered under my breath: 'There's a queue even here.'

And the people waiting patiently heard me. One fellow, as far as I could see, someone from the provinces and so more patient than us Muscovites, commented pertinently upon my dissatisfaction: 'Once in here, there's no need to hurry any longer. The slower, the better.'

There once existed the following medical maxim: 'If a patient does not feel better after a conversation with the doctor, then the doctor is no good.' What are we to think, now that doctors virtually do not talk to their patients? Without saying anything, the first thing they do is to send the patient off for X-rays and tests. Without tests the doctor of today is deaf and blind. One's way of life over recent years, any possible deviations from the normal pattern of life, the shocks which, these days, we call stress, permanent inner disquiet, if it is present, its causes, our positive and negative emotions, food, place of work, material discomfort or possible complexes – all these are areas which the doctor has neither the time nor the wish to inquire about. No matter what you complain of you hear: 'Tests, X-rays, electrocardiogram'. With a piece of paper showing the results of tests, the doctor in two minutes decides on treatment, writes out prescriptions and, most important of all, makes out a medical certificate. Perhaps they are right: why feel the stomach or the liver with your hand, when an X-ray will show up everything as clear as day? Why make the effort to find out the details of how a patient feels when a test will show beyond a doubt that the level of bilirubin in the blood is higher than normal? Two years ago I suffered a sharp, though admittedly temporary, loss of weight. In a month and a half I lost seven kilograms without trying and, naturally, started to worry. I went for advice to a large gastroenterological institute.

They did all the tests, found a little too much bilirubin in the blood, made recommendations as to how I should treat my liver, how not to overtax it, what I should take to improve its condition.

'But what about my loss of weight. . . . Can the liver really be the cause?'

'It isn't very likely.'

'Then what is? Perhaps the thyroid gland?' By now I am offering suggestions to the doctor myself.

'Perhaps, but endocrinology is not our field. With the thyroid you have to go to a different institute.'

And none of them (and they were all important professors and top men) thought of asking me in detail how I felt, or about the weakness which at times would suddenly come upon me, when all I wanted to do was lie down with my eyes closed, or about the times when I would break out in a sweat in my sleep, even when it was cool or cold in the room. And further (after all, seven kilograms could not have disappeared for no reason), no one thought of inquiring whether I had anywhere on my skin a little black thing the size of a pea. A doctor these days really should know that just such a thing can cause a temporary but sharp loss of weight at some point over the many years of its slow progress towards maturity. I know that – now. And I would have carried on treating my liver with cottage cheese and Borzhom water until I no longer had any need for a liver at all.

In Room 206 the doctor, a woman of about thirty-five, turned out to be more terse than the other doctors.

'Show me what you've got there.'

She moved it from side to side with two straight fingers, felt the area around it and pressed on it from above.

'I don't think it's anything VERY terrible. You'll have to undergo a three-day isotope investigation. After that we'll decide what to do with it. I'm giving you a letter for our laboratory. You could get there along the street, but to do that you'd have to get dressed. But you can also get to it by the ground-floor corridors. It's a long and complicated way, though. But if you ask, you'll make it. In the laboratory they'll offer you a wineglass of radioactive phosphorus, which you'll drink. Then you'll go three days in a row for the investigation. It's a pretty accurate and fool-proof method of diagnosing surface tumours. So in three days we'll know everything. I don't think it's anything very terrible.'

Underground passages from one block to another, ground-floor corridors, yellow in the poor light, tiled, with thick, asbestos-covered pipes overhead. If they made a film of my passage through these corridors, they would acquire a symbolic significance. At first I was walking a little bent, the fat-looking pipes hung so low, but then I became more courageous, stood up straight and discovered that I could walk freely without bending and that there even remained a small gap between me and the pipes.

Although I am walking alone through these monstrous, seemingly 300-metre-long passages, I am still part of the general flow. Patient No . . . (I had forgotten the number) – and nothing more. I put behind me all the corridors and turnings, mounted a staircase and found myself in front of a door marked *Radioisotope Diagnosis*. In front of the door is a table, paper, a telephone and a girl in a white coat. I show her the letter. She makes an entry about me in some sort of book and advises me in a businesslike manner: 'It's not worth your drinking it today. There are two non-working days in front of us. You must drink it and come on the next day for the investigation. So, come here on Monday. We'll treat you to some isotopes, and then the following three days we'll do the counting.'

'Will you be on duty here on Monday?'

'It makes no difference.'

I went back along the same purgatorial passages (I still found myself bending). For no particular reason I remembered and started repeating over and again to myself (as happens if poetry is your profession) some lines of a poem by someone (Leonid Martynov?). I walk along and half sing them to myself, getting them mixed up with my own practical considerations:

> I shall buy a present just for you
> In the isotope department.

I shall not manage to get back to Karacharovo today. In Karacharovo my papers are set out on the table, a book lies open at the half-way mark. In Karacharovo there is a fresh covering of snow on the paths in the park. Squirrels dart along the footpaths there.

> I shall buy a present just for you
> In the isotope department.

I shall not manage to get back to Karacharovo before Thursday, or even Friday. You can consider the week lost. But I have things to do in Moscow. All right, I'll drop in at the television studio, take an icon back from the restorer's, ring up the Contemporary Publishers.

> I shall buy a present just for you
> In the isotope department.

Damned passages. Tiles and pipes. But, more to the point, they will fill me up with isotopes on Monday and then start counting. What are they going to count? Isotopes? It's all rubbish. But the main thing is to wait until Monday. No, until Tuesday. They will begin to count only on Tuesday. No, wait until Thursday. After all, they have to count for three days. I shall not get to see the doctor in Room 206 before Friday, perhaps not even before the following week. And in Karacharovo the papers are set out, the book lies open at a page half read.

> I shall buy a present just for you
> In the isotope department.

When I went out at the gates I was met in the street by the same dank November day, with early slushy snow on the ground, a gloomy grey sky and a piercing wind; only the day was even viler than it had been in the morning.

'Ah, Boris Aleksandrovich,' I had said that time in the car, the day I made such an important aquaintance, 'here I am in the same car with a surgeon such as you – and there's nothing that needs cutting out! But when the need arises, a person of your stature will be way out of reach!' And that is what happened. Professor Petrov lies buried, and I am left wandering nameless and faceless in purgatory, in its outer circles for the time being – and it will be a fine thing if that is where things come to a halt.

Thinking about Boris Aleksandrovich, I remembered Tatyana Sergeevna and rang her immediately, not envisaging any concrete gain but simply for her kindly and experienced advice.

'My dear Vladimir Alekseevich! How are you?'

'That's just it. I said to Boris Aleksandrovich that time when we were coming back from Zagorsk . . .'

'Why, what's the matter?'

'Nothing very terrible. But I still need a check-up. And an operation is not out of the question.'

'Wait. . . . You say it's your skin? Well, as luck has it, Agnessa Petrovna is head of that department in the Herzen Institute.'

'Who is Agnessa Petrovna?'

'A professor. A friend of mine. Boris Aleksandrovich did not think of surgery as a woman's profession and was always, well, let's say, paternal towards women surgeons. Only Agnessa Petrovna was an exception with him, he thought she was doing the right job. She's a very energetic woman. Sometimes we jokingly call her Agressor Petrovna. As it happens, she's a reader of yours. Only the other day she was asking if she could get hold of your latest book. Do you want her telephone number? And I'll ring her as well. It will be treated as a top-level case, with first-class service.'

'What sort of institute is it? Why "Herzen"?'

'Herzen, since you ask, is the grandson of the Herzen you know. He founded the Russian school of oncology. It's an oncological institute, you understand. It's in Begovaya Street.'

'But that's next to where I live! I won't have to cross the whole of Moscow for the tests. And the name "Herzen" makes it more interesting.'

'Why?'

'My literary life really began in Herzen House, the Literary Institute. We poets like that sort of finished quality in composition, a circular form like that.'

'Well, that's enough of that! Ring Agnessa up, and everything will be all right.'

7

From the sky the white snowflakes fall –
Flowers, the dawn and the snow –
May your heart but the good recall,
This I ask you to do.

From the sky the white snowflakes fall,
Burying all the ways.
May your heart but the good recall,
How we were in past days.

From the sky the white snowflakes fall,
As we finish the wine.
May your heart but the good recall,
To the rest be resigned.

Time despite us deserts us all,
And in anguish we go.
May your heart but the good recall –
This I beg you to do.

May your heart but the good recall –
Pain and torment endure,
For the coarse food of life is all
By the soul rendered pure.

Neither joyful nor effortless
Is her task, yet she will
Conquer life's cloying formlessness
And her purpose fulfil.

As in youth she'll be cleansed once more,
Yet within will keep fast
All the gold, all that's fine and pure,
All the light of the past.

From the sky the white snow cloud falls,
Dark the sky in its haze,
Yet my heart but the good recalls,
How we were in past days.

From the sky the white snow cloud falls,
Life is bared to the bone.
Yet my heart but the good recalls,
And the dearest alone.

From the sky the white snow cloud falls,
Though my hand cannot touch.
Yet my heart but the good recalls,
Mindful not of so much.

In the midst of the snow and wind
Is no light, is no light.
You remain in my heart and mind
Always pure, always bright.

I'll remember your goodness when
At the end I must leave –
In the forest of life you shine,
As in Eden did Eve!

8

Everything was different for me in the Herzen Institute. Agnessa
Petrovna with open arms instead of the head of the clinic, who did not

even look up at me, the instantaneous, even hurried completion of medical documents, and the loud, energetic voice of Agnessa Petrovna, who personally examined my sore spot. And only Agnessa Petrovna's final words astonishingly coincided in meaning (and even literally) with the, albeit quietly and wearily spoken, words of the doctor in Room 206: 'I don't think it's anything very terrible. You'll have to undergo an isotope examination. After that we'll take the final decision on what to do with it. I'll ring our laboratory now.'

I walk about the yard asking 'Where's the building here they call The Tower?' I passed a two-storey building which, even through the walls, smelled of animals living crowded together. The vivarium. This is where they inject them (the rabbits and mice) with illnesses and then irradiate them and stuff them full of chemicals. And then after all that they dissect them and look at them under a microscope. Do not forget what yard this is and where you are going!

However, the laboratory on the second floor of The Tower greeted me not simply warmly, but even in a very unhospital-like manner. One of the staff of the laboratory, Zhanna Pavlovna, started to talk first about literature, and not about my illness. Then I noticed that the people working in the laboratory had small, flat black instruments fixed to the front of their white coats – radiation detectors. And when I commented delightedly on their luxuriant Christmas cactus, saying how surprised I was that it was flowering earlier than usual and not in December, on the day of St Barbara the Martyr, and in general showed surprise at the abundant growth of the flowers on the window-sills and along the walls of the laboratory, Zhanna Pavlovna explained: 'Yes. Here the people are ill, but the flowers are bursting with health. The raised level of radiation has a beneficial effect on the plants. But, of course, only in such insignificant doses as we have here.'

The laboratory assistant, Rita, took me to a bunker in the basement, where behind a heavy lead door, all alone on a large table, there stood a small conical cup made of thick green glass. In the cup there were about fifty grams of transparent liquid. I was told to drink it and I did so, trying to catch a suggestion of taste (I had never in my life had to drink radioactive phosphorus before!), but I discovered no suggestion of taste. It was just ordinary, pure water.

'There we are. Come tomorrow for the whole day. Bring a supply of reading or work with you. The thing is, we'll be counting your isotopes every two hours, from nine in the morning until five in the evening. At nine, eleven, one o'clock and so on. Bring some work. We'll give you a separate table and you'll feel as though you're in the House of Arts.'

'But won't all the isotopes fly out of me by tomorrow?'

'Phosphorus has a half-life of fourteen days. That is, you'll be radioactive and irradiating for fourteen days.'

'Is it dangerous for those around?'

'No. It's a tiny dose. And the irradiation is tiny. But our meters catch everything.'

At nine o'clock the next day I was with Zhanna Pavlovna again. I should say that she was between thirty and forty, with a kind face, but it had a sort of permanent tension, as did her voice. At first I could not understand why this was, but, while the preparations were going on near the apparatus, a young girl with a bandaged leg and a single crutch came into the laboratory.

'And who is this come to see us!' All the people working in the laboratory were joyfully surprised. 'Nadenka has come to see us!'

Nadya gave Zhanna Pavlovna a box of chocolates.

'The girls can all have these with their tea.'

'What are you thinking of? Take them back! Well, how was the operation? How do you feel?'

'All right. Only my leg is swollen, as you see. Now I've come to find out. . . . But all the same you won't tell me.'

I guessed that Nadya had undergone tests in the laboratory (as I would undergo them today), then they operated on her, and now she had hobbled over from Surgery to pay the laboratory workers a visit and at the same time to find out the results of the analysis of the tumour that had been removed – that is to say, her histology. I shall have to get used to this strange-sounding little word.

'Well. . . . Let's see about you. . . . With you . . . everything is all right.'

'But I heard things were not quite all right.'

'Where did you hear that? There is a small complication, but it's very superficial. And how are your stitches? Is it healing? How do you feel in general? You'll go home soon.'

A conversation about literature, flowers and plants prepares one for greater confidences. When Nadya left, I asked Zhanna Pavlovna: 'Do you have to deceive people all the time?'

'Sometimes we say things so well we even believe them ourselves.'

'What's wrong with Nadya?'

'She had something here on her leg, too. . . . But a real melanoma. And the operation was more complex. After all, she is a girl, and the appearance of her leg is not unimportant. Apart from the basic operation they also did some plastic surgery. They took some skin from her stomach and put it on the place of the operation.'

'You think that the stomach's appearance is less important than the leg's?'

'But just the same . . .'

'Did you say that the operation was more complex? Than what? Than my operation will be?'

Zhanna Pavlovna faltered: 'I was speaking in general.'

'In general, you are right. There won't be any need to make my leg beautiful.'

'What are you talking about! You haven't got anything. I said that quite without thinking. Sit down next to the instrument. Internal tumours are, of course, quite a different matter. But our instrument gives a sufficiently accurate diagnosis of external tumours. Uncover your bump. A typical angiofibroma.'

'What's the principle of the instrument?'

'You irradiate radioactive particles. Every part of your skin irradiates them. But malignant cells have the property of accumulating these particles and so they irradiate more of them than other areas of skin. We'll put the meter against your innocent fibroma . . . like that . . . and then in four minutes we'll put it against the corresponding place on your other leg. And then we compare the number of particles that jump out there with the number that jump out here. It's simple arithmetic.'

'And what difference is considered significant?'

Zhanna Pavlovna was embarrassed. She did not want to answer my question. And she did not answer it.

'You know, it varies a lot. It depends on many factors. And then, we have our own sort of arithmetic. We divide, multiply, subtract . . .'

'Extract square roots . . .'

'Don't laugh, better show us your fibroma.'

Next to the instrument with its dials stood a hospital bed. They were supposed to put me on the bed, and then I would lie and look at the ceiling, and Zhanna Pavlovna and I would chat together during the four control minutes and I should not be able to see the dials on the instrument or the notes which Zhanna Pavlovna put down in pencil on a piece of paper. But they felt awkward about putting me on the bed and sat me down on it sideways in such a way that made sitting uncomfortable. Then they brought a chair and I ended up facing the instrument. The sheet of paper, without any numbers on it as yet, lay on the bed before my eyes.

They put one end of a metal tube to my 'pea', moved a lever and at once an oval green light started to flash on a glass screen on the instrument. I watched carefully. Sometimes the light flashed two or three times in a row, at times intermittently, sometimes even more slowly, then again quickly, almost falling over itself. With every flash of the light a needle on a dial would move forward one mark.

Possibly realizing she had done the wrong thing, in order to divert my attention from the dial, Zhanna Pavlovna asked me: 'So you are at a rest centre now? What is it called? Karacharovo?'

'Yes. Right after these tests I'll be back there again. Or will it have to be removed?'

'It will have to be removed anyway. But not in a hurry, I think. Later. When you return from Karacharovo. They will probably remove it for you in the out-patients' clinic.'

'How's that?'

'So you don't have to come into the hospital. They'll pluck it out and you'll go home. Now then . . . what have we got there? Four hundred and ninety. Now let's have your other leg. The same place. Let's put this on.'

We involuntarily grew silent, staring at the little screen on the instrument. There the light jumped and flashed infrequently, with wide, distinct spaces in between. Even without the meter you could see that there would be far fewer flashes than the first time. The conversation dried up immediately. In Zhanna Pavlovna's face and intonation there appeared the same tension I noticed in the first minute of our acquaintance and which I began to understand during her conversation with poor Nadya.

Zhanna Pavlovna took the sheet of paper and pencil and was about to go and sit at the table so that she could write down the second figure there rather than in front of my eyes, but she suddenly realized that, just the same, she would not be able to hide the paper from me for three days. And then what is the point of hiding it if all the dials are straight in front of me anyway? She put the paper back on to the bed. At the head of two columns (which would become long in the course of three days), there appeared on the paper the figures 490—80. As if by chance the head of the laboratory, a young professor called Agranat, came in and stood behind my back.

'Well, what have you there?'

'On the whole. . . . Now we'll try again.'

The second result turned out to be 500—110, after which I could get on with something of my own whilst waiting for the next session.

Zhanna Pavlovna was crestfallen. Professor Agranat left the

instrument-room without commenting on our figures. A sense of misfortune surrounded me, but I (perhaps some people will not believe this, yet it is true) settled myself down at the table they had given me and started to translate the prose sketches of Abutalib: little stories, parables, fables in prose. I had long since noticed about myself that I worked with fanatical zeal during times of great trouble and personal catastrophe. But what sort of personal catastrophes had there been earlier? Unfaithfulness, break-ups, quarrels? I could do now with a few more catastrophes like those instead of the misfortunes that now hung over me – we shall not say yet 'had befallen me', though possibly it had indeed already befallen me.

Between sessions I sometimes sat writing at the table, sometimes installed myself at the telephone and rang round about one thing and another; sometimes I would go home for lunch. The little columns of figures on the page grew longer: 400—70, 420—75, 390—60, 360—70. At this point the first day's tests finished.

I did not know whether my figures were good or bad, but I saw that in the laboratory they were expecting a different result, that Zhanna Pavlovna would not look at me, that her face grow longer from session to session and that, however much they might hide their alarm, a sense of alarm was in the air, and afterwards made itself felt even in what was said.

The next day began again with 'good morning'. I gave Zhanna Pavlovna a book she had asked me for the day before, and we sat ourselves down once more next to the instrument.

'So you are working at the rest centre now?' Zhanna Pavlovna asked as she put the tube to my leg. 'What's it called? Karacharovo? Is that far from Moscow?'

'A hundred and fifty kilometres. On the Volga.'

'You were going to go back there, then, after the examination?'

'My papers are all set out there. There's a story stopped in mid-sentence. As soon as you finish counting my isotopes, I'm off there. Or have you different ideas about that?'

'No. But . . . perhaps you could get rid of it first. Why take it with you wherever you go? It's not as if you need it!'

'Get rid of it how? An operation? But that takes a long time. Or, as you said, as an out-patient?'

'Perhaps it's best to get rid of it once and for all. Properly. I don't decide anything. Agnessa Petrovna will decide. It's just a suggestion.'

'And if I don't come as an out-patient, how many days will it take?'

'It depends how it heals. Two or three weeks. Let's see. . . . What have we today? Good, 300—70. The ratio is stable. Go and work for now. In two hours' time. . . .'

Professor Agranat came into the room where I was translating Abutalib.

'Vladimir Alekseevich, what is that I hear? Do you mind if I interrupt you? It seems that when you were talking to Zhanna Pavlovna you put forward the idea that cancer is not a disease of the lungs, the liver, the skin or the stomach, but a disease of the entire body. And where the disease manifests itself – the stomach or the skin – is neither here nor there.'

'Well, yes. I did say that. It's the same as metabolism. With diathesis a pimple can pop up on your ear, your nose, your head – but isn't it all the same? You must treat the metabolism, not the pimple. It's the same thing here.'

'But that's how I see it! It doesn't solve the problem, of course, because the nature of the disease affecting the entire organism is not clear to us. You are made up of thirty billion cells. Just imagine. Each cell knows its job. Or, rather, it obeys something in the body of which we as yet know nothing. For example, suppose you grazed the skin on your arm. A superficial injury. Straight away the cells of the skin begin to divide in order to cover over the wound and restore the torn area of skin. Once it's restored, the cell division stops immediately. Somebody gives the order for the cell division to stop there, and the cells submit to the order.'

'But they divide even without any injury. When they wear out, others replace them. And that happens everywhere – in the brain, the blood, the spleen . . .'

'Quite true. But they divide according to iron rules just the same. The same quantities of chromosomes, an established pattern of division and, in general, order. But then a few cells stop obeying this SOMETHING which determines their life in the body. They begin to divide not in the designated manner but as they like. They begin to divide irregularly. That puts them out of the game, out of the overall, sensible and purposeful process of life.'

'But what does the body do? Surely it must have some means of defence, of suppression and interception?'

'Yes. A disease-carrying cell – a bacillus or a virus – has only got to find its way into the body for the legions which guard the body to throw themselves into battle, into mortal combat, and more often than not they overcome the uninvited newcomers.'

'So what happens here?'

'This disease is so insidious because it involves not foreign or alien bodies, not evil-doing newcomers, but its very own cells, only they are degenerated. Mutant cells. The body does not react to them – after all, they're its own! But at the same time they excite to anarchy a greater and greater number of cells, influencing them in some way and causing them to degenerate. And the body begins to die.'

'But do the evil ones die too? Or, rather, the malignant cells?'

'Alas, that is the only solace for the dying body.'

'Let's return to the beginning of our conversation. Who should we blame – the cells which have become insubordinate or those control centres which allowed the insubordination? Have specific areas weakened or let something slip? Or, perhaps, they have lost the ability to control with accuracy and exactness precisely as a result of a general disease?'

'We don't know that. There is a great deal we don't know about this disease. Take, for instance, a tumour on the skin. . . . A small percentage of patients get quite shot of it after the operation. No relapses nor metastases. Nothing. They live to be a hundred. But why one managed it and not another – that we don't know. But, generally speaking . . . people have an exaggerated fear of the disease.'

'Why is that?'

'You tell me why. Death from cardio-vascular illnesses occupies first place on this earth, right?'

'Yes. I know the statistics too.'

'But you tell a man he has a bad heart and he won't take it as a death sentence, he carries on living and often couldn't care less. But you have only to tell a man he has cancer and immediately there's horror, panic, tears. But death from cancer is only in second place.'

'Wonderful, professor. That piece of knowledge is quite sufficient for me. Why, do the figures really show cause for alarm?'

'What figures? Oh, yours! We haven't analysed them yet. I don't know anything yet.'

'I have read that in America they tell a patient if they suspect he has cancer. And you, too, sometimes rely on the body's own ability to survive. Well, it's still not clear when the body puts up a better fight – when the brain knows or when it doesn't know.'

'Yes, they have their own way of looking at things there.'

'That's it. For instance, in France . . . it's amusing, really. They have the highest rate for cirrhosis of the liver in the world. You can see why. They always drink wine with meals. Well now, our patients with liver disease are only allowed to eat boiled meat, but in France boiled meat is forbidden.'

'Then what do they eat? Surely not fried meat?'

'No, they use a grill over coals, without fat or a frying-pan. They think that that's the least harmful way. They're great eccentrics, aren't they?'

After this rather less disquieting conversation about the eccentric French, the professor retreated from the room and I sat down to the next of Abutalib's parables.

During the session that followed Zhanna Pavlovna said this: 'An operation is necessary, of course. But, to be quite sure, it's a good idea to irradiate the area before the operation. Only one has to choose which method to use . . .'

'What methods are there?'

'You can irradiate just once with a heavy dose, but one which won't penetrate far. Or you can irradiate daily for two weeks.'

'They'll doubtless choose what's best. It's not for me to decide.'

'But don't start worrying. It's only a precautionary measure. Nothing more. Just in case. You know, so that it heals up better after the operation.'

That evening I felt a kind of strange, cautious atmosphere surrounding me, even at home. My wife suddenly informed me: 'Kolya rang. Some acquaintance is offering him natural balsam. Twenty roubles for ten grams. Perhaps we'll take a couple of portions? They won't take up much space.'

'Didn't Kolya suggest some quack or fortune-teller, then?'

'There's no quack.[1] But there in Sambor they have a spring in the forest with a little chapel over it . . .'

'It sounds as though Agnessa Petrovna rang. And what did she say?'

'She didn't say anything. I thought I'd just mention it.'

. . . When we finished work on the figures (they had continued all the same way: 300—60, 290—56, 310—70), Zhanna Pavlovna sent me on my way with the remark, dropped with apparent casualness: 'Our figures mean nothing in themselves. There will be a clinical discussion tomorrow when the final diagnosis will be made.'

'The final diagnosis, as we know from the novel of that name, is made only at the post-mortem.'

Zhanna Pavlovna was pleased by my happy, carefree joking. But perhaps she was even more pleased that I did not recall, at least aloud, a certain thoughtless remark she had made before the tests began: namely, that their method recognizes and diagnoses external tumours with some degree of accuracy.

9

So, supposing we admit that I am sentenced. But by whom? The machine? Or Zhanna Pavlovna? Perhaps tomorrow's clinical discussion will pronounce the sentence. It would be unfair to place such a responsibility on them. And the sentence was pronounced much earlier anyway. But for what?

As I see it, in the life of every person today there would be a sufficient quantity of facts for which one could be virtually canonized, and, on the other hand, a sufficient quantity of facts for which one should be immediately pulverized. I shall not insist on the 'every', so as not to offend, however unintentionally, the odd righteous one (let each one look within himself), but in my life there is enough of both types.

A few years ago I began to write a novel in which I have attempted to evaluate my actions specifically from this point of view; specifically to sort them to right and left, like sheep and goats, but I immediately came up against insurmountable difficulties. An action which at first sight seems magnanimous and kind can sometimes have the bitterest results, whereas an action which seemed bad, egotistical, and even malicious, turns out to be good and a blessing for all concerned.

Actually, the novel is making slow progress, not because I have become bogged down in it, but for other reasons. We are not going to mention them here. The point is that I heard no inner protest within me against the sentence. And it would be senseless, anyway, to complain even to oneself about something that is not subject to complaint. After all, you will not start shouting: 'I am good, I am kind, I am needed, can't you see, I have talent!' No, you will not shout that.

'We shall say nothing of other qualities, but talent really was given to you.'

'What do you mean by that? I tried to use it for the good of . . . I have twenty thousand readers' letters.'

'But how much of it did you use? A tenth at the most. The rest you wasted on committees, out wandering, asleep, eating, waffling at meetings, chasing after nothing, you strewed it about and let it blow away.'

'Give me time and I'll prove . . .'

'You were given time. You should have been killed in the autumn of '42 together with your contemporaries Valka Grubov, Borka Grubov, Serega Chernov, Boris Moskovkin, Ivan Kunin. . . . Now add up how much time you were given to show yourself at your best. More than thirty years.'

'But I have managed to do something. I haven't been lazy or idle. I have written a large number of books. I began as a village lad and became a Moscow writer. They publish my books abroad. . . . Do you think it's easy and simple for a kid from Alepino . . .'

'They expected more of you. And you had your chances.'

'What chances?! If you knew the conditions, the surrounding circumstances . . .'

'You were alive – that's the condition. Once you were alive, then you could do it. Only death takes away all opportunities.'

'All right. I'm to blame. But why so early?'

'It's neither early nor late. How old are you? Nearly fifty? Of course one could creak on to a ripe old age. But, you know, many people have died younger than you. We won't trouble ourselves with the millions. We'll take the well-known names. Pushkin – 37, Byron – 36, Lermontov – 27, Mayakovsky – 36, Esenin – 30, Belinsky – 37, Blok – 40, Nikitin – 37, Pisarev – 27, Petöfi – 26, Khristo Botev – 28, Dobrolyubov – 25, Gogol – 42, Jack London – 40, Griboedov – 34, Maupassant – 43, Chekhov – 44, and Dante, of course – 56 years. . . . And yet we do not think of many of them as having gone particularly early, before their time. At least we don't think of Dante, Chekhov, Gogol or Maupassant in that way, not to mention people more or less the same age as you: Lomonosov – 54, Molière – 51, Bulgakov – 49, Coster – 52. . . . I don't remember exactly, but even Napoleon managed if not entirely, then almost entirely to put the time allotted to him on earth behind him before he was your age. So you mustn't complain.'

'I'm not complaining. But isn't the means too cruel? If only it were quick . . . like a heart attack.'

'You should be ashamed! Anyone would think you were going to have your lower jaw blown off with a mine like Valka Grubov. Will you have to wander about, surrounded and starving, in an autumn forest before dying? Or lie in a goods wagon full of typhus? How about wading across a vast, ice-cold river? Or the blockade? Do you feel like sitting in a concentration camp until starvation finishes you off? Don't you have an urge to dig earth under the noses of guards or fell a few trees? How would a couple of good trials by ordeal suit you? What about burning on a fire in a large square? Or standing against a wall in front of rifle barrels? Or sitting on a stake? How about putting a noose round yourself with your own hands? Obviously we are not talking about the end in itself. The end itself is absolutely the same for everyone. Strictly speaking, it doesn't exist. As far as our senses are concerned, it doesn't exist at all. Obviously, we are talking about the transition. So, then, you won't be tied to galloping horses, or pushed into the furnace of a locomotive, or have lead poured down your gullet. You won't watch your children die of hunger, you won't be put into an arena to be mauled by lions, or nailed to a wall. . . . Well, what other kinds of terrifying transitions are there? Those listed already are not simply made up. All of it has happened to living people. That is the sort of transition they chanced to get. You can't do anything about it. And anyway, one must say, not the worst things possible have been listed. If one were to make a collection of the different forms of human agony that some people have had to suffer before death. . . . People have had to eat their own children, saw off their own hands to free them of shackles. But you are going to lie in a fine ward. You will be surrounded with attention. Pain-killing injections, sleeping pills. An interesting book. They'll let you have a drink when your friends visit you.'

'I don't want any of it!'

'Now that's totally stupid. You are not being asked anyway. And as far as sudden death is concerned, I should not insist on it in your place. Perhaps you are being given a last chance. Not a big one, but you have time to think about things. Perhaps you will have time to take some step, and that step will turn out to be very important. In the event of a heart attack, though, which is instantaneous, you won't have time to do anything, as you well understand.'

'What step can one still take? I know of no such step.'

'Think hard. That is why you have been given a little more time.'

'But why pick on me?'

'I don't understand you.'

'Why not? The thing is, my friends will still be here. How are they better than me? What have I done wrong that they haven't?'

'Who will still be here?' At this point, although the person I was talking to was imaginary, even in his voice there appeared a tone of genuine astonishment and a sort of alarm. 'Who will still be here?'

'Well, they will be. . . . The people with whom I live on earth.'

'Not one. Not a single one. Of all those with whom you live on earth, not one will remain. I give you my hand and word of honour on it.'

'But for some time . . .'

'So that's what you mean! And I took you for someone serious. Do you really attach so much significance to the microscopic difference in

the time at which various people leave this life? Louis XVI and his
executioner stood on the scaffold. Nearby stood the judges who had
sentenced Louis. Louis had his head chopped off, the executioner went
home to his supper, the judges went off to their duties. But where are
they all now? Are they not all now in the same place? First, they are all
there in the eighteenth century. And even for us, the living, the
difference of a few years between each of them completing his time here
has no significance. And it's even more the case for them. So be of good
heart. Nobody wants to trick you. This system is more conscientious
and reliable than others. Moreover, tomorrow there will be the case
discussion. . . . Who knows, perhaps you'll get a decent respite. But if I
were you, I shouldn't chase after it. And then, if this disease turns out
not to be terminal, what are you going to die of in the end? You will
have to submit to some other illness and, you can rely on it, it won't be
one whit better than this one. And it won't be in three hundred years,
but much, much sooner. The respite, as you must understand, cannot
be so decent as to make it worth talking about seriously. Well, ten to
fifteen years. . . . When did you move into your new flat?'

'Twelve years ago.'

'And it seems like? . . .'

'It seems like yesterday.'

'Well, that's just it. An instant, a breath of time. Now measure off
just such an instant, only forwards. There you have all the arithmetic
of it. And take into account that, as you get older, the years fly away
faster and faster.'

10

How I wished to
Be, be, be.
Sail across the
Sea, sea, sea.
Scale the mountains
High, high, high.
Over others
Fly, fly, fly.

How I wished to
Do, do, do.
Tread upon the
Snow, snow, snow.

See the lilac
Grow, grow, grow.
Feel my loved one's
Glow, glow, glow.

How I wished to
Sing, sing, sing.
So my throat would
Ring, ring, ring.
In that song was
Strife, strife, strife.
In that strife was
Life, life, life.

How I wished to
Fight, fight, fight.
Raise my hand for
Right, right, right.
Cares all in the
Past, past, past.
And my sword held
Fast, fast, fast.

How I wished to
Dare, dare, dare . . .
But before me
Death, death, death.

11

I came to the case discussion at exactly twelve o'clock, as I had been told. However, the room – I glanced in – turned out to be empty. Pacing about the corridor of the Institute clinic, I met Agnessa Petrovna. She let fall on me a deluge of optimistic feelings.

'How are things? How do you feel? And in yourself? I think it's all nothing. I'm sure of it! But I want others to see it too. So as to confirm my view. I think it's simply a fibroma. An angiofibroma. They'll come now. Wait just a little.'

With these words she went into the room and I remained outside. Zhanna Pavlovna appeared in the corridor with an official-looking folder in her hand.

'Oh, it's you! And here I am carrying all your isotopes. Our laboratory's conclusions. They'll look at them now and form their own opinion.'

'But what have you concluded?'

'In that bump of yours there could be a large number of blood-vessels. We've got a misguided impression because of them. But don't you worry, they'll get to the bottom of it now. They have called in Professor Larioshchenko. She's our big name. She's already retired, but they asked her and she promised to come.'

They finally called for me. Everything after that happened so fast I could not even get my bearings.

'Lie on your back and show your thigh. Colleagues, please look and state your opinion.'

The doctors, all without exception women, came up to me one after the other. Each in turn looked at my tumour for a few seconds, felt it with two fingers, moved it from side to side, pressed down on it, hastily asked questions.

'Have you had it a long time?'

'A few years.'

'Has it ever bled, cracked, left marks on your underwear?'

'Never.'

'Does it hurt or bother you?'

'If I knock it, it hurts. If I lie on it, it begins to ache after about five minutes.'

At this point the door opened and an elderly lady entered the room. Judging from the fact that she was late, this was the professor who had come specially from home. She came in and, without greeting anyone, went straight up to my thigh. She bent down and touched it.

'Has it ever bled or cracked?'

'Never.'

Suddenly all the doctors in turn pronounced some abstruse medical term, each the same one.

'I am very glad, dear colleagues, that your opinion is the same as mine. Vladimir Alekseevich, you don't object to an operation? Sign here. On Monday you'll give a blood sample for a rhesus factor test and other tests. On Tuesday we admit you, and on Wednesday we operate.'

'I must go to Karacharovo. I have my papers set out there. A story in mid-sentence . . .'

'What are you suggesting?'

'To leave it for a couple of weeks more.'

'Weeks are out of the question. I'll compromise and give you a day.

You come on Wednesday and on Thursday we operate. . . . There you are. I said it was nothing terrible.'

A nurse with my case record in her hand asked the professor: 'What shall I put down as the name of the operation?'

'A broad excision about a pigmental growth on the skin of the upper third of the left thigh. Goodbye, Vladimir Alekseevich. Go and finish your story.'

12

Strange as it may seem, this firework of a discussion put me at ease. I forgot about the laboratory, about Zhanna Pavlovna's strained look, and about the lights flickering on the small screen of the machine. That very day I went off to Karacharovo and, after the journey, went swiftly and soundly to sleep. But I awoke during the night and grew restless; something at the back of my sleepy mind would not go away, when suddenly and abruptly I surfaced from sleep. I felt fresh and totally awake. I saw the day's discussion in a new, clear and sober light and realized the mercilessly obvious fact that they had made their diagnosis before the discussion, basing it on the laboratory data which, of course, they knew. Agnessa Petrovna had rung the laboratory three times a day and asked about the results of the tests. And that whole discussion was nothing more than a good show put on to set me at ease before the operation. If it was a pitiful benign fibroma, then why the hurry? Why was a single day so important? Why the broad excision? I had no clear idea of what a BROAD excision was, but the very phrase itself spoke of alarm, danger, extreme measures.

What is a man most saddened by having to leave behind on this earth when he has to die? Strangely (and there is a paradox here), he is more concerned about leaving behind things he has already come to know, see and experience, than about the things which so far had remained uninvestigated and unknown. And of course a man cares less about the fact that he never managed to see icebergs being formed in Greenland, sliding and breaking away from the ice mass and plunging into the water, than about the fact that he will never again go mushrooming on a short and misty autumn day, never again swim in clear river water at the start of the day, or pick flowers, or watch the clouds, or kiss women.

Certainly I never caught sea-turtles, hunted for whales or crocodiles, bored into the earth, drove locomotives, I was never a test pilot, never built houses, bred rabbits, did clever things in chemical laboratories, was never in the Solomon Islands, never worked for Criminal Investigation, nor ate bison's lip, nor fought sharks, never went on strike with dockers, never had any part in government, never went to La Scala, never flew in a balloon, never tried the ski-jump, nor played goalkeeper for the USSR first team, never went underwater in a bathysphere, never stood beneath sequoia firs, nor saw the Cathedral of Hagia Sophia or the Egyptian pyramids, never travelled in Japan, India, nor in many other countries. I have never been to Kamchatka or Baykal. . . . Now is the time for a bitter sense of regret to well up within me, regret over not seeing, not doing, not trying. But no, I felt a lump in my throat when I remembered the rain in Batumi and thought that, perhaps, I should no longer hear its incessant, unbridled noise, or plunge myself into dark-blue salty water.

Yet something I had managed to see; in fact, not so much that the world had begun to seem trivial and boring, but sufficient to understand the beauty and variety of the earth's blessings. I have seen Paris, London, Budapest, Warsaw, Sofia, Munich, Bonn, Edinburgh, Berlin, Dresden, Cologne, Hanoi, Peking, Tiranë, Shkodër, Bucharest, Cracow, Copenhagen, the Island of Bornholm, Nice, Aix-en-Provence, Marseilles, St Michel, Tyrnovo, Belgrade, Ljubljana and many other cities in countries which I have had occasion to visit. But even there. . . . Take Paris, for example. . . . There is plenty in Paris that I have not managed to see, that I cannot even guess at. But I am sad not that I shall never see certain things, I am sad that I shall never be seeing Paris again from the top of its famous hill, that I shall walk no more along the narrow Rue du Bac, at which all my Parisian pedestrian excursions began. You do not go a hundred steps along this street before it turns into the Boulevard St Germain, and just there, right on the corner, near a café entrance, stand baskets of oysters strewn with sharp-smelling seaweed. If you go to the left now, you find other cafés and small restaurants, and not far away the Church of St Germain-des-Prés. But if you go down the Rue du Bac, you will come out on the embankment of the Seine and, looking right, you can already make out the huge building of Notre Dame and, straight opposite, across the Seine, the Louvre itself.

No, at the bitter moment of parting (or, at least, of realization that parting is at hand), you are drawn not to the Solomon Islands, where you have not been, but to some place, some Saranda or Sozopol, where you have been. Lord, I need no Saranda even! I should like to walk on our hill at Alepino in April, from the village to the meadow, clearing the way with a stick for a small stream of water. The stream is still only just gathering a little strength, though already in places it runs into a channel it has made in the snow, whilst in others where the snow is thicker, it is lost altogether. If you draw your stick across such a place, where the mass of snow is bulging with water, the water runs off down its new and unexpected channel, creating a sense of great joy and relief, gurgling and glistening in the sun. And the bulging snow at the sides of the channel whitens as you watch, with the water draining out of it until there is none left. But the channel is there now, though already blocked by a frosty heap of shattered ice, so now there is the pleasure of breaking down this barrier with the stick and giving free flow to little ice-blocked lakes. Below the blockage the stream immediately overflows its banks, rushes along faster than before until at one bound it fills up a little lake near another blockage. You go up to it with your stick, and so on down the sun-warmed slope of the hill, where there are more thawed patches than snow, so that you bring the stream down to the meadow and then on until it falls into the river, which is already swollen and pushing up the heavy winter ice.

Lord, I do not even need to set free a stream! That is, I do – but that is really a huge treat, a great blessing. Once, this was in April too, I took a handful of snow from a place where the sun was particularly warm, and it was made up of tiny lumps that glittered in my hand like large crystals of salt, and pleasantly cooled my burning palm. So I kept hold of it until the translucent granules in my hand became fewer and fewer. I should like to hold just such a handful of April snow once again. But the Solomon Islands – you can have them. Probably they are wonderful, but it is not them that I miss now.

Yet, within us, complex and clever mechanisms are at work. Between two particular sections of the body, between two assemblies, as an expert on cars would say, there should not perhaps be any direct link, any wire or means of communication. On the contrary, it is as if some insulating padding has been put in, and, if it is broken, all sorts of manias, complexes and psychoses break out and life becomes intolerable.

Everyone knows that he will die. No normal person wants to die. Then why does the thought of death not torture us throughout our lives? Why do we speak easily of our death, even laughingly, as if we are not talking of our own death? Because there are areas of insulating padding placed in the necessary parts of the body. There he goes, the lover of life, jolly, active, fit.

'You know you'll die,' they tell him.

'Me? Of course I'll die!' he laughs. He laughs louder. He opens a new bottle of wine. Kisses his woman. Moves off with her and turns round laughing. 'We'll all die!' How funny. It is all a joke. You could split your sides. A flashing smile. Life overflows. He repeats the question: 'Me, die? Of course! We'll all die.' And he laughs loudly once again.

In the body, in the psyche, somewhere there in the hidden depths of the brain, a slender little wire is purposefully left out. The connection is missing. That is part of the defensive mechanisms of the human organism. In just the same way women forget about labour pains, become pregnant again and give birth, although during the birth they swear it will be for the last time. They remember this afterwards, but it is as if it does not concern them. The insulating padding has come in between.

When you are fit, it is good to laugh at death. But what if things get dicey? If you suddenly get a nasty shock? If, as they say, you begin to suspect the worst? Then the body turns out to have further defensive functions. During a dangerous illness, and during a terminal one even more so, it is possible (I am only guessing) that somewhere there in the adrenal glands are formed and secreted into the blood certain substances that dull the sharpness of the possibly approaching end. And even reconcile one to it. There sets in a certain necessary degree of indifference, depression and tiredness, when simply to lie and think of nothing is more pleasant and desirable than to bustle about once more, run off on business, struggle and push and engage oneself in general activity.

As I recall, I had earlier been subject to waves of tiredness and grey, colourless indifference coming over me, but they never absolutely swamped me. I simply caught myself thinking that I did not really want to do anything today. There was nothing outstanding in which I should have liked to get involved; no course of action I should have liked to carry out, no state of mind in which I should have liked to find myself. I could have gone for a walk – but I did not want to; lit a bonfire in the wood – but I did not want to; had a game of chess – but did not want to; gone to Paris – but did not want to; set off in search of relics from the past – but did not want to; sat with friends and had a drink – but did not want to. . . . The point is that, after thinking with some sense of alarm over all possible activities, I always found in myself a vital spot: I found what I should like to do. That means that my tiredness was still not complete, not terminal. I have never yet not wanted to write. Work always saved me. Sometimes what I wanted was far off, something impossible to fulfil immediately. I would want, say, to walk beneath the warm rain in a pine forest, while the Moscow winter lay outside the window. But that does not matter. The main thing is to find something in life to cling to, to want something, even if it cannot be fulfilled at that precise moment. The main thing is to have that vital spot within you, the means by which you might feel yourself a living person. But sometimes I would have an alarming presentiment. Supposing, I would think, there suddenly came a day when I wanted absolutely no more than to lie down, shut my eyes and think of nothing?

13

Not for me the ways I wandered through,
Nor down new paths shall I stray.
'Madame, let me give my thanks to you' –
From now on is what I'll say.

All the gifts of life what we accrue
Disappear like fallen tears.
Madame, let me give my thanks to you
For these few and final years.

All but lost the light that once I knew,
Faintly shine its shrinking rays.
Madame, let me give my thanks to you
For these few and final days.

How a woman's beauty pierced me through –
Joy and passion both were ours.
Madame, let me give my thanks to you
For these few and final hours.

Even now the scythe has struck the dew
And its blade the grass disturbs.
Madame, let me give my thanks to you
For these few and final words.

Now the sun burns low and fast ensue
Shadows, for my day grows short.
Madame, let me give my thanks to you
For the final warmth you brought.

Much was given me, much less was due:
North and south and east and west.
Madame, let me give my thanks to you
For the final bloom, the best.

Take my gratitude and ever reign,
Think of me in later years.
Though the thanks I offer once again
Disappear like fallen tears.

14

In the house at Karacharovo nothing had changed during the preceding days. The open book lies where it was in the main room, on a low table in front of the settee. Joyce Cary, *The Horse's Mouth*. A wonderful book. Near the book a cup with the remains of some green tea. The remains in the cup are covered with a kind of greasy stain. On the chessboard there is a three-move problem set up, which I had not managed to solve at the time. On the table in the study lies a routine page of work, half covered with writing. At all costs I must finish this story, which is to have the title 'A Robbery'. I must.

Everything here is as it was. Life had been hurrying along, hurrying along in a number of channels, and then it had stopped and stood still. As in the fairy-tale everything had stopped when the Princess pricked her little pink finger on the spinning-wheel. Then the Princess received a kiss and everything spun into motion again, bringing to completion half-made gestures, half-spoken words, half-taken steps. The same with me here: I had to pour fresh tea into the cup, turn over a page in the book, make a move with the rook and finish writing a sentence. The flow of life had not broken off, it had stopped for only a moment. And only about a week had gone by. But my life here a week earlier now seemed so idyllic and unreal. As if I had glimpsed my things, set out here and there, from the distance of a different era.

Three days. . . . I had managed to get out of Agnessa Petrovna Saturday, Sunday and Monday. Three extra days on the banks of the Volga, in the old park, in the comfortable settee, at my desk. As if no purpose, the weather was such as I had never seen in fifteen years at Karacharovo. Unexpectedly (on 17th November) the first frost pierced the air, which was completely windless and shot through by the low sun. A black mirror of ice, four centimetres thick, had formed on the Volga, and fluffy hoar-frost had settled on the trees, though there was still not a single snowflake on the ground: just the black earth and yellow leaves, recently fallen. But the leaves were covered with hoar-frost, and every blade of grass, and even every stick that lay on the ground. Through the ice you could see everything in the water: the sandy bottom with its shallow undulations, dark yellow in colour as if one were looking through coffee, the weed and the small perch swimming amongst it. One could move about on the ice only with small, slippery steps. The ice was sagging and twanging melodically. It seemed as though it was not the cracks that were running off in all directions in a spider's web, but the sounds themselves. But the ice still supported you, so that you were able to slip and slide across the whole, kilometre-wide mirror of the reservoir. But a good blow with a stick would break the ice right through. The distant wooded patches on the far edge of the mirror, covered in hoar-frost, looked more fantastic and inviting than the frost-covered trees on the near bank immediately overhead. The state of nature was that which is usually described, without looking further for epithets, as fairy-tale. It was a fairy-tale, and in the mood I was in I took it as a farewell gift.

But, really, why farewell? The operation after all is not one of life or death. Nobody has yet died after the excision of a tumour on the thigh. That is as may be, but still, if the sentence has already been pronounced. . . .

Many of my friends advised me to refuse the operation outright. Their arguments were always the same: 'A lady acquaintance had had just such a thing all her life. Then she decided to have it removed. Three and a half months later it was all over with her.' 'Someone I know had an apparently innocent mole removed. Four months later he was dead.'

A former fellow student and poet spoke more persuasively than the others: 'I know that Institute like my own home. A friend of mine and two women I know passed through it. I took them there. Carried gifts from people to them. Got them discharged. Buried them. Take even the poorest book on tumours, they all say first and foremost in black and white. It' – here he meant the melonoma – 'fears the knife. Like no other tumour. After the surgeon's knife its cells run off into every part of the body. Straight after the operation you seem to feel all right. Your strength returns, your mood and physical state are good. . . . Then after three to six months your temperature goes up. They begin to treat you as if you had pneumonia – and that's that. Zhora, my friend, knew how these things go. He started to have a good time and throw parties. I told him off. . . . After an operation you need peace, a regular pattern of life. And do you know what he answered? He asked: "Which one of us is dying – you or I?" I did not say another word to him. You see, old fellow, that thing can be dormant for years. The surgeon's knife sets a clock going in the body. Get it? The clock starts to tick. Like a bomb. And it's too late to stop it. They can tick from three months to three years. So everything depends upon whether the clock starts up after the knife. I know one particular case. In this very Institute. The diagnosis could not have been worse. And the woman was suspicious of everything. If you irradiated her, she would have guessed everything straight away. I took the responsibility upon myself – no radiation, no medicines. I trusted to the body. They discharged her and said: "You have nothing wrong."

'"But can I go to the South?"'

'"Go to Africa if you want."'

'"Can I sunbathe?"'

'"Fry yourself in a frying-pan if you like."'

'It's over nine years now, and she's forgotten all about her operation. But that's a case in a thousand. Usually the clock starts to tick.'

'So why the operation, if you know beforehand? . . .'

'How could you do otherwise? Supposing you were in the ocean trying to save yourself on a piece of broken mast. You sight land. You know that it is dangerous to go ashore there. There are wild animals, malaria-carrying mosquitoes, tsetse flies, cannibals. Your chances of being rescued are nil. But just the same you try to reach land and won't push yourself away from it to float off again into the boundless ocean on your piece of wood.[2] But how have you come to be stuck with it?'

How indeed? There, in Karacharovo, I had time to reflect upon this, when all is said and done, unanswerable riddle. There could be no question of its being inherited. All of the ancestors that I could recall from family stories and legends had lived a long time and died a normal, quiet death between eighty and ninety years old. It is true, they did not write poetry, were not members of a Moscow writers' organization, did not live in a vast city.

As I went along the hoar-frost-covered walk of the old Gagarin estate, I mechanically prodded with my stick at the oak and lime leaves, which were hard with frost, and went over in my mind all my, as they call them now, negative emotions – though not those which suddenly burst upon you in life and then disappear, but those which gradually, slowly and surely would have stifled me over a period of many years, bringing my inner condition to such a degree of emotional fatigue, that the struggle against this stifling gives way to indifference and capitulation by the body.

There is always something on one's mind. All right. I do not work in an office or in some place of business, I do not receive a salary. I am a freelance artist. I write a book, they publish it. I get the money. A book takes a long time to write, from a few months to a few years. True, such a long period does not remain completely empty from the earnings point of view. I might write an article, do a radio broadcast, give my opinion on somebody's manuscript for a publisher. But that is all irregular work, there is nothing permanent about it, it comes and goes. Apart from that, a book which you have been writing might not be published, either in a magazine or as a book. It did not strike them favourably, it's on the wrong theme. There is no shortage of reasons for turning down a book. My novel *Coltsfoot* had a spell in the editorial offices of three magazines before it saw the light of day. *Letters from the Russian Museum* visited a few magazines before they were published by *Young Guard*, and *Black Boards* was rejected by *Young Guard* even.

For how many years now have Sundays, May Day, Easter and my own birthday ceased to exist for me! In the morning, whatever the day, I have to sit at my table and write. No leave, no holidays, no days off. And even if days do crop up without the writing-desk, it is because those are the days when I sit at meetings, visit editorial offices, engulfed in fuss and bother.

I mentioned this permanent lack of rest only as a single factor. I do not think that it alone could make a man overdo things and fall ill. Especially as I had never been brought to the level of starvation: only the threat of misfortune hung over me, misfortune itself there was not. But, conversely, there were other, permanent worries, whose very permanence, and at times hopelessness, were capable over many years of wearing down, as they say, even a stone, let alone the vegetative, is it, or central nervous system of a person of today who has, apart from that, to stand up to noise and smoke and speed and vibration, various chemical poisons, the whole unnatural, feverish pace of life. What wears one out, if you like, is not the actual process of working at a desk (my work always brought me nothing but joy and satisfaction) but the sensation of lack of time, a sensation that one is using more time than allowed, like breaking the rules of a game. If there are five things you have to do within a certain space of time, and you feel that you will only managed to do three, you naturally begin to feel on edge. An involuntary state of tension arises within your body. A fifteen-minute nap refreshes a balanced, even if very tired man wonderfully. But try and drop off for fifteen minutes if you know that you are late for everything and not getting necessary things done. You will lie for fifteen minutes without moving, as if you were resting, but you will feel hot, you will even start to sweat, as if you were hurrying about seeing to your business. The sense of falling behind time, even when short-lived, is bad for the health. But when it goes on for years, it is ruinous and fatal.

All you hear about nowadays is negative emotions, negative emotions. Avoid negative emotions! When you wake up, try to smile before doing anything else. And in general smile and laugh as much as possible. But, most important of all, avoid negative emotions.

They talk as if negative emotions were simply a quarrel, an unpleasant piece of news, heated words with a shop assistant, with the boss at work, a drunken husband, an unfaithful wife, a poor mark in your daughter's report book, a broken television, a jumper burnt through with an iron, a laddered stocking, a lost game of chess, forfeited bonuses, your teenage son taken off to the police station – and all those unpleasant occurrences which may be unexpected but are none the less everyday for that.

I am convinced that if you see a beautiful tree out of your window every morning, a beautiful street, a beautiful building or beautiful view, even if it be of a town, you feel better and live longer. If, on the other hand, you see out of your window every morning a rubbish pit, a dirty yard, gloomy grey buildings, stunted and dying trees covered with a layer of greasy, black soot – these will be your negative emotions, the more so for not being occasional, but permanent and somehow even unnoticed, but no less destructive, at least oppressive, which is the same thing.

Usually our glance falls indifferently upon the monotonous, standardized buildings that block the horizon on the outskirts of towns, upon villages hideously churned up by heavy tractors, upon huge heaps of agricultural machinery, rusting under the open sky, upon green hillsides covered with red, clayey sores, upon the earth, torn up and turned inside out by bulldozers, upon rubbish-filled, if not demolished forests, upon blackened rivulets where there is no sign of life, upon decapitated churches like skeletons with the light shining through them. But do we just glance? And are we indifferent? Does there not arise in the soul an ache, at first not noticeable, like a hairline crack in a monolithic stone. But once the crack has appeared, be it less than a hair's breadth, then the stone sooner or later will fall into two along the line of the crack. . . .

But I must admit that all these reflections concerning the origins of

disease, which came to me on the frost-covered walk in the park at
Karacharovo, are fine but hardly true. Medical knowledge states that
melanoma in particular is found more frequently in horses than in
man. So I should have to make out that even horses possess negative
emotions, which hypothesis would be, as men of learning say, not
totally correct.

15

What is the flavour of emotion –
That bread of anguish which we eat?
Can it be really so, the notion
That pain is bitter, love is sweet?

For sadness' taste is to be savoured,
Its bitterness a gentle thing.
But slights we find less kindly flavoured,
Like salt upon a wound, they sting.

More passionate my life than placid,
I clearly feel the difference
Between contempt, so sharp and acid,
And sourish, limp indifference.

The sunset is both sweet and galling
And, black against its lighter line,
The wine of rain and leaves is falling,
Like sorrow's harsh, astringent wine.

Yet nuances are nought, and muted
The mouth of him who has to quaff
The spirit pure and undiluted
Of jealousy, one hundred proof.

It is so; let it be so ever.
The sweetness and the salt I'll take.
But, God, oh spare me and deliver
From one thing, for thy mercy's sake:

Where there is neither storm nor summer,
Where there is neither found nor lost,
Where there is neither taste nor colour,
Where there is neither fire nor frost!

16

It was as if a glass curtain had come down between me and the rest of the world. I could see everything, and even very clearly, even in greater relief and more brightly than usual, but everything was somehow distant, existing all on its own, and I, too, existed all on my own. I felt neither fear nor pain nor distress nor hopelessness, but as though I were at a distance. There was nothing that I could complain about. If indeed there was something that had given me life fifty years earlier, and now had decided to liquidate me, it would be despicable to feel offended. The crystallization of this sensation of mine was helped by one of the ten or so unread letters which in passing I had taken from my desk and pushed into my brief-case as I left for Karacharovo. These letters were all from that other world on the other side of the glass, but just the same I started to tear open one envelope after another and run my eyes over what was written there in different hands:

. . . This is my third letter to you already. I urgently request you to send me the address of the old woman Sofya Pavlovna, whom you describe in your book *Grass*, My son is incurably ill. . . .

Today mother read me a passage from one of your works. In it you pity people who do not understand the feelings of a passionate collector. . . . I am writing all this because, if ever you visit our town, you are invited to come and see us. My husband was a keen collector of many different things: stamps, coins, medallions, icons, weapons, pipes, postcards, books. . . .

Over a year has gone by since I sent you my definitive work entitled *Collectivology*. You have expressed no opinion on it to this day. Can it really be that a Soviet writer . . .

. . . If you recall, in your *Autumn Leaves* you assert that religious believers turn to God with various requests: 'Have mercy', 'Save and protect', 'Help, o Lord', 'Send, o Lord', etc., and that were you a believer, you would address God with but one phrase: 'I thank Thee.' But it seems to me, Vladimir Alekseevich, that saying that is fine for one who is not, as they say, in a sticky situation, who enjoys excellent good fortune, health and general success in every respect. If, on the other hand, a man is torn apart by illness, family trouble and suffering of any kind, then your formula is hardly suitable.

Yes, I should go to Yaroslavl, the antique collections left after the husband's death drew me there, I should send the man my opinion on his ridiculous, three-volume – two thousand handwritten pages – *Collectivology*. But all that in some strange way remained on the other side of the glass, and reading letters did not stimulate in me any desire for action.

However, I stopped to think about the last-mentioned letter. Was I right when I expressed that thought in *Autumn Leaves*? Or was it just a passing mood, incapable of withstanding the test of time? The test has come. The disease, and an operation in two days. The sentence has been pronounced and is about to be carried out. And on top of all this, a mass of everyday problems. I place all this on one side of the scales, and of course it plummets down into an abyss. To the Devil. And I do not know what I must put on the other side of the scales, if not to achieve a balance, then at least to stop the plummeting of the first.

But there is no need to put anything there. I do not divide my life into separate events. I somehow see it all at once, in an instant, cognizant of the not unimportant fact of my birth, of my appearance on earth, and I really do not find I have any other emotion than sincere and heartfelt gratitude, which suddenly sweeps and washes over my soul like a warm, bright wave. As I see it, it is like this. If a man does not exist (and he does not exist if he has not been born), or if his existence is but a state of black muteness and, as I look at it, if you were to take this man out of his condition of non-existence for the sake of nothing more than the warm rain, a piece of bread, a single kiss. . . . There goes another list! What for? If you were to wake the man up for an instant, just to show him a blade of grass sprinkled with dew and nothing more, as I see it, he should already be grateful; after all, there might not have been this blade of grass sprinkled with dew. And now let us recall what there has been. Yes, yes, that is it. The scale stopped and slowly but surely started to rise.

17

Let life hold for me only malice,
I know I am weak and will fall.
Yet your golden love is my solace,
From heaven the last gift of all.

Your skin which is golden and burnished,
Your eyes which are light as the sky,

The couch which you carefully furnished,
The tear which at parting you'd cry.

It is not by chance we're together,
So all idle chatter rebuff!
But is it a gift I am given
Or punishment in your young love?

As punishment have you been sent me
That, when my life's thread is cut through,
It may the more surely torment me
To go from this earth and from you?

18

I wanted to write one more poem before leaving Karacharovo. A sense of its imminence was already troubling me. That, as I knew, meant it was there within me, had already set itself in motion in the depth of my soul, was already making its way upwards to show itself on the surface, just as the flower of the wild celery floats up from the river-bed when the time comes for it to be warmed by the sun and offer itself to dragonflies and butterflies.

I usually take one particular route there. From my little house straight down to the Volga, then left along the river-bank to Uncle Vanya's house (that is, Ivan Sergeevich Sokolov-Mikitov), then, taking the left turn past Uncle Vanya's house, along the woodland avenue until it comes out on a grassy, sunlit clearing. And it had happened already five or six times that it was precisely on that woodland avenue that a poem I had felt coming and troubled by burst into the light. That is to say, the theme of the poem would spring up and its first lines be born, in my head now and not just in my heart. I recall that 'Men', 'I Have Killed No One on This Earth', 'Falling Leaves', 'The Alder Tree', 'Blue Lakes' and 'Argument' had appeared on that very path. I had come to believe in there being some fortunate reason for this, so this time too I decided to go along the route I had so grown to like. Of course, it does not always or inevitably work. If it did, collections of verse would be flying out from under my pen like lightning. But just the same, just the same. And so now the hoar-frost is crunching under my sturdy shoes and the dead leaves rustle as I automatically stir them about with my stick. At first the poem wandered about in circles. Round and about. It caught itself up in the famous line from *Terkin*:

'And at least spit in her face, then, if it's all come to an end!' And it
began to knit and weave along, taking that line as its starting-point:

> No, there no need to spit upon her,
> But try to die with dignity,
> Accepting as one would an honour
> The gift of death awaiting thee.

But there was no way forward in that. The verse had no germ or
shoot in it, it exhausted itself, and was complete in itself. It could be the
end of a poem but not the beginning. But it was an end over which I did
not feel like going to a lot of trouble.

I soon lost its thread, sinking into thoughtlessness as I walked upon
the crunching leaves, but when my mind stirred and I looked about, I
found I was already in the woodland avenue, beneath the tall, arching
trees of black woodland alder, and a poem had clearly formed in my
mind. All that was left for me to do was to sit down for half a day and
write it down on paper. That is, all the rest was, as chess-players like to
say, a matter of technicalities. These were the lines I put together:

> Life is like war. And, wounded now, I stumble.
> A fatal wound. Such is the soldier's luck.
> A generation's remnants onward stumble,
> But I shall fall, flung down upon my back.
>
> But I shall fall,
> Not wrathfully or boldly,
> Accepting calmly my appointed end,
> As fell a friend who on my left lies coldly,
> As soon upon my right shall fall a friend.
>
> A ceaseless bustle weakens in the distance,
> As like a weight life's clamour falls away,
> How strange it seems, in these remaining instants,
> That there's no part in it for me to play.
>
> A wood, a path, a river, house and village,
> A spelling-book, a blackboard, pencils, pen,
> The flowers, bees, the birds and trees in foliage,
> Amid the depths of lilac – summer rain.
>
> The crackling of the logs throughout December,
> July, when woodland strawberries are picked,

The naked foot in fields of green and amber,
The rusty nail with which that foot is pricked.

Small boys and books, and catapults and toadstools,
The term, reports, attendance rather thin,
And foodstores, railway-lines, and tents and work tools,
The roaring, gnashing, shuddering and din,

The fences, chimneys, mines and courtyard mazes,
The meetings, hostels, smoking night and day,
The tightly puckered lips, the smiles and gazes
(Though nowadays they kiss another way),

The fevered verses, poets, and editions,
The trolleybuses, parties and events,
And Homer, Shakespeare, ballets and musicians,
Then till the dawn the fruitless arguments.

The towered stairways and the urban babel,
The sun of Bukhara and Georgian wine,
The sleeping pills, the lamp upon the table,
The heat of flu and sulfadimidine,

The herds of cows in fields and hobbled stallions,
My children's lively voices as they ran,
Museums, churches, dark and ancient icons,
Polluted rivers, forests spoilt by man,

Viennas, Londons, Parises and tyrants,
Receptions, telephones and large hotels,
Bananas, cognacs, *biftecks châteaubriand*,
The ocean's surf and resonance of bells,

A woman's moans in nights of adoration,
And films and skis and chess and market scents,
The triumph all, and all the tribulation,
The upward flights and violent descents,

Advances, books and critics, dissertations,
The papers in the morning, gold and lead,
Then China, problems of Near Eastern nations,
And what awaits my Russian land ahead,

And even you, your body warm and slender,
You and your beauty with its regal pride,

Who will the world but love alone surrender,
Yes, even you, the flesh personified,

And all the world of things, events, emotions,
Of future plans and worries of today,
Of some inspired, and some more humble notions
Which, like a whirlpool, spun me every way,

This world like some lost vision fast clouds over,
The battle sounds of life grow distant, die,
The sky and I remain, and nothing other,
I on the earth and over me the sky.

And now before the light of ideation
Should flee my eyes,
A single wish I own,
Beneath the watchful visage of creation
To be, if but an instant, quite alone.

Well, Agnessa Petrovna, the poem I needed to write is now written. The walk around the avenue at Karacharovo has been taken. Pick up your scalpel.

But I have not admitted until now that I asked them for an extra day, not only for the sake of collecting together my papers which were set out in the house at Karacharovo. There was another reason, a lyrical one. In order to explain it, I must make a small digression and go back two years. Literary theorists would call this section a story within a story.

19

That day an important trade-union activist came on a visit to Boris Petrovich from Moscow, and Boris Petrovich decided to treat him to the Art Gallery, which was situated not far away in the largest town of the region. They invited me to go.

The black Volga rolled smartly up to the main portal of the former Putevoi Palace of the Tsar, and we confidently started towards the entrance. Behind the dark glass of the door a board, hung crookedly on cords, announced that today was a day off at the museum.

'So much the better,' said Boris Petrovich, not at all stuck for words. 'The day off is for the visitors, but not for the staff. So the halls will be empty, we will ask to be shown round, and they will do so.'

The thought that they might refuse us did not occur to Boris Petrovich. We knocked and rang. Seeing three respectably dressed people, a simple woman door-keeper, the duty caretaker, opened up, but we could not have asked permission of her to view the Gallery. She went off dragging her shoes along the ground into the depths of the corridor, which was curved, and soon out of those depths there came a tall, slim dark-haired girl of sixth-form age, with grey-green eyes and somewhat prominent cheek-bones. She was in a white blouse. There was a flush on her cheeks (as they used to say in olden days), the colour of poppies. She timidly inquired as to why we had come. At once our Moscow guest got out his little brown book with the gold stamping, opened it and held it out for the young employee of the Gallery to see.

'I am sorry, but it is our day off. The director is away, and I cannot help you. I am a junior employee and, really . . . I am sorry.'

'And we have a writer with us, too. Perhaps you have heard of him?' Boris Petrovich let fly his last trump. 'Perhaps you have heard . . .'

The girl quickly asked the name of the writer.

'Oh, then please come in. I will take you round myself, only I cannot be very long.'

I had always been sure that I was completely free of vanity. But, my God, what a wave of nothing but satisfied vanity suddenly engulfed me at that moment. No articles in my praise, no prizes, not that I ever won any, could bring me greater joy than that surprised cry of the dark, red-cheeked girl. And at what a moment! What a triumph, how I grinned to myself! I felt a rush of gratitude towards the girl, I wanted to do something nice for her, and I told myself I would send her a book with a friendly inscription, let it come as a little surprise for her.

We walked about the empty halls of the palace. The girl told us about everything. The tour took no longer than thirty minutes. But during that time I had to find out her Christian name and surname in order to carry out my intention, otherwise, to whom would I be sending my book? I had to engage her in conversation about something other than the tour. The girl, though unwilling and more than reticent, told us she had finished secondary school but had not managed to get a place at an institute. She had not got through. She had come here and found work for the time being. But in the summer she would try again.

'Where?'

'Leningrad. The Faculty of the History of Art at the Academy of Art.'

Well. . . . I did not say anything, but thought to myself that, most probably, she would find it quite difficult to get a place. Leningrad, the Academy of Art! That is no joke.

Evidently the look of concern in my eyes did not escape our guide's attention. She said sharply, as if she were arguing with me: 'But I shall try just the same!'

Anyway, during the tour I noticed that the girl had talent, worked there with a sense of vocation, talked passionately about art, and to my earlier, perhaps unfounded impulse was added the conviction that it would be a good thing to help such a talented person.

The whole episode gradually grew dimmer in my memory and faded away. A few months went by. The Congress of the Russian Society for the Protection of Cultural Monuments was under way in Leningrad. But going to Leningrad is important anyway. You can, of course, forget the reason for going once you are there. The telephone calls begin, the encounters, walks and conversations. In this way my Leningrad friend, the artist Evgeniy Demyanovich Maltsev, and I happened to be having breakfast as guests of another major Leningrad artist. In compliance with our host's age we ate cottage cheese (with sour cream or honey as desired), enthused over his huge Newfoundland dog, then went into his studio to look at the artist's latest canvas: a naked woman lying next to a lake. The picture, executed boldly and brilliantly, delighted us, our unaffected delight overjoyed our host and the atmosphere became most warm and friendly.

Suddenly in the conversation between the two artists, who were discussing in my presence their Leningrad business affairs and problems, there was a mention of the Academy of Art. It transpired that our generous host worked there and, as luck would have it, was at the time preoccupied with allotting places for the new intake; and I immediately remembered the girl from the regional museum, how she had emerged from the depths of the building along the curved corridor, in a white blouse and with bright red cheeks . . .

'Listen now. . . . The intelligentsia is born of the intelligentsia. What chance has a girl from a village or regional school, from somewhere like Melenki near Vladimir, Balanda near Saratov or Vesely Farm, of going to the Moscow Conservatoire, the Institute of Telemechanics and Communications, or to your place, the Academy of Art? The girl dreams passionately of gaining a place in your establishment. She has tried once. No success. She's trying again. She does not know we're talking about her now. She's cramming away somewhere at home, in the town park or on the sofa, whilst all the while here, over a cup of this superb coffee, as if in heaven itself, her fate could be decided in a single instant. All she wants is a place as an external student.'

We again looked at the pictures, again enthused over the Newfoundland dog, scratched him behind the ear, shook hands with each other before taking our leave. And Zhenya and I had already stepped out of the front door when our host, who was seeing us off, suddenly asked: 'And what is the girl's name, just in case? Would she really like to study with us?'

I recall I stayed rather a long time in Leningrad and the time had come when it would be possible to find out about the success of the young school-leaver, but I did not want to involve myself in a second conversation about it, and I decided to go to the Academy of Art myself and look at the list of accepted students, which was displayed in the corridor.

I should doubtless have found those lists somewhere in the corridors but, by coincidence, I had only just reached the Academy when I caught sight of my protégée, who had just emerged from the building. She stopped in front of me, blushed as red as the three plastic cherries pinned to her grey frock, her greenish eyes flashed angrily and she very nearly stamped on me with her little foot in its provincial-looking shoe.

'How could you? Who asked you to? It's a disgrace, a disgrace! Did you think I wouldn't find out? But they as good as told me. . . . They dropped hints to me, mentioned your name. I understood everything straight away! . . .'

'But were you accepted or not, for heaven's sake?'

'That's just it, I was accepted.'

'Well, what's up then? Where's the tragedy?'

The girl said, lowering her voice: 'How am I supposed to know now how much of a right I have to study here?'

'What do you mean, how? As soon as the examination period comes round, it will all become clear. If you are not up to studying in this Institute they will expel you.'

'Really?' The newly fledged student seemed overjoyed.

'Really. But it's time for lunch now, and I want to invite you to join me.'

When we were alone at the restaurant table (beneath the dome of the Neva Restaurant), we found ourselves in a difficult situation. Neither she nor I was able to strike the right note even for those two or three hours. To distract attention from the agonizing awkwardness of the situation, I talked without stopping, saying perhaps not the silliest things, but the feeling never left me that what I was saying was of no interest whatever to my companion. She ate and drank absolutely nothing and looked at me all the time with her enormous green eyes, trying perhaps to get across some thoughts of hers, or to find out, perhaps, what I wanted of her.

I did not want anything. Or, more accurately, I wanted nothing of her when I decided to help her, nor on that day when I invited her out to lunch. But, despite that, her youthfulness, beauty, nervousness, those unblinking eyes looking at me constantly from such a close distance, the situation itself – a table in a restaurant, a glass or two of brandy which I had already drunk – all this interfered with reality and gave rise to indistinct fantasies, sending out feelers into the distant future. Finally we both realized this, so that, in order to make things clear, I was forced to say: 'Do not imagine that I need anything from you. You found out about my help by chance, and today we ran into each other by chance outside the entrance to the Academy. Now we will finish our lunch and go our different ways for ever.'

But just then I looked at her and suddenly felt a sharp, burning desire that it might not be for ever. I wanted something to hang on to, a straw, a little ray of hope. So, turning aside from the short, straight path of the sentence I had begun, I made a zigzag and started off verbosely: 'You see, the years will pass, you will study and become quite grown up . . .'

'I am grown up . . .' she interrupted impatiently.

'You will become quite grown up. Should you ever wish, you can ring me up or send a letter. Just one sentence: "I want to see you." Agreed? Let it be in a few years' time. That's not important. The main thing is that you should really wish it.'

I was leaving Leningrad and she accompanied me to the train. At the carriage door which I was about to enter, she suddenly and for me incomprehensibly burst out in anger. Instead of calmly bidding farewell and goodbye (and, hell, it would not have been out of place to say 'thank you'), she suddenly let fly in a voice broken with agitation and even malice: 'I shall never phone you or write to you. And don't you ring me, understood? And don't write. Give me your word that you won't phone or write. Give me your word!'

'As you wish! Who said I was going to? . . . Just as you wish.'

She blushed again and that blush made her even more beautiful, and an inner voice told me quite distinctly that I must immediately, in answer to her outburst, tear up my ticket, throw it down under the carriage wheels, stay there – and take whatever came. But instead of that, rather sternly and even displaying a slight feeling of offence, I said, as I took hold of the iron handrail: 'All right. I promise not to write or telephone. Live in peace and work at your studies. . . .'

The train moved off.

A great deal happens in two years of a man's life. A great deal happened with me. But in spite of all those events (books, journeys, meetings, mountains, the sea), there still remained in the end a deep-seated ache; that section of the mind which was in charge of my relationship with that girl would not forget her and was waiting for something. So somehow I was not even surprised when the occasion came and I opened an envelope, addressed in a hand still schoolgirlish, and read there on the top few lines of a page taken from a square-ruled exercise book: 'You gave me the right to write to you should I wish to. I want to see you. I want your advice. Come to our town. I'll be waiting.'

I received the letter the day before my visit to Professor Agnessa Petrovna Bazhenova. Then the isotope examinations began and after that they set the date of the operation. But it was because of the letter that I asked them for an extra day. . . .

Who would believe such a coincidence! Two years. Seven hundred odd days, and everything happened on the day before my operation. If one were writing a novel, putting together a plot, one could never think of such an improbable coincidence. But life is bolder than our creative imagination because it is not afraid to appear improbable or contrived.

So then, I shall see you after all? I shall collect up my papers, write the poem, and I shall have a whole day left. An enormous free day. The journey to your town takes an hour and a half. Can you call that a journey! It is an instant compared with eternity. So perhaps it is true that someone (under the name of fate) creates our lives. And there you have it – a present in the midst of those dark days. On the day before the operating-theatre of an oncological institute, on the day before a hospital ward, a nurse, bedpans, thermometers, soporifics, injections and the whole feeling of hopeless frustration that one has in hospital – a burst of life and light. The buffeting speed of the car, the unusualness and poignancy of a meeting after two years, wine and a smile, green eyes and black hair to the shoulders. Isotopes. . . . Isotopes, the liars! What have isotopes to do with anything if you are here, alive? You sieve through time like gold dust in which every other grain is a speck of gold. And then suddenly there is a nugget as big as a walnut!

But some damned wall kept me strangely separated from life. It was as if a sheet of glass really had come down between me and the rest of the world. Everything is visible, and even very clearly so, the relief is even greater and brighter than usual, but everything is somehow distant, existing all on its own.

I was now coming nearer to the crossroads where I could turn left to Moscow, or right to another town, her town. I had the firm intention of going right, but I found with horror that I felt neither excitement at the impending meeting nor nervousness, nor even any desire for it. On the contrary, it meant two extra hours behind the wheel and tomorrow two hours back, in addition to the inevitable road to Moscow. I was tired and it was all the same to me, I was bored with sitting at the wheel, bored with the journey, bored with watching the trees as they flashed by and the ugly mounds of earth pushed up by bulldozers, bored with looking at the grey sky and the hungry black birds sulking under a November wind. I was just bored with watching. You might imagine a film in which a gold prospector spends his life panning sand, hoping for a gold nugget, and then, when he gets the nugget in his hands, he no longer has strength enough to lift it to his eyes, or else his eyes are too weak to look at it. And everything turns misty, runs together and then goes dark.

The crossroads appeared before my radiator more quickly than I expected. Someone else switched on the left-hand indicator for me and turned the wheel to the left. Someone else experienced for me an unusual, tickling sensation on my cheek, felt with his fingers and saw that his fingers were wet. Someone else did that, whereas I was simply going to Moscow, nearer and nearer to the Herzen Oncological Institute in Begovaya Street, and farther and farther away from a young, green-eyed woman who had written on a page from an exercise book: 'I want to see you. . . . Come to our town. I'll be waiting.'

20

At Reception they had obviously been told beforehand that I would come at twelve o'clock. In any event the woman in the white coat, before filling in my papers, took a book out of her desk drawer and again, as in the laboratory a week earlier, asked me to write something in it. 'Upon entering purgatory. . . . Abandon hope outside the doors, ye who enter here.' I should have written something of that sort. But I wrote my usual: 'To dear Nadezhda Ivanovna' (let us say). 'Hoping you will remember kindly of me.'

I had to undress at once and receive for my temporary use a genuine linen nightshirt with long sleeves, a primordial vest such as I had not worn since my days as a soldier, and a pair of dark-blue, worn-out and washed-out fustian pyjamas. My new uniform. Since she had got my autograph, the woman in the white coat really could not forbid me, albeit against the regulations, to take in a grey casual shirt, so as to avoid sitting about in the fustian jacket, and also (what is far more important), a little black case of the type called 'diplomatic', full of clean paper, the half-finished literal versions of Abutalib's writings, and books.

When I had changed (the blue fustian trousers barely reached my ankles and the jacket sleeves came just a tiny bit below the elbow), they led me up the stairway to the second floor. As I went, I managed to catch a glimpse of the notice on the toilet doors: *Not for the Use of Patients*. And I am a patient. Now I am at the other side of the fence from these sisters, doctors and nurses. From now on we are divided by an invisible line. I am ill, and they are healthy. I am in a dark-blue jacket, a patient from Ward No. 60, one of the, say, forty patients occupying the second floor, and nothing more. The diagnosis has been made, all the analyses are done, the operation is set, and a bed in Ward 60 has been allotted me. One of the four, the one next to the right-hand wall, in the corner farthest from the door.

Just as a cat investigates every corner in an unfamiliar place, I walked around the corridors to see where everything was. A hall, four dining-tables, a serving-hatch, closed down at the moment. Here the patients take their plates of food, at these tables they eat. Here, too, is a refrigerator full of bags, packets, jars, bundles, bottles of milk and yoghurt. And I, too, will store here everything they bring me from home to add to the hospital diet. There is a television here also. After the evening meal they all sit down and watch it, just like in the most innocent of rest centres. A corridor leads off the hall. To the right there are medical rooms, a room for applying dressings, a treatment-room; there, too, are the medicines, linen and toilets. To the left are the wards. Not many of them on the one floor, ten in all. Their doors on to the corridor are nearly always open. That way there is more air, and lying there is not so tedious; although on our floor there are few bedridden patients. Only in the next ward but one from ours there is a woman who never lifts her head up from the pillow. Her face has turned yellow. Looking at her arm, which is stretched out above the blanket, you can tell just how limp her body is, you can see it has become resigned to the bed and only wants to lie motionless. Well, they say that on other floors they are all bedridden. One floor is for tumours of the uterus, another for stomach tumours, another for tumours of the lung. But then the sixth floor is common to all – that is where they do the cutting. Yes now, that is what they say, the seriously ill patients are on the other floors. Because even if we do have in common but one illness and one kind of death, still, when they cut out some skin and lymphatic nodules near the groin, it is not the same as when they clear out your abdomen, a breast, or do away with your stomach, gullet, or half a lung.

I had provided myself with three good detective novels to last me the first few days at least. Perhaps waiting for the operation would in the event be hard to bear, perhaps after the operation it would be nice to take my mind off things with a light adventure story. Quite apart from the problem of the operation itself, there were three others in the ward: it would also be better to leave them and go off somewhere like the London back-streets, Parisian cafés, fashionable modern hotels, large airports, international express trains, suburban villas, banquets, parties, the cabins of gigantic transatlantic ships – anywhere the author's imagination leads you.

In recent years my life had worked out in such a way that I did not have to live in hostels of any kind. Oh yes, there had been the Blue Basement, the Literary Institute's hostel, where sixteen future prose writers and poets lived together in one room. And we felt fine there. There had been times when my own family of four, or five (if my mother-in-law came), had had to settle down in one not particularly spacious room. I had also spent the night in farm-workers' hostels on one of six beds smelling of paraffin, where one inhabitant has the radio on as loudly as possible, another is asleep and snoring, and a third arrives when we are all sleeping and at once switches on the light and the radio again.

But gradually over the years (as my nerves wore out?) I started to look upon living with other people as an undeserved punishment. It began to seem absurd that they could put me in an hotel room, just like that, together with any stranger who had chanced along. And I am obliged to stay with him in the one room, chat and listen to the rubbish he talks (I am in luck if he is not drunk), listen to him puffing and coughing and sneezing (and he is obliged to put up with the same from me), but why? And I have quite ceased to understand people who go to rest centres (!) and sanatoriums (!!) in order to relax (!!!), and then live a few to a room.

Not long ago I read a scientific article about animals kept in captivity, about how large their cages or compounds should be. It seems that the important thing is not the size of their living space. You would not like to live in something the size of a factory shop. It seems as though it is more important for the animal to have a refuge where it can be alone. Without such a refuge the animal perishes very quickly, even if its compound is full of space. The animal has to hide away, sit out for a bit, and only then will it need the surrounding space.

With the passing of the years I have noticed that my whole life is subjugated (aside from various literary designs, ideas, plans, trips and enthusiasms) to two opposing urges: the urge to be alone when I am surrounded by hustle and bustle, and the urge to throw myself into hustle and bustle when I am alone.

Our human community is fine, going to the theatre, the stadium, out visiting, going to meetings, grand literary evenings, dinner with friends, art exhibitions, the beach, meetings of the editorial board. . . . Our trolleybuses are fine, the buses, the metro, the shops full of people, the cinemas, cafés, post offices, restaurants, simply the streets. But, when all is said and done, I have to remain in my room alone, sit down in a comfortable armchair and switch on the table-lamp. Complete isolation would probably make me scream in a month or so; the impossibility of solitude would finish me in three days. This is what I was thinking when they put me in the ward with the four beds. And for this reason I armed myself with the trusty detective stories. I saw my refuge in those three books which I had smuggled in in my little contraband case.

But on that day I simply never got as far as reading. Not because the people interfered, but because . . . it somehow worked out that the need to seek refuge with the help of books did not arise.

A particular rapport sprung up between me and each of the three patients. They were all different, if one did not count the common feature – the illness by reason of which we had all come to be here.

Victor Mikhaylovich, the person in the bed opposite mine, who has had one leg amputated at the groin and, naturally, uses crutches (which turned out to be very convenient for me during the first two days after my operation), is a man of about fifty-five, on the small side, but robustly built. He is an executive with responsibilities throughout the rural district. Straight after the war, when they needed personnel, it is possible that he worked even as secretary of the District Committee. But then his inadequate educational qualifications caused him to be moved back into secondary posts, then came the loss of the leg, the pension and this illness. At home he runs a Zaporozhets. He frequently quarrels with his wife, because, he says, of her temperament.

'I tell her: "Galya, bring some water for me to drink with my tablets during the night. I forgot." And she answers: "You go and get it. You think too much of yourself." '

'And what do you do?' I ask, seeing that the story is not continuing.

'Well, what? I get her with a crutch.'

'And what does she do?'

'Runs off to complain. But what's the point? I'm an invalid. They won't put me inside. Or we go off for a ride in the Zaporozhets and settle down on the edge of a wood. It's a place for sitting about in and relaxing. But no, she starts to nag: "Let's go back home." What sort of relaxation is that?'

But, as I saw it, he was recalling all these annoying trifles because there had been a more recent and greater cause for offence. He has been in hospital for a few months already. He is bored. His illness, as they say, is hanging fire. He has long understood that he should go home. It is the same wherever you are, once you are ill. He wrote a letter to his wife to come. Without her he cannot even be discharged, because he was admitted in the summer wearing a suit, and now it is the end of November, he needs warm things. And his wife has not come. Now he is pinning his hopes on his brother. He is lying and waiting for him to bring him his hat and coat. He was always the first to start a conversation with me.

'Well, tell me. If you write a book, do you hand it over for checking?'

'What is there to check?'

'What do you mean? You could write anything. Perhaps something which doesn't measure up.'

'Measure up to what?'

'Well . . . instructions, regulations.'

I was starting to describe the path by which a manuscript makes its way into a journal or publishing house, but soon our conversation of its own accord began to skip over on to subjects which really did not comply with the theme and character of this essay. Two Russians (and they knew this even a hundred years ago), once they have become acquainted and got talking, are unable to resist immediately discussing the main political problems facing, if not humanity, then at least their own people.

But gradually conversation between us grew easier, a great deal became clear and now Victor Mikhaylovich was able to open with the most unexpected questions.

'Now then. You have travelled abroad. Is it true that you have to pay for a spell in hospital there?'

'I haven't been a patient in foreign hospitals. But they do say that you have to pay. And a great deal too.'

'Well, how much?'

'I don't know exactly. And they have different types of hospital there. Some are more expensive than others.'

'Let's say a hospital like the one we're in now.'

'We are in. . . . We are in. . . . In the USSR there are only two such institutes. The Kashirka and this one.'

'And so?'

'Let's consider my case, for instance. The operation will be performed by a professor. Not less than a thousand dollars. The anaesthetist stands to get, let's say, three hundred. All the tests and investigations – about fifty dollars a time. And occupying a bed – a hundred dollars a day.'

Victor Mikhaylovich even jumped up in bed.

'What are they charging all that for?'

'Sisters, nurses, duty doctors, medicines, expensive apparatus, equipment in general. If it's a private clinic, it's got to justify its existence and show a profit as well.'

'So what happens? You spend twenty days there and it costs a few thousand? And I've been here for how many months already! . . .'

'Well, there you would not stay for months. Your Galya would soon come running after you.'

We might be silent, or I might be dozing, face to the wall, or reading a book (now I am recalling the questions which Victor Mikhaylovich asked, not necessarily on the first day of my stay, but on other days, too) when, without any preamble, but in a voice loud enough for me to understand that I was being drawn into conversation, Victor Mikhaylovich would utter: 'How is it that there are so many learned people around, science, so to speak, has put us on the moon, yet many people think that some part of a man remains after death. The soul, for instance. What sort of darkness must you be in to believe that!'

'You and I won't remain. But perhaps *something* will remain of us,' I said, egging my partner on.

'How's that?'

'You know bubbles in water? In the rain or at the edge of the sea in the surf. There are big and little bubbles, but every bubble is a bubble, nevertheless, right?'

'Of course.'

'But what are they made of?'

'Air and nothing else. Air and a thin envelope.'

'Right, a membrane. Now let's imagine that the bubble bursts. It's disappeared, died, ceased to exist. The bubble is no more. The membrane has disappeared. But of course its contents have not disappeared. They merge in with the rest of the air, with the atmosphere, the great ocean of air. Well, some people suppose that there is perhaps an ocean of the spirit. Bubbles appear and burst, appear and burst, but the atmosphere as a whole, from which they are made and which they merge with again, continues to exist. . . .'

After that Victor Mikhaylovich was quiet for a whole hour. I thought his next question would be about Paris, about the food there, or something different, like collective farms. But my amusing idea about bubbles had evidently become firmly entrenched in Victor Mikhaylovich's head.

'But the envelope, where does it go, then?'

'The envelope is made of water. It merges with the puddle. Or the sea. You are taken from the water and must return to the water. The envelope goes downwards, but its contents go up. . . .'

Another inhabitant of our ward, Yakov Vasilyevich, came here with a relapse. A few months ago in Yalta he had a small black thing (like mine) cut out, and now just a few days before my arrival they had removed the lymphatic nodes in his groin. He had a pale-pink face and his grey hair produced rather the impression of a rain-cloud than a coiffure. He did not take part in our discussions and in general spoke little, although he did get round to saying that his wife had left him, that he now lived alone and that if they discharged him now he would be unlikely to go straight to Yalta. There he had to keep his stove going and, in addition, cross the entire yard to the toilet, and walking was difficult for him. So that, perhaps, some distant relatives in Moscow would take him in for a time.

In his relations with each of us he had little to say but much to do. He was the first to save a place for all of us, both in the queue for meals and at the table. When Victor Mikhaylovich was running a temperature, without asking anyone at all he brought him his food into the ward. He did the same for me on the first day after the operation. He unobtrusively tidied up if any of us was careless enough to leave any litter in the place. He had made friends in other wards and would go off to them for a couple of hours.

In all that time I came to know nothing about Ivan Adolfovich: neither who he was, nor what he was or had been. We knew about him only what it was impossible not to know: he too was a 'relapser'. A few months ago they had cut out a black thing (like mine) on his upper lip. Now he was being prepared for an operation to remove the lymphatic nodes around the throat. He was a Muscovite. Every day his wife or his daughter would come and he would sit for a long time with them in the hall. The rest of the time he was ready to play chess, over which he forgot all about himself and played fanatically. Without noticing how, I found myself facing him across a chess-board within the first fifteen minutes. And when they brought me back after the operation and I could not yet turn over from my back to my side, I still played chess with him before an hour had passed, squinting and awkwardly pushing the chessmen about with my left hand. In twenty days I think we must have played about a hundred games or more.

Such was the crew of our doleful Ward No. 60.

21

In the evening they injected me with a sedative so that I would not be anxious before the operation and would sleep better. In spite of this I had a terrible dream. I dreamt that they had trained dogs, Alsatians, to sniff out cancer tumours inside the human body, just as they find narcotics in Customs, even when they are hidden in car tyres. And so there I lie, naked, and a large dog is sniffing me all over. My lungs, gullet, stomach. Having reached the liver, it started to sniff with particular intensity, and suddenly, pushing its nose under my ribs on my right-hand side, started to whine. I woke up. The large rectangle of the window had turned from black, through the lilac stage, to grey. The window had two long lower portions and two short upper ones. So the vertical bar and transom rose above all of us who lay in Ward 60, like a correctly proportioned graveyard cross, only without the small lower crossbars. And so I lay beneath this cross until the light was put on. A nurse came into the ward and thrust us a thermometer each.

At eight-thirty they gave me another injection, and at nine precisely both halves of the door opened wide and Nurse Galya, small and nicely proportioned, in a shining, crisp coat, pushed in a tall, long and narrow trolley. In fact, a stretcher on wheels. She told me to undress completely, lie down on the stretcher and cover myself with a sheet.

'But I can go up to the fifth floor myself and then lie down on the operating-table. Why on earth cart me on this trolley whilst I am still mobile and strong?'

'It's procedure.' And off she went.

I quickly lay down under the sheet and Galya reappeared straight away. She pushed me to the lift under the sympathetic and understanding glances of the patients at breakfast, then up and into a room glinting this time with the nickel of surgical instruments, where there was a huge round lamp above the so far empty table and a large number of people in green surgical coats waiting for me around it.

'Well, how do you feel?' Agnessa Petrovna blasted off. 'How did you sleep? Never mind, everything will be fine. Lie down here now.'

There immediately appeared at my head a young woman, the anaesthetist.

'Are you my guardian angel or a Valkyrie?' I joked.

'What's a Valkyrie?'

'A receiver.'

'Receiver of what?'

'Of my soul.'

'Then I am your guardian angel.' And she started to apply to the veins in the bend of my right elbow a rubber tube with a needle on the end, leading upwards to some glass containers. They tied my left arm down to the table. They also tied my legs.

'Don't worry, Vladimir Alekseevich. Now I shall start the anaesthetic. Try to breathe as deeply as possible.' And she opened the valve on the rubber tube so that, apparently, some sort of liquid would run into my vein. I conscientiously started to breathe as deeply as possible and once more heard a woman's voice above me: 'Can you hear me? Can you hear me? Open your eyes!'

With some difficulty I opened my sticky eyelids and perceived that there was now no operating-theatre, and that I was lying in another room altogether, and that in my thigh there was a dull, drawn-out ache.

'Now then, wake yourself up properly. I'll be back in about two hours.'

In America now they put certain millionaires into deep-freeze so that later, in a hundred or two hundred years' time, they can bring them back to life and cure them. Does that mean that for them, too, there will no interval between the closing and opening of their eyes? In my case one and a half to two hours went by. And it would have been just the same if there had not been so much as a moment, just as there was no break at all between the two phrases of the anaesthetist: 'Try to breathe deeply' and 'Open your eyes.' Not even a second went by. Nothing at all went by. No time at all. Zero. Absolute zero. Sometimes they do not wake up after the anaesthetic. . . .

Although I had opened my eyes, I must still have been half asleep. I did not move my arm at once, nor did I immediately start to shift about a little to make myself more comfortable. Something glimmered at the back of my mind, some blue flashes of ideas and notions, but they were all in a mist, made little sense and did not trouble me at all. Just one thought stood out brighter than the others: a single moment had not passed and they had already done everything that they wanted. They had chopped away half my thigh. That is not so bad; you could wake up with the thought that there is no, let us say, stomach inside you. How does that strike you?

Nurse Galya appeared once more, trundled me to the lift and down into the ward. She helped me to move off the tall trolley and lie down on the low bed. I lay down and settled myself in. Out of sheer joy that my stomach was still whole I immediately drank a bottle of milk. Ivan Adolfovich quickly sat down near me, moved up another chair and put the chess-board on it. Squinting and with an awkward pushing of my left hand, I moved the king's pawn.

22

Once in an electric train, somewhere between Serpukhov and Chekhov (I was travelling back after staying with Serafima Fedorovna and Nikolay Ilyich), I could not help overhearing the conversation going on behind me, on the two carriage seats backing mine.

'If only one knew beforehand that, for example, one was going to die in a month's time or, say, in a week.'

'What would happen?'

'Well, what? There'd be no end to your power and freedom.'

'What freedom, if you die in a week?'

'This freedom. I could, let's say, go and kill somebody I hate. They'd put me on trial, in prison. But me? After a week it's all over. I am protected from them by knowing when I'll die.'

'Who, then, would you kill?'

'I'm not talking about myself, just in general. Right now in the train I could go and kill five or six people. Great! They'd handcuff me, prepare to shoot me, but I couldn't care less. I'd die in a week just the same.'

'What weird thoughts.'

'Oh no, I'm not serious. Just wondering. What if you were to take that view. Or you could set fire to your neighbour's cottage. That would be a fine sight too. Imagine it burning up. Expensive books, his grand piano . . .'

'Murder and arson – I think that's pointless. It's going too far.' A third person had entered the conversation. 'But now if you were to sell your belongings, everything you can, and spend the money on as much pleasure and drink as you can squeeze in, that's the thing! Sell everything except the clothes you stand up in and calculate things according to your remaining days. Say you are supposed to die on a Monday, then you spend your last twenty copecks on drink on the Sunday.'

'But why spend it on drink?' put in a man with a quiet but confident voice. 'You should give all your possessions away to other people. It's all the same to you, you are dying, but it's a help to them. . . .'

At this point, before anything else was said in answer, I turned the whole conversation over in my head, and I realized that it touched upon, albeit in so simplified a form, two major aspects of human behaviour, two basic, if not philosophic, then moral areas. If a man lived alone (Robinson), then the formula 'give and take' would have practical significance for him only in relation to nature. But man lives in crowded conditions. Every day and every minute he enters into various relationships with those who live with him in one family, in one apartment, one town and, of course, in one society. However varied the actions a man performs amidst his fellows, however complex his behaviour, all the same there is no escaping his two basic functions: 'I give' and 'I take'.

We shall not touch upon the relationship between these two functions in working life, which is systematized in one way or another, particularly as in the sphere of work they frequently do not enter a man's consciousness. He works eight hours and receives his pay. He does not think about whether he gave in those eight hours more or less than he received in the form of pay. We shall take it that in this case the proportions are balanced by Gosplan. And, anyway, that is not the point because we have here a kind of obligatory giving and obligatory taking. We are talking not about a man's behaviour at work, where things are determined in large part by regulations and life's necessities, but about his moral, voluntary behaviour, about the properties and qualities of his soul.

It is not difficult to notice that people's tendency 'to take' is developed a little more than the tendency 'to give'. Many philosophers have seen in this fact the human race's basic evil, its basic vice and the basic cause of its future perdition. Indeed, there are people who profess and even teach others: 'Take, grab everything you can.' Money, a factory, a group of businesses, power, a neighbouring state, a country house, an apartment, women, all the good things of life. As a half-way stage, some people say: 'Yes, I'll take money, factories, businesses, neighbouring states, millions of human lives. I'll take them – but why? In order to give them away to people. I'll take from some and give to others. In this way, in doing evil, I shall be creating good.'

Oh, that age-old question of good and evil! It is obvious to all that good is better. People think that man may achieve the highest joy only by doing good – that is, by giving in the widest, moral, psychological (yes, and also literal) meaning of the word. They think that to do good to others is a purer and deeper joy than doing good for oneself alone. That is the basis of the idealistic concept of Christianity. If all (ALL) give away everything (EVERYTHING) one to another, a blissful golden life will begin. That is, if there are on earth only sheep alone, the threat of being eaten or killed and made into shashlyk is reduced to nil. But what if just one man on earth were a wolf? What if everyone gave over and again, and that one man busied himself all the while with the opposite activity? Would he not in the end gather everything into his own hands to the point that the others would have nothing left to give each other? And what if there turned out to be a number of such gatherers? And could ten thousand sheep re-educate a single wolf and make him a sheep? And what if the gatherers were in the majority? So the theory might be correct, but humanity has somehow not yet matured enough for it, and there is no danger of its maturing enough for it in the near future.

I do not know if I should once more repeat that I have been speaking here not about giving away property and money in the literal sense, but about one's psychological attitude in principle, and that only occurs in two forms: with a plus sign or with a minus sign. Imagine that you have felt a cold sensation about the heart: go and get on with giving things away. Make peace with those people who (as you think) are your enemies. Instead of not greeting them when you meet, write articles in their praise. Renounce love (not in the philosophic, but in the biological sense of the word), renounce collecting old works of art. Reject your spacious apartment. Renounce all action that might cause others even the slightest bit of unpleasantness. Replace all the joys of life (perhaps indeed imaginary, illusory, tawdry) with the joy of self-denial, the joy of GIVING.

But you, perhaps, like humanity in general, have not grown into this ideal state and, whilst you are alive, will remain a human being and cer-tainly not an angel. But, possibly, just during the last minutes. . . . But will you know that they *are* the last? Whilst there is breath, there is hope.

I went over all this in my mind after the comment, as you will remember, of the fourth speaker with his quiet but confident voice: 'But why spend it on drink? You should give all your possessions away to other people. It's all the same to you, you are dying, but it's a help to them.'

Perhaps I would have developed my ideas further, but at that point one of those arguing answered, and I was struck by the simplicity with which he destroyed in a moment the fine concept of the one who was for giving one's possessions away.

'So what?' he countered. 'If you give them to others, they'll sell them for drink. There are no longer people around who need saving from death by starvation. . . . Perhaps in other countries. We may say someone is poor, but he watches television every evening. So you give them to him. He'll say "thank you", but he'll be laughing at you inside. Look what a saint, he'll think, not like ordinary people. A weird one. Or off his head. He went and gave me this out of the blue. A weird one! Go on, go on, give it away, empty your purse, take off your shirt. . . .' He argued more and more heatedly, noticing that his opponent was sitting with downcast eyes and not speaking.

But at this point the station at Chekhov came up and the 'philosophers', who had given me a few interesting minutes, got out.

23

My time in hospital dragged on. At six o'clock in the morning they tap you on the shoulder and give you a thermometer. You push it under your armpit and drop off again. Once a day the doctor treating your case drops in and and asks how you feel. The rest of the time is free. At first the arrangement was that relatives and friends could visit the patients at any time during the day. I rang a friend of mine from the Interns' Common Room and explained how to find me.

'Of course not. You don't need permission to come. You can bring that too. We'll celebrate my operation. Of course, I haven't had so much as a sniff of it for a whole year because of my liver, but listen. . . . With the disease I have now, what am I going to do with my first-class liver? Take it on outstretched hands to show to the Lord God? "Look what a wonderful liver I managed to preserve. I did not touch a drop of wine and lived on cottage cheese and honey." No, bring it along. Any time. There are no restrictions here. We're like condemned men here, we're allowed everything.'

I was joking, of course, when I said that. But Dr Olga Aleksandrovna was put on her guard and started to listen in to my babbling. She pricked up her little ears. Probably at the morning five-minute meeting she reported on what the patients felt about their (on the whole correct) regulations, and from the next day the patients were allowed visitors only from four to six.

Being at the very bottom of the hospital hierarchy, as a run-of-the-mill patient, I could understand the majesty of the professorial rank. The patients look upon the arrival of the doctor in charge as a great event, a gift of grace; but when Agnessa Petrovna's voice boomed out in the corridor, a reverential whisper passed along the wards: 'The General has come. The General . . . Agnessa Petrovna.'

Run of the mill I might have been; nevertheless, I persuaded matron Valentina Aleksandrovna to give me the key to her room, and when she went home (about five) I had a superb refuge. A large study, a writing-table with a telephone. Now for a few hours a day I could work, although I was not used to writing in the evening.

Seeing that the days were slipping by in hospital anyway, I asked if they would give me a general examination at the same time. So that during the day I sometimes pattered along the corridors to be X-rayed, to have my kidneys examined or my liver scanned.

A few events occurred in the ward. Victor Mikhaylovich nearly surrendered completely to depression. I saw he had tears in his eyes. He wanted to tell me something, but his lips trembled and would not obey him.

They performed an operation on Ivan Adolfovich and he could not play chess for two days. He did not feel so good. At night he snored unbearably because the operation was near his throat and his larynx was swollen. After the operation they prescribed drugs for him.

Usually they say this: 'Well, congratulations. You turned out to be perfectly all right. But to reinforce the result, to make it fully guaranteed, so that you never go through it again, we have prescribed radiation treatment for you.'

Radiation and drugs. Radiotherapy and drug therapy. Patients, however poorly they understand the details of their illness, nevertheless know that if radiation and drugs are prescribed, then it means they have really got it. But they know this so long as radiation and drugs are being prescribed to other patients. When, on the other hand, it is their own turn, they look at the doctor, their eyes large and full of hope, and listen to what he says as if bewitched.

'You are quite all right. Everything is as it should be. But to reinforce the result, as a further prophylactic measure. . . . Exclusively for preventive purposes.'

So that, when after the operation I spoke on the telephone to a surgeon acquaintance, the first thing he did was to ask me: 'Have they prescribed radiation?'

'No.'

'Drugs?'

'Not that either.'

'Has the histology come through already?'

'That's the thing. It's eight days now and their is still no histology.'

When patients wait after their operation for the histology, that is an investigation under the microscope of the tumour that has been removed, it is just like those agonizing minutes when the Court has retired to deliberate and soon the cry will ring out: 'All rise. The Court is in session!' And a solemn voice will be heard announcing the sentence. Only here those agonizing minutes go on for a few days.

I do not know what peculiarities there are in my personal make-up such that I felt no anguish whilst waiting for the histological analysis. I could not wait for them to take out the stitches, could not wait to be discharged (actually, I was somehow not particularly impatient about that); nevertheless when ten days had passed and there was no histology, I inquired of Olga Aleksandrovna what, after all, was happening there.

'It is not a quick business. You must realize that they first remove the fat from the tumour, then they saturate it with paraffin, then take some thin sections. Ten days, that's quite normal. It's never any faster.'

I thought that the professor would come with her entourage. Or she would summon me to her office. Or that during the medical round there would be a grand announcement. . . . But just before noon, at a most inconvenient time, when Ivan Adolfovich was setting in motion against me an attack of pawns on the king's flank, in his enthusiasm not noticing that by so doing he left his king unprotected, the duty doctor, a man still very young, dropped in to the ward for a minute as if by chance, in passing. Without any sort of preamble he reported: 'Well, I can congratulate you. You are quite all right. The histology is fine. Congratulations.'

At that moment I was making a move with a knight and, before I had completed it, the young man had disappeared.

On that same day, whilst I was having my dressing changed, Agnessa Petrovna's deputy, Leonid Danilovich, told me as I lay in front of him: 'Consider that you have won a lottery. The chances were one in a hundred thousand. We didn't tell you, but the diagnosis was the worst possible. And now the most important thing is not to think about it at all.'

'Aren't you going to prescribe radiation and drugs, then?' I said, testing things out a little.

'We rely on the body's own defence mechanisms,' Olga Aleksandrovna was quick to answer, but Leonid Danilovich gave her such a look that she immediately bit her lip.

'But what about the isotopes? I thought there were a good many of them jumping around in there.'

'Did they tell you how many?'

'I don't know the significance of the figures, but I understood a thing or two from their anxious expressions.'

'Oh, those laboratory people! Your isotopes were higher than normal evidently because in that thing of yours which we removed the blood-vessels were terribly thickly knotted. And so it's because of them that the mistake in diagnosis occurred.'

They talk convincingly. 'Sometimes we say things so well we even believe them ourselves.' A sick man becomes so suspicious! Tone of voice, comparisons between what the doctor said yesterday and what he said today – for the patient everything is an object of attention and reflection.

'We rely on the body's defence mechanisms.' If the histological analysis showed that the tumour was not malignant, why, one wonders, rely on anything? You do not have to rely at all. I shall somehow survive without your relying on anything. If, on the other hand, you are relying. . . .

And here is another revealing episode. To have my liver scanned I went to the same laboratory where they did my isotope examination, only it was in a next-door room. When I left, Zhanna Pavlovna was talking on the telephone in the hall.

'. . . Not at all. I saw it myself. It turned out to be so small without the fat. The isotopes? Simply a large number of small blood-vessels had knotted together there. No, no. He's fine. I am certain.'

'Oh, it's you!' Zhanna Pavlovna put the receiver down and turned towards me. 'As it happens, I was talking about your tumour.'

'I realized that. Who were you talking to?'

'Leonid Danilovich.'

'Ah . . .'

'So just carry on. The main thing is, don't think about it. And everything will be as it should be.'

Everything will be as it should be, or everything is as it should be? And why is it that they are always advising me not to think about it? I remember when Nasreddin promised a merchant some buried treasure, he put him in a sack for a whole day and said that the treasure would be found on condition that the merchant did not think of a monkey.

And so, Zhanna Pavlovna had no other time in those ten days to talk about me, except for the moment when I could hear her conversation? Anyway, they had already discussed and gone over everything twenty times! And why should she be explaining to Leonid Danilovich about the blood-vessels if he had only just been explaining them to me himself? But they deserve to be thanked, of course. It's the thought that counts.

When I was going home and saying goodbye to Olga Aleksandrovna, the doctor in charge of my case, I made her a promise: 'I'll write a short account. I'll put down all I went through because of this.'

'But what did you go through? After all, you didn't know the danger, the abyss you were hanging over.'

'And what if I had known?'

'And you still kept so calm?'

'What else was there for me to do? . . .'

The days passed, the stitches were healing, I was beginning to forget the hospital. Was the clock at work inside me? Did it start up, switched on by the surgeon's knife? That would become clear in the course of a year. In each of us there is a clock. The only difference is in the figure at which the extra hand of the alarm is set.

For some reason even before the operation I had not been too worried about my misfortune, but now I was completely at ease. They did it, after all – the doctors sold me the idea. And I, in my turn, began to sell it to all my friends and acquaintances.

'You know, the diagnosis was not confirmed. They were very alarmed after the isotope tests, but the histological analysis . . .'

'Yes, they cut out a very large piece of me. They were too careful. A very wide excision. But you can understand them. You know, after the isotope tests they thought. . . . But everything is all right now.'

'Why are the stitches healing badly? The skin is stretched a great deal. They chopped out a kilogram of flesh. But it will heal. The chief thing is that it turned out to be a false alarm.'

'Why the anaesthetic? Well . . . I don't know. They spent a long time exploring, they were probably checking the lymphatic nodes.

Yes, thank God, it looks as though I came through safe and sound.'

Future plans began to glimmer in my head about where to go in April or May. What should I do with the coming summer? How should I continue my novel? And, in general, what should I do next in life? A few people, to whom I spoke about this, thought I was putting it on and being hypocritical, but there was a moment, I distinctly remember, a moment when I realized with palpable annoyance (let us put it less forcefully – with some annoyance) that I had once more to hitch myself to the cart of life and pull the load. Perhaps for that reason I finally went to a library to search out a book I had been meaning to find for a long time. How strange that, with all those masses of conversations about isotopes, I still had not got around to discovering what is considered normal in such tests, what is looked upon as an alarming deviation from the normal, and what would mean illness. The difference between my unhealthy and healthy places was, if I have not forgotten: 400—70, 420—75, 390—60, 360—70. And then there were the figures for the second day: 300—60, 310—56, 290—70.

But what do these figures signify? Are they good or bad? How bad? Tiny blood-vessels. . . . Thousands of patients pass through their laboratory, and not one with tiny blood-vessels? No, I must get hold of the book and find out once and for all what the figures mean.

I put a pile of specialist books down in front of me and started to thumb through them quickly. The ghastly details of tumours I could do without. I knew what I was looking for and soon wrote out conscientiously and painstakingly on a piece of paper, as if I were preparing to write a polemical article and had hit upon a very effective argument which would slaughter my opponent:

Professor R. Raychev, VI. Andreev, 'Malignant Tumours of the Skin', *Medicine and Physical Training*, Sofia.

Together with R. Lazarev and P. Penchev we also investigated the test with radioactive phosphorus (P^{32}). 44 patients were investigated with various skin tumours, including 31 with malignant melanomas. The average size of the RV factor in melanomas is about 4.0; in spinocellular carcinomas, 2.1; in basocellular carcinomas, 1.5; and in benign pigmental formations, 1.0-1.8. The RV factor is the relationship between the impulses received from an area of the tumour under investigation, compared with a symmetrical area of healthy skin.

24

It's June in your life, though
September in mine.
Where you're green and youthful,
In silver I shine.

Each life something loses
And something receives.
Now – you are white daisies
But I am dead leaves.

The bright gulls are flying,
My eyes are like lead.
On grass we were lying
So late out of bed.

But now let the gloom
And the darkness entwine,
While here in this room
We'll have warmth, we'll have wine.

To life when it loses
And when it receives!
To your field of daisies
And my falling leaves!

25

'Eve? Hello, Eve.'
'I can't hear you.'
'I'll ring again.'
'There we are. That's better. How are things with you?'
'What do you mean?'
'How do you feel?'
'Splendid. . . . Can you drop everything and come away with me
for a few months?'
'Where to?'
'We'll think of somewhere. Kamchatka, Tobolsk, Lake Baykal, the
Caucasus, Samarkand, Dushanbe, Moldavia, Susamyr, Leningrad,

Beloe Lake, Warsaw, Paris, the Solomon Islands . . .'

'Today's Tuesday? On Wednesday I'm having a fitting. I'm sorry, but I can't leave before the day after tomorrow.'

NOTES

[1] The business did get as far as a quack in the end. Much later I had to go to Bulgaria. There, in Sofia, I found a fellow sufferer – the remarkably gifted writer and poetess Blaga Dimitrova. She had also had an operation, one similar to mine, only cavitary, so the complications were multiplied. Someone recommended to her a folk doctor, Petr Dimkov, a revered ninety-year-old. When she was about to visit him for the first time, Blaga suggested I go as well, and I did.

Dimkov has a diagnostic method all of his own. He sits the patient down before him on a chair and with the help of a magnifying glass looks into the pupil of the eye; on the wall there hangs a map, looking like the two hemispheres. It is a diagram of the eyes. The eyes are speckled with hundreds of dots. Each dot is supposed to correspond to one or another illness.

His flat is modestly furnished. Petr Dimkov treats people for nothing. I have heard he has written a book a thousand pages long on folk, or, more precisely, his own medicine, and they say that the book will soon be published.

He looked into both my eyes too.

'I'll give you a little jar of jam. But that's only to start you off. For a full course of treatment you will need a good deal of it. This is how to make it: you take some wild elderberries [the unpleasantly smelling grass elder, *sambucus ebulus* – V.S.], spread them out evenly, one finger thick. You pour on to the berries a layer of granulated sugar to the same thickness. You have to wait for all the sugar to dissolve. Then you strain it all and the syrup is ready. You don't have to turn it into jam. The course of treatment is as follows: ten minutes before meals you drink not quite a glassful of distilled water (150 grams), and after the meal, for dessert, you eat a tablespoon of the syrup.

'If you continue like that for six weeks, you'll be as fit as an Eskimo,' Dr Dimkov concluded, 'and as slender as a soldier of the Queen's Guard. If everyone ate this syrup, there would be eighty [eighty!] per cent fewer malignant diseases. If you had come to me at the right time, even an operation would not have been necessary.'

By way of lyrical digression he told me a few details about the elder. Swallows fill themselves with wild elderberries before flying across the sea, and then without resting conquer huge distances with ease. A weasel will attack snakes: if a snake bites the weasel, he stops fighting, runs off, quickly eats his fill of elderberries and immediately returns to vanquish his foe.

'But what is the point of the distilled water?'

'It cleans the blood – when taken together with the elderberries. If you drink a glass of ordinary water, at least a third of it is retained by the body. If the water is distilled, then not only does that water itself all pass through, but it will take out with it a third of a glassful of other water from the body too.'

At this point Dimkov showed us his portable apparatus for distilling water, which operated non-stop and produced up to a litre in twenty-four hours. These pieces of apparatus are apparently sold in Sofia and cost fifty-five levs (about sixty roubles), but they are not readily sold to private individuals, as they are very good for making plum brandy.

I have not yet embarked upon this course of treatment. In the first place I have only just returned from Bulgaria. Secondly, wild elderberries can be gathered only in areas more to the south, they do not grow in our country. Thirdly . . . thirdly, not one of our reference books recommends it as a medicinal herb, and the *Great Soviet Encyclopaedia* mentions it only as a means of getting rid of mice and bed-bugs. Fourthly . . . fourthly, it would all be somehow too simple.

[2] Fate gave me the chance to see a case in which a man decided against an operation. I had a guest at home – a writer and poet from a small town. I told him about my operation (it had already been done by then). At this the guest unbuttoned the top buttons of his shirt and showed me something without saying a word. In the hollow of his chest there sat a black, flattish, plate-shaped thing (I shall not try to find another word), in comparison with which my pea was rather like a chick alongside a full-grown turkey. It was about the size of a three-copeck piece and, furthermore, a few lentil-like bits had sprung up around it.

'What? Has it been there long?'

'Eighteen years. For fifteen years it just sat there and didn't grow. It was like a pea. For the past three years it has been growing. I think I'll last about another five years.'

So, eighteen plus five – twenty-three years. That is the lot of a man who 'pushed himself away' from the dangerous shore. For no patient lives for so many years after the operation. If he does, it means his tumour was not malignant. They frequently die during the first months after the operation and rarely (10 per cent) make it past three years. There is a decision for you – put in at a shore with crocodiles and cannibals, or make away from the land to the open sea. Unfortunately the episode with my guest and his illness took place after my operation. Anyway, I should not have refused the operation even so.

TITTLE-TATTLE
Small Unintentional Mystifications

During the summer months in the country you cannot help relaxing; you dress casually in loose-fitting clothes, so that you can sit on the ground, make your way through the scrub and nettles on the river-bank, get wet in the rain and then dry out again in the wind and sun. The same thing with shaving. You tire of shaving every day as you do in Moscow, and you give it a miss for four days. A reddish stubble appears on your cheeks along with a great many whiskers which have lost their colour. You do not look quite like a convict on the run, but you are no angel either.

A research worker from one of the literary museums, Svetlana Efimovna Strizhneva, who had come as it happens to our village in search of some manuscripts, was spending the night at Alexandra Kuzminichna's. Over tea they began to talk about the local writer.

'Well, and what's he like?' asked Svetlana Efimovna with interest.

'He's all right really. Only he's not very well turned out.'

'What do you mean?'

'Well, he is from Moscow. He's sometimes on television. Well, he should dress accordingly. A hat, sandals, some sort of tie, a nylon shirt. But he puts on some baggy thing over his trousers and struts about like that.'

My car with its tarpaulin roof (that old runabout of mine, that same old Jeep, the old goat) was getting worn out and scruffy. Scraps of tarpaulin were hanging down in places, there was a draught coming in through the rents and they dripped whenever it rained. In the early days we washed it perhaps twice a day, but now I do not even remember when I last did so. I might well have not washed it for a couple of years now. How does it look when an unshaven character peers out of that sort of a banger, especially if, in place of the hat recommended by Alexandra Kuzminichna, he has a scarf with blue spots tied about his head like a pirate? I love walking in a headscarf – it does not slip over your eyes, catch on to branches in the forest, get blown around by the wind or slip about.

This 'external appearance' has given rise to a number of small amusing leg-pulls, albeit unpremeditated. A couple of them are even worth writing down.

1

When you drive over our way, after leaving the Moscow road, here and there where the side-roads emerge on to the asphalt from the hinterland of fields and paths, people are standing, two or three people trying to get a passing car to stop. I have made it a rule not to stop when I see their raised, beckoning hands. First, you cannot pick them all up. Secondly, there is a regular bus which will collect them all anyway. Thirdly, you have thoughts of your own and sometimes you are stumbling through a poem. Fourthly, there is that absurd moment when they begin to push fifteen copecks towards you for the lift. You do not take the money, the passenger insists, you begin to get angry, you raise your voice and end up swearing at him. And so, in place of simple gratitude, he goes away swearing back at you.

But at the turn of the road there stood an old woman, as the poet said, 'in an old-fashioned shabby coat, with a bundle in her arms'. She was the traditional sort of old woman and I stopped to let her get in. Businesslike, not in the least bit shy or timid, she removed a parcel which was lying on the seat, settled down and made herself comfortable and, since I hesitated whilst I looked at her, ordered: 'Well, what are we waiting for? Put your foot on the accelerator!'

I did and off we went. What a good opportunity to have a talk with an elderly person, to ask her about things and see what she had to say! But the old lady was first to take the initiative.

'Who do you work for?'

'I'm from Forty Octobers.'

'Ah, what a stroke of luck. First and foremost I'm from your area. From Burdachevo. Perhaps you've heard of it.'

'How could I not have? That's our area.'

'The second thing is, our Bykov is deputy director of your collective farm.'

'Of course, of course. Bykov's our deputy director. And so, you say he's yours?'

'That's right. He's from Rozhdestveno. His house is three houses along from me. Tell me, does Burdachevo still exist?'

'Burdachevo has gone to ruin. It's just deep holes and apple trees now. I passed through it not long ago.'

'It was a fine village. What a pity. You could go into the fields and smell the clover.'

'Doubtless it still smells of clover even now.'

'But there is no one to smell it. So Bykov, you say, is with you? Well, what's he like? All right?'

'He's fine, fine. He's a hard-working fellow.'

'He doesn't swear at the workers?'

'Not that I've heard.'

'But how can you manage without it? Without swearing nothing gets done by our sort of people. That's what they're like. Go and try talking to them without it. They just won't listen.'

'Well, I haven't heard any.'

'Now don't you go defending him – don't now, I shan't tell him. Now, does Ostanikha village still exist?'

'Yes, it does. Only none of the original inhabitants of Ostanikha live there now. They're all holiday-makers.'

'Do you mean they've bought the houses?'

'Yes. Out of the twenty-two original houses only five remain. Two have been bought by holiday-makers from Moscow, and three are boarded up.'

'Well, well! What a long way to come from Moscow!'

'But it's good there! The central buildings on our collective farm are surrounded by cars, tractors and people. They rattle around, the earth gets churned up, when it rains the tractors get stuck in the middle of the village. Really, it's not a village but some sort of motor depot, you can't tell. But over there it's quiet, with grass everywhere. There's just a little narrow path through the village. It's a haven of peace.'

'Yes, nowadays the smaller villages are disappearing and the central farm buildings are growing bigger,' the old woman summed up. 'Well, does Bykov drink, by the way?'

'Not that I have noticed.'

'But again, how could he not drink? These days you can't manage without it. Nerves. Get a move on! And all round you everyone is the same.'

'I haven't seen Bykov drinking myself.'

'Don't you go defending him. What do you do?'

I kept silent, pretending to concentrate on avoiding the bumps.

'All right, don't tell me. Now then, does the village of Negodyaikha still exist?'

'Negodyaikha has also disintegrated. Kostya Kamynin has gone off to Vladimir. Two houses have been bought by holiday-makers. It's even quieter there than in Ostanikha. And the forest is nearby.'

'And have you heard them say that they want to increase the pension for old folk?'[1]

'I haven't asked. I've still a long way to go for my pension.'

'They keep putting it off, holding it up. This is the second year there have been rumours. Perhaps they're waiting for some of us to die so there would be fewer of us?'

'What is the sense? As you die, others grow old.'

'That's true. And do you see Bykov often?'

'I do. How could I not?'

'Well, and what's he like? Not too strict? He doesn't shout at you?'

'Not at me. As for others, I haven't heard him shouting.'

'Now then, does the village of Krutovo still exist?'

And so we talked until we arrived at the turning to Rozhdestveno, or the Lenin State Farm as it is now called. The old woman tried to push a ten-copeck piece into my hand but I refused it.

'Take it, take it. I won't tell Bykov. You've earned it.'

'Put your ten copecks away. I am used to earning money another way and you haven't had your pension increase yet.'

'Well, thank you.'

The old lady climbed out of my car, which was rather too high up, given her lack of agility, took one step away and cast a critical glance at the car and me and, hoping to amaze me with her perceptiveness, feeling triumphant that I had not managed to trick her and that she had seen through me, said sarcastically: 'You reckon you're Bykov's driver, but the car is not good enough.'

'The car suits its owner,' I answered with a joke and set off.

The old woman remained behind at the crossroads.

2

On a small hill, fifty or so paces from the road (on the side of which their car was standing), three soldiers had settled themselves down to break their journey in the open air. They had spread a cape on the warm June ground and laid out on it some things to eat: lightly smoked sausage, bread, pieces of fish such as are usually sold ready-cooked in

---

[1] The conversation took place before the pension increase.

railway buffets. A bottle was lying to one side already empty and they were just pouring the other one into those paper cups which have the strange property of making any form of drink poured into them tasteless, whether it be beer, lemonade, coffee or plain water.

I had at that time set myself a task. An hour earlier I had finished writing a story and had now decided to exercise myself with a good circular walk before lunch. Usually when out for a walk I go straight forward without using the road, between fields, over sprawling hillsides, along the edge of ravines, skirting the forest land and sometimes crossing fields if they are even – for example, if the crop is clover or buckwheat. By coincidence I clambered out of a ravine at just the spot where the officers had their magic table-cloth and at the very moment when the drink was about to be splashed out into the paper cups. I turned to the left to avoid disturbing the meal but they immediately called out to me.

'Hey, man! Come and sit with us awhile. Come on, don't be shy. We'll pour you a glass.'

I went up to them and lay down head on hand next to the cape. In my hand there appeared a paper cup, the weight of its contents unpleasantly incongruous with its flimsy construction.

There was nothing unusual about the officers. Evidently they had come out here to check the line of communications and so had decided to sit a while in the bosom of nature. They consisted of a major, a lieutenant and a second lieutenant, but I did not notice any reflection of rank in their behaviour or conversation. There they were with their snack, just like equals. The second lieutenant spoke least of all, though perhaps out of some sense of tact, as the one with the lowest rank. The major, too, was not very talkative (was it beneath his dignity?), and so the lieutenant turned out to be the biggest talker. He it was who had called me over to the group when he shouted: 'Hey, man! Come and sit with us awhile!' And it was he, too, who began asking me about everything.

'Well, and how are things with you on the agricultural front? They say it's not a bad harvest this year. But will you be able to get it in? You won't leave it to get snowed under? Aren't you short of people on the farm?'

'They'll bring in the students or the factory workers. Or else they'll throw in your soldier-boys. We'll be all right.'

'So you're counting on the town? Very clever! And what do you do yourself?'

'Not much. This, that and the other.'

'I see. So you didn't want to study?'

'To become what?'

'An agronomist, an expert on livestock . . .'

'I didn't manage to become an agronomist. But I don't complain. Any one of our herdsmen or milkmaids on the farm makes more than your agronomist. So, of course, I get quite enough . . . for the kiddies' milk.'

'Just the same, how much?'

'What do you mean, how much?'

'How much do you get a month, on average?'

'I don't have a regular wage. You see, I'm a very rare sort of skilled worker. Not everyone is able to do what I do. I might produce one particular thing and in one go they'll hand over a thousand . . . or more.'

After I said that (and, God knows, I did not invent anything, as a writer I really do not have any salary and I receive money only for a published book), they looked at me suspiciously; or perhaps not quite suspiciously yet, but closely. At any rate when I turned away and then at once looked quickly back in their direction I managed to catch in the corner of my eye an expressive gesture of the second lieutenant's. He was making a circular movement with one finger near his temple. Everyone knows what that gesture means. However, the lieutenant carried on talking with me no less seriously.

'What sort of skilled work is that, then? Are you a carpenter, a cabinet-maker? Or some sort of fancy stove-builder?'

Instead of answering I reached out for my cup, took it, gestured as if to clink glasses with them, the conversation was interrupted and, after we had drunk, the subject changed. But just the same their earlier confidence concerning me had gone, I noticed. It is well known that in village life you sometimes come across born simpletons or people who have gone crazy as adults. They are quite harmless people and can be normal at times. But suddenly in the middle of a conversation they begin to talk some nonsense about having drunk tea with Kalinin or being the best of friends with Voroshilov. Or you meet braggarts like our Vladimir Postnov (may he rest in peace) who, having lived a time in Moscow, returned to his native village and declared that he had been Dzerzhinsky's personal chauffeur, and not an ordinary chauffeur but one kept for special occasions when reckless speed was required.

'They only got in touch with me for one reason, Vladimir Sergeevich would say. 'Oh yes, the other drivers would be out working – there was plenty to do – and I would sit and smoke and take things easy.

Suddenly there's a shout: "Comrade Postnov to the Chief!" That means they needed some lightning-fast, breakneck driving. I start up the car straight away and I'm off! That's me! They kept me specially for that sort of driving. Others couldn't take it, oh no.'

And now it was my officers who were deciding whether I was a braggart or crazy. Meanwhile the conversation continued.

'Is there game in these parts? Hares, for instance?'

'What 'ares! All those chemicals in the fields kill 'em off. There are no 'ares at all now.'[2]

'A pity. Because if you fry one of the beggers just the right way . . .'

'An 'are needs to be stewed and served in gravy. Now, I remember in Paris . . .'

'Where? Where?' The lieutenant choked on a half-chewed piece of sausage.

'I said that in Paris they do a nice 'are in gravy.'

The officers glanced at one another.

'And how did you happen to be there?' Now it was the major himself who tentatively inquired.

'Oh, I have a friend there . . . de Gaulle's personal interpreter. So he got me invited.'

'Who . . . invited you?'

'It was done through the Ministry of Foreign Affairs. There's a certain Mme Longchamp there.'

'Longchamp, *cochon*. . . . *Pip sil tre, Ivan telya passé*,[3] is that it then? Now, fellow, lie if you want to but know when to stop.'

'Why should I lie?' I scratched the unshaven stubble on my chin. 'I have plenty of friends. Zhivkov's deputy in Bulgaria is also my personal friend. If I wanted, he'd send me an invitation right away and off I'd go to Bulgaria.'

The second lieutenant even started up in anger but the lieutenant stopped him as if to say it's all right, let him fib a bit.

'Well, and what other governments are you friends with?'

'I was a guest of Ho Chi Minh's. It was good fun. I went to Hanoi on some business of mine for a month. Well, they met me, welcomed me and put me in a house on its own. Everything was fine, only I noticed that the food was like ours, chicken, fish, nothing interesting. I said to them, feed me Vietnamese-style. I want, I said, to get to know your

---

[2] For a long time, even in the Literary Institute, I could not rid myself of those ' 'ares' and ' 'ands' and now I pronounced that word with particular pleasure.

[3] This is a humourous transcription of a Ukrainian saying ('The priest grates the salt, Ivan tends the calves'), which in general has a French sound to it.

food. They said it was quite impossible because the European stomach is not used to Vietnamese food. But I kept on and even started to get angry. We argued for three days.

'And later when I found myself a guest at Ho Chi Minh's he asked me – he was a very well-mannered, warm-hearted man – he asked me what requests or wishes I had. I answered that I had no requests, only let them give me Vietnamese food. All right, said Ho Chi Minh, I'll arrange it. After that I ate only the local food. And I ate some good-tasting food that month!'

My simple tale amused the soldiers.

'What a one the man is!' The lieutenant was nearly in tears with laughter.

'What a one!' repeated the others.

But I must say that nothing in my stories was invented. They appeared fantastic to my listeners only in conjunction with my appearance and the unusual situation. An unshaven country yokel is stretched out on the grass, lying through his teeth about stewed hares in Paris.

Concerning the episode in Vietnam everything is true as well. Really, when I was sent to Hanoi by the *Literary Gazette* to work on a book (see my *Post-Cards from Vietnam*), I insisted on Vietnamese cuisine and only after our Vietnamese comrades had hesitated for three days did I get my way.

'What a one the man is! Well, and what did they feed you on?'

'It was good. You sit down to dinner and they put twelve dishes in front of you. If you like, you can choose what you want from them, or if you feel like it you can eat them all, one after the other. It's mostly fish, pork, pigeons, only they are cooked in a special way, and then there are frogs, snakes, dogmeat, grasshoppers . . .'

'Grass . . . hoppers? Dogmeat? Ha! Ha! Ha! Ho Chi Minh says . . . I'll arrange it. . . . In a house on its own. . . . Ha! Ha! Ha!'

'Why are you laughing? It was a fine detached house. True, it had only one floor.'

'Ha! Ha! Ha! And then there was that . . . that about Zhivkov's deputy. . . . Ha! Ha! Ha!'

'What's funny about that? He's my personal friend and comrade, Georgiy. But I call him simply Gosha. Like mates. How are things, I say, with my friend Gosha? All right, he says, OK. He's a great character!'

At this point my acquaintances had a chance to think and suspect a trick. When I quoted Gogol I opened for them a small window on to the genuine situation. But they could not have seen a performance of the *Inspector General* for a long time and they were even less likely to have reread it. Well then, so much the worse for them.

'So, you get to see mostly presidents and prime ministers? What a big man! Well, and who else have you met?'

'I've been to Hungary too. Budapest is a fine city. It's on the Danube. I went there on business. And there, in the evening, there was a huge reception in the parliament building. I must say, it's a most beautiful building. There were thousands of people at the reception. Ambassadors of all nations, various attachés, correspondents, the Hungarian intelligentsia. And Voroshilov represented our government. Now in one hall they all started to dance the csardas – it's a Hungarian folk-dance. A wonderful dance. The music simply makes your feet move. You feel good, lively, happy. And it's easy to do. If you don't know how, you just see it once and off you go. They had their dance and stopped. Then Voroshilov – he was a lively old man, dancing the csardas had made him go red – said: "Well, who will help me with a Russian dance?" And he looked at me, because I was standing nearby and talking in Russian with a diplomat. "Are you Russian?" Voroshilov asked me. "Yes," I answered, "what else could I be?" "Come on then."

'And then off he went, kicking out his legs. Well, I'd drunk a bit and I couldn't let him down. But then two women ran up, our own Soviet artistes, probably. Well, they went slowly and gracefully round Voroshilov and I got more and more to one side and disappeared into the crowd . . .'

'Ha! Ha! Ha! So you danced Russian-style with Voroshilov? In Budapest? He! He! He!'

Again, nothing had been invented in that episode. I was in Hungary in April 1955. They were celebrating the tenth anniversary of the Hungarian People's Republic. Klim Efremovich Voroshilov went to the celebrations. As correspondents of *Ogonyok* Kolya Drachinsky and I were invited to all the receptions connected with the celebrations.

Suddenly the lieutenant abruptly stopped laughing, as if he had been switched off.

'Now, you there . . . you know what . . . be on your way . . . off you trot.'

'You invited me yourselves. And now. . . . But why?'

'Never mind. We've had a laugh and that's enough. You mustn't go too far. Be on your way now.'

'That's not very polite of you. It's not good at all, you're offending me. I can see your car number. Now, the next time I play rummy with your general, I'll make a point of telling him that you were drinking here on the grass instead of attending to your duties.'

(And in this, for them, sensational and shattering piece of news there was nothing I had to invent. About two months previously I had been enjoying myself at the university celebrations of a regional Party worker. Everyone of importance in the region was present, including General N. During the lengthy interval in which they cleared away the food and laid the table for tea, we were all in another room feeling a little bored and there were some cards lying on the radio. I picked them up and started to shuffle them as if inviting people to play; and there were in fact two volunteers, one of them the general. We managed to play three games, two of which I lost. They then invited us back to the table.)

'I'll go if you want to get rid of me. But it's not good. You called me over yourselves. And I'll tell your general a thing or two.'

'Wait! Wait!' the major suddenly blurted out. Something was dawning in his head. 'Which general are you thinking of?'

'General ——. And I clearly stated his surname, first name and patronymic. 'And his wife is called ——.' And again I came out with the information smoothly and correctly. 'Is that not correct?'

It was a big shock. I crossed to the other side of the ravine and stopped there in safety, but they were still sitting motionless, looking at me. Just then a shepherd came by ahead of a small village flock. I saw the lieutenant questioning the shepherd, pointing at me, and the shepherd explained something to him in detail. The officers jumped up and stared in my direction, and I blew them a kiss.

UNDER ONE ROOF

We happened to live for some time in the village of Svetikha, where we occupied a semi-detached house. The two halves of the building were totally separated from each other: we left the house on our side, the neighbours on theirs. But there was still the common wall. Through it into the corridor there came to us the smell of potatoes frying in vegetable oil, of fried onions, fried cod and even of the oil-stove itself.

Sounds also penetrated it. You could clearly hear Nyushka, the woman next door, chopping up nettles for the ducks; her father, Uncle Pavel, snoring as he slept in the corridor, the yapping of their stupid little dog called Rubicon, an absurd name in a village, and the daily quarrels between father and daughter.

They lived together on their own because Uncle Pavel's numerous other children had all gone their separate ways. Nyushka alone had become thoroughly attached to the village house. She had been widowed during the first days of the war and had lived without a man since then, something which, probably, also had its effect upon her already difficult character.

Uncle Pavel received a pension of twenty-seven roubles. Nyushka earned much more on the farm. Probably this material inequality was the chief source of contention between father and daughter. Nyushka removed Uncle Pavel from her dining-table and organized things so that they ate apart. That would have been all right; an old man of eighty does not need much. The twenty-seven roubles' pension would have been just about enough for village life. But Nyushka was superior in one other way, apart from her wages. She was a woman, a cook and mistress of the house. It was more convenient for her to heat up the stove, make soup and fry the potatoes in vegetable oil. It would have been impossible for them to work together at the single stove. And, on top of that, Uncle Pavel's easily offended nature would not have allowed any joint activities. And so it was that the old man took to living on cold food.

Nyushka spent half the day on the farm. During that time Uncle Pavel sometimes lit the oil-stove if only to heat up some tinned fish – sprats in tomato sauce. They say that in old age when the blood gets sluggish people particularly like something hot. But more often than not Uncle Pavel would stand in front of the house, hunched up in his padded coat, looking along the line of the village with tearful eyes and chewing bread which he broke into bits in his pocket and pushed about in his mouth with its toothless gums. Sometimes the old man would treat himself to biscuits, which he also broke up in his pocket. This was not from greed and not so that people should not see, but, at the same time, why stand in the middle of the street with a paper bag full of biscuits or a chunk of bread in your hand?

During such times it was quiet behind the wall. But as soon as Nyushka came back from the farm, the noise and bustle started up. You might hear the mistress of the house saying something to Rubicon in a kind voice. Perhaps that was the only creature in her house to whom she spoke kindly, with the possible exception of the duck with the lame leg. To Rubicon Nyushka spoke like this: 'Well then, are you fed up, you silly thing? It must be boring sitting chained up all day. I'll untie you now. Ah, it's got through to your doggy brain, you're pleased. Go and run about a bit.'

After that she began the feeding of the ducks.

'Ah, you dear thing, my little lame one, here, this is just for you. . . . And where are you trying to get to? Go and eat with the others.' This was addressed to some duck who had decided to eat from the lame duck's dish.

A piglet, sensing the food, would begin to squeal piercingly and heart-rendingly.

'You darn nuisance, your time will come. Be quiet, or I'll start shouting at you. I'll shout at you!'

If Nyushka had possessed any other form of livestock, probably she would have piled on some loud language and choice words here. But there was no other livestock. There remained Uncle Pavel.

In no way do I think that Uncle Pavel came in for some abusive language because his daughter thought less of her father than of Rubicon or the piglet; but after all, Uncle Pavel, unlike the dumb animals, could answer back and usually his oaths were equally sharp and well aimed.

After each of these regular fights the old man came over to our side. He would greet us from the doorstep, take off his hat and sit down on a chair which he would move from the table into the centre of the room. We would try to persuade the old man to sit with us and drink a cup of tea, but the more we tried, the farther away he moved his chair.

At first the conversation would be about this and that – again there's been no rain, or, on the contrary, again it's rained all day – but after that, Uncle Pavel would switch decisively to the main topic.

'The bitch. Where do such people come from? Look what she's doing to me! She won't give me plain hot water! Oh, it's not that, not the hot water. If only she didn't shout and swear at me in the worst possible way. I remember when I lived with my elder daughter. It was heaven, not ordinary life. She would come home and I'd be sitting at the cottage window. She'd look in at the window from the street and laugh: "Well now, you old rooster, you're still there, the fox hasn't taken you off yet?" She'd make a joke like that and straight away there'd be a feeling of real human life. But this one . . .' – Uncle Pavel's voice would change – 'she should be crushed underfoot. . . .'

We were embarrassed to hear such blunt outbursts from a father about his daughter, the major part of which I cannot reproduce here because they would be censored.

'Now, you wait,' Uncle Pavel continued. 'God punish me if I'm wrong, but she'll make life impossible for you here too!'

This suggestion seemed strange and unlikely to us. How could anyone behave badly towards us if we behaved well towards everyone ourselves or, at any rate, did not interfere with anyone? But Uncle Pavel's gloomy prophecies unexpectedly began to come true.

The inhabitants of the village make a practice of pouring their dishwater on to the road. If you think about it, you could not invent such a repulsive habit if you tried, because, should there be any source of infection in the discarded water, there is no surer way of spreading it throughout the district than to deposit it on to the road. A cart or a car passes by and the infectious material sticks to the wheels and is carried here, there and everywhere. Nevertheless, this strange practice exists in Svetikha. Every housewife carries the dirty water out on to the road opposite her windows and pours it into a shallow ditch.

There was no road outside the semi-detached house in which we found ourselves at that time; it was situated away from the main street. In front of it there was flat green grass. It was pleasant to walk barefoot on it and to lie on it in the shade of a big old lime. In the middle of this little glade, about seven paces from the windows, there was, not exactly a ditch, nor was it really a small hollow: once someone had dug a small ditch but by now it had filled in and become covered with the same silky grass as elsewhere. The tiny depression that remained was of great use. During a summer downpour or miserable daily rains the water did not collect into a puddle in front of the windows to become stagnant, but rushed along the length of the depression into a distant pond.

And now suddenly through the window we saw Nyushka carrying a large bowl of dishwater, which she poured on to the lawn straight in front of the windows. In the first place, there would be no more lying on the grass under the lime tree; secondly, the flies would multiply and come in through the windows on to the bread and sugar; thirdly, when it rained, the dirty water would be swept along into the pond where people rinsed their washing, cleaned their feet after the day's work and where the children sometimes swam.

My wife, who studied sanitation and hygiene at the Medical Institute, could not bear the sight of dishwater in the middle of the village, especially just beneath our windows. Nyushka, on the other hand, for some reason took to the lawn and started to bring the dishwater every day and pour it out in exactly the same place. A foul-smelling black ulcer appeared on our clean, green lawn.

Two crows were constantly stuck there, picking in the dirt at the remains of something rotten; something, however, which was evidently still edible for crows.

During one of Uncle Pavel's usual visits to us we asked him to persuade his daughter, perhaps even mentioning our name, to take her slops somewhere out of the way.

'God forbid! I won't even hint at it. And you had better not, either. Do you think one can possibly say anything against her? You can't know her yet.'

We could not bring ourselves to believe this and went like some kind of delegation to the other half of the house.

Nyushka was busy at the stove. 'Hello,' she blurted at us rather snappily in answer to our own completely timid 'hello'.

We sat down on the bench near the door and began waiting for the mistress of the house to appear from behind the partitioned wall of the kitchen. The lady appeared. It was the first time I had looked at her properly. She was a woman of about forty-five, short, with a round face and traces of a certain attractiveness, but at the same time she had a sort of gloomy, unfriendly expression. In general everything about her appearance was ordinary: thin, faded hair of an indefinite brown colour, little eyes which you could not say were grey, but neither were they blue, an expressionless, small mouth – in short, everything was commonplace and unexciting. In spite of all this, when she smiled, coming out from behind the partition, a dimple appeared on each cheek and I could imagine that twenty-five or so years earlier she might have looked quite attractive.

The smile encouraged us and we set about our business. We talked about the harmfulness of flies, about the ferocity of summer diseases, about one's feeling for beauty and its meaning. It was a detailed lecture on sanitation, hygiene and nature conservation all in one. Nyushka listened in silence until we came to the actual dishwater. Finally I plucked up courage and said: 'So we ask you, Anna Pavlovna, to take your dirty water somewhere out at the back, any convenient spot.'

Mostly I expected her to agree. At worst she could come up with some practical objections – who knows what she might have in her head? But the most unexpected thing happened. Anna Pavlovna told us to go, really quite some distance, spelling out the address exactly and unambiguously. Having uttered her energetic four-word phrase, she went behind the partition and we jumped out of the house like scalded cats.

The next day in the village shop, according to detailed accounts, the following episode took place. Our neighbour entered and, in the presence of seven people, eight counting the saleswoman, right out of the blue announced loud and clear: 'All sorts come here and we have to put up with it. Now what have they thought up! They want to buy their half of the house outright, make it impossible for me to live in my half and then get their hands on it. Of course they're townspeople, they know all the ins and outs. And am I, a poor widow, then supposed to wander the streets? Where would there be a corner for me? How many more years will Father live? Is there really no justice on earth? Well, I'll go tomorrow to the Rural Council or the militia. They can be thrown out instead. I, too, have a head on my shoulders. The Soviet Government won't allow it.'

We were astounded at Nyushka's imagination. Never, even in a dream, had we intended to do anything of the kind, the thought had not even crossed our mind, but in five minutes she had outlined a complete programme of action for us. At first I simply laughed. But I suddenly thought of Nyushka going to the Rural Council, the militia and somewhere else too, making up tales about us all the way. I began to feel uneasy. The next day at the well, with three women around her, Nyushka became even more inspired in her fantasies.

'They're sending spiders through to my house.'

'No!'

'There are cracks between the boards in our corridor. I look and see one spider creeping through from their half and then another. That means they're catching them in their place and then sending them through the crack to me. And perhaps the spiders are poisonous. . . .'

I pictured myself and my wife in the guise of saboteurs, releasing poisonous spiders into foreign territory, and felt both amused and sad at the same time.

Meanwhile there were further developments. In order in some way to neutralize the action of the dirty water under the windows, my wife sprinkled insecticide over the rotten black ulcer – after all, it is a disinfectant. Not every fly would alight on it and not every one that did would fly away again. Nyushka, it seems, observed the sanitary and hygienic measures of the enemy camp from her window. I do not know what sort of fantastic imaginings the sight might have prompted in her, but by coincidence on that very same day Nyushka's cockerel died. I do not think it was the result of the insecticide; because why, then, did not all the other chickens die? But in Nyushka's imagination the fact of the matter received its own interpretation; she understood that not only had war been declared on her, but that it was being waged by impermissible chemical means. We had to wait for reciprocal action.

During the quiet hour before evening, when I had just got into a book I found interesting, my wife rushed into the room in a flood of tears. She threw herself on to the bed face down, her whole body shaking. I rushed off to the kitchen for the valerian drops. For a long time she could not explain to me what had happened, but finally she blurted out: 'Go and shoot Rubicon this instant.'

It is true that I have a gun and shooting the little dog would not be so difficult, but first I had to find out what it was all about. It appeared that, a mere five minutes earlier, Nyushka had beaten to death with a stick our Afanasiy, a wonderful fluffy kitten.

Before setting off to the village we had gone into the Bird Market in order to wander about there between the rows of aquaria which looked so beautiful with their fantastic tropical fish sparkling and shimmering like precious stones, no, even more beautiful than precious stones. I have not had an aquarium myself for a number of years: constant absences from Moscow prevent me, but it was and still is a treat for me to admire those of others.

When we had wandered long enough about the market we saw at the market exit-gates a girl of about nine holding a charming creature in her arms. She was pressing to her breast, or rather not her breast but her throat, a tiny but already fluffy and alert-looking little kitten.

We were not intending to buy any pets but it would be interesting to know what kittens were going for in the Moscow market.

'I am not selling him,' answered the girl, overjoyed by our question, 'but please have him for nothing.'

'Why do you want to be rid of the kitten?'

'I overheard a conversation. Grandmother wants to leave him somewhere in a doorway but I'm sorry for him. Supposing nobody takes him and he'll be feeling hungry and miaowing? I want to give him to somebody myself so that I know who it is. Please, please take him, he's lovely, really lovely. Please. . . .'

Obviously someone had given the girl the idea of going with the kitten to the Bird Market in particular. It was surprising that no one had taken the kitten from her before us. One look at his funny little face and you could not refuse him. The girl made us promise that we would feed the kitten every day, would not beat him and that we would sometimes play with him, using a twist of paper tied to the end of a thread.

And now this same kitten, our dear Afanasiy, had been killed with a stick by that wicked woman, Nyushka.

My wife was sobbing and telling me to shoot Rubicon without delay. I felt unbearably angry myself. So, then, things would go like this: in response to her evil action I kill Rubicon; our sheets, hung out to dry in the garden, she tramples in the mud; I destroy all her chickens and ducks, perhaps the piglet, too, with rapid fire and she scalds our children with boiling water. . . . My imagination stopped here, but who knows the limits of Nyushka's imagination and ingenuity! Of course she would not have been able to take the biggest step and set fire to the house, because she herself lived under the same roof. . . .

Probably that is the way history began on earth. A wrong is repaid with another wrong, always with that, albeit little, extra bite. A grain of evil gave birth to a pea-sized act of evil. The pea led to a nut, the nut to an apple, the apple to a melon. . . . And so, in the end, an ocean of evil has formed, into which the whole of humanity may sink. Things have gone right up as far as setting fire to, or, more exactly, incinerating the house. The only good thing is that, as in our microscopic case with Nyushka, everyone is living under the same roof, and setting fire to your neighbour's house means setting fire to your own.

Any number of outlandish comparisons might have crowded into my brain, but the reality of the situation was that our Afanasiy had been killed with a stick, that my wife was in tears and that I had to go and shoot Rubicon.

'Well, what are you sitting there for?' said my wife. 'Today she killed the kitten, tomorrow she'll break your daughter's leg and you'll still be sitting there. You must pluck up courage and go and shoot it.'

Since I remained seated and said nothing for the moment, my wife continued: 'And anyway, whether you shoot Rubicon or not, let's leave at once today. I can't live under the same roof with her. Not for another minute, do you understand?'

We could not leave for quite a number of reasons and so I still remained silent.

'Why don't you say something? You are the man, the head of the family. You must find a way out of every impossible situation. If you can't pay her back for Afanasiy and if we can't leave, tell me how I can go on, what I must do, how I must behave. Tell me!'

'You see, you are telling me to be courageous. But the thing is, shooting a little dog. . . . You might say it wouldn't need any courage in the strict sense. But you have the opportunity, if you want, of doing something which is courageous in the real sense. Go ahead and do it.'

'Strangle it with my bare hands?'

'No. Take the packet of yeast which I brought from Moscow and give it to her. Say it's a present from us both.'

My wife gave me a frightened look, as if I was out of my mind. For a split second her expression was vacant, like that of a man who has just been hit on the head. And that is hardly surprising, for during that split second her racing thoughts, her state of mind, her anger and thirst for revenge – all these had to stop as if an iron brake had been applied and then start to move in the reverse direction.

'Are you being serious?'

'Very. That is, if you were seriously asking me how to go on, what do and how to behave. I've thought about it and consider the only proper thing to do in the situation is to take her the packet of yeast. Let's see what comes of it.'

'Oh no! Then you'd better shoot me instead of Rubicon. To humiliate oneself like that . . . in front of that heap of malice.'

'Right now we are a heap of malice ourselves. What's more, I don't see any other solution. If we were to continue any further on our present course, this is what would happen: I'd shoot Rubicon, she'd trample our sheets in the mud. I'd kill all her ducks, she'd break our daughter's leg. . . . In the end there'd be only one thing left, to set the house on fire – we'd have to see which of us got to do it first. But in our case that would be senseless because we live in the same building, under one roof. We can't leave. We can't drive her out. So I really don't see any way out. But still, there is a way out and I am suggesting it. Pick up the yeast and take it to her as a present from us both.'

'It would be better if I were to hang myself in the loft!'

'Pick up the yeast and take it round.'

'Not if I live to be a hundred!'

'Pick it up and go.'

We wrapped the yeast up in newspaper, otherwise everyone outside would see what was being taken. My wife wiped away her tears, tidied herself up and set off.

I realized she was now performing a heroic, in a way even a great act. Because, given that it is more difficult to go up a step than down one, given that it is more difficult to climb out of the mire on to dry land than to step off dry land into the mire, then the most difficult thing for all men throughout history has been to step across one's own limitations.

I did not know what was happening behind the wall. Perhaps Nyushka had dashed the yeast into her face. Perhaps she had gone further and spat at her as she left. I was prepared to ask my wife's forgiveness for such an interesting but taxing experiment, when suddenly my wife came into the cottage. She was full of excitement, as if she had just received the most joyful news of her life. Her eyes shone and her voice when she began to speak was broken by a feeling of joyful agitation. There was a trickle in my own throat and I realized that we had just touched on something very central and important, perhaps the most central and most important thing in human behaviour.

After she had calmed down, my wife told me what had happened. When she entered the house, Nyushka had reached for the oven prongs, thinking that some sort of revenge for the kitten was on the way. And really she might have been expecting anything at all except the peaceful arrival of a representative from the enemy camp. But my wife unwrapped the packet of yeast and put it on the table. My wife had had the courage and ingenuity to say, calmly and quietly, that today was Sunday and we had decided . . . because there was more in our house and this would be left over anyway and go to waste, because it was hot and you cannot keep yeast for long. . . .

I gather Nyushka burst into tears and rushed forward with open arms. Then my wife burst into tears, too, and they both wept on each other's shoulder. They both said something at the same time, but exactly what, in detail, my wife could not repeat because she herself was talking more than listening.

We had not yet calmed down after this event, or rather, after this change of events, when Nyushka appeared in our doorway. In her hands she was holding a large sieve, full of choice onions.

This means, I suddenly thought, that the spring had begun to unwind in the opposite direction, but also, strange as it may seem, in an upward direction: we give her a packet of yeast, she gives us a sieve of onions; next time we shall give her an expensive cake and she will give us an oven-ready duck; we shall give her some material for a dress, she will give us a whole piglet; we shall give her some roofing iron, she will suggest taking down the partitions in the house. . . . Again my imagination ran away with me.

I would rather not recount how much unpleasantness occurred after that between us and our neighbour before the autumn, or what she said about us outside the shop and at the well, or what Uncle Pavel would say about her when he came round to get things off his chest. All that did happen later, and probably would happen again if we decided to revisit the village. But still, I shall never forget my wife's shining eyes after she returned from Nyushka, or Nyushka herself standing timidly in our doorway with a big sieve of choice onions.

THE FORTIETH DAY

At noon one Sunday, when I had just got ready to take a walk to the river to see if the winter ice had buckled up, Shura Toreyeva dashed in on us.

'Aunt Agasha's giving a dinner in memory of Ivan Dmitrievich. She is asking for you to come. What shall I say to her?'

'Say we will come right away.'

'Then come as quickly as possible. Everyone's there already. They're at the table.'

Aunt Agasha's is the humblest little house in the village. You could say that in our village there are no poor houses: the worst ones have either been demolished or renovated and painted. If there are new planks lying in front of a house now, they must be for a bath-house. Some people are getting round to garden fences.

Aunt Agasha's little house was once also new, well maintained and stable. Only two people ever lived in it: Ivan Dmitrievich, in whose memory we were to gather today, and Aunt Agasha. They never had any children. The absence of extra mouths, thrift and hard work – these are the reasons why the doughnuts and pies in Ivan Dmitrievich's house were of the finest white flour. Their stores of white, even slightly yellow-looking, 'privately made' flour lasted them pretty well up to the war.

Gradually the little house grew shabby and one corner began to sink into the ground. And its inhabitants were growing older too. The old folk were often told it was time to pull it down or it would flatten them. But Ivan Dmitrievich and Aunt Agasha accurately reckoned it would hold out for the rest of their lives.

As for Ivan Dmitrievich, he worked for many years as a night-watchman: he would walk about the village at night and give a ring on the bell near the fire-fighting equipment once every hour. At first the old man carried a Berdan rifle which, however, was not likely to be loaded, but then he started to wander about simply with a stick.

I cannot say whether Ivan Dmitrievich was a kind man because I never once had anything to ask of him. But any of the villagers will confirm that he was an inoffensive old soul. He was somehow clever enough to live through his seventy-five years without giving offence to a single living thing, let alone a human being.

Once when I was a lad I climbed into Ivan Dmitrievich's orchard after cherries. Having eaten all I could of the black berries, pecked about as they were by the sparrows, I started to make my way through to the gap by which I had entered. In the gap stood the owner of the orchard, with a stick. He was waiting for me, smiling beneath his red, close-trimmed moustache.

'Well then, caught red-handed? Have you taken a lot with you? None at all? Good boy. Come and eat again, only don't take any away with you.'

As I went past Ivan Dmitrievich I was afraid it was a trick just the same; perhaps he would do one on me with the stick. He did not. That was the last time I climbed into his orchard for cherries.

During his last years Ivan Dmitrievich was watchman not for the whole village but for the church only. It was he, too, who lit the stove in the church, swept up and lit the candles. In the spring he would clear away the rubbish from around the church.

But they closed the church. It was turned into a farm storehouse. In place of the icons and brass plate appeared heaps of oats, peas, mixed feed, boxes of nails, carcases, hacked-off heads and legs. In place of incense and hot wax it began to smell of ageing salt beef.

Ivan Dmitrievich's activities switched over to our little village shop. There, too, he gratuitously and selflessly swept up and helped the assistant to sort out the goods as they were unpacked, but more often than not he sat on a sack of salt.

There were people and chatter all day in the shop. The old man was not bored. Watching through the window, you could see Ivan Dmitrievich in his felt boots and galoshes, shuffling along twenty or so times a day from the shop to the house and back, from the seat in the wall of his house to the shop. True, the distance was no more than about seventy paces, but in that way the day passes.

More and more frequently the old men in our village live to be eighty, and for some reason increasingly often die during the winter. You spend the winter in Moscow, come back to the village in April and it seems incredible that you will no longer run into, say, Sergey Vasilyevich Baklanikhin on some pathway or other. Over the past three years there have died in this way Ivan Vasilyevich Kunin, Sergey Vasilyevich and Kuzma Vasilyevich Baklanikhin, old Auntie Marya Baklanikhina, all of them over eighty, and Olena Grybova – well, she was past ninety.

In the village they do not talk about it aloud but they all know in themselves roughly whose turn it is to die, who at any moment is the oldest and frailest inhabitant. That is why Ivan Dmitrievich's death at seventy-five surprised everyone. They said, shaking their heads: 'He was too quick. It wasn't his turn.'

He died virtually in the course of an hour. One morning his head started to ache. He came back from the shop and slumped down. His legs went numb, his tongue was paralysed. It is true that he breathed for as long as twenty-four hours after that, but he did not come round even for a moment.

All this happened at the beginning of February. When the forty days were past, Aunt Agasha gave a meal in his memory.

Now I have to say why it was Shura Toreyeva specifically who came to fetch us. In the first place the Toreyevs are Aunt Agasha's neighbours. But that in itself is not the whole reason. The fact that Sergey Toreyev is a very decent man (although not without his weaknesses) was probably nothing to do with it. There were other decent folk to be found in the village, especially as Toreyev (or, as we all say, Torev) is not one of our Alepino men but joined us from somewhere else. Now, of course, nobody considers him an outsider. His house is known nowadays by his name, as Torev's, whereas it used to be Moskovkin's. Younger generations, most likely, do not know that Sergey came from elsewhere. But now, Ivan Dmitrievich in seventy-five years could have nurtured some kind feeling in himself for someone a little older and better established. There must have been something else, something more important to and decisive for the Toreyevs.

Aunt Agasha had withdrawn eighty-five roubles for various necessities from her savings account. She had put the tight roll, wrapped in a handkerchief, into some sort of secret pocket she had in her skirts and had taken herself off home. Some time later Shura Toreyeva came round to see her.

'Well, tell me now, what have you lost?'

'I haven't lost anything.'

'Guess what it is you've lost, or I won't give it back,' laughed Shura.

Aunt Agasha felt her pocket through her skirts, not wanting to look directly: we do not like to count money when there are onlookers. Finally Shura took pity and gave her the roll of money, eighty-five roubles – no small amount in village terms.

From that time on Ivan Dmitrievich would say: 'Listen, old lady, I'll die before you . . .'

'That's enough, be quiet now. Look how old I am. I can hardly walk, but you're just the same as ever.'

'Don't contradict me. Listen. I'll die before you. So I have to tell you what to do – keep hold of Torev.'

It soon became known that Ivan Dmitrievich was leaving his lopsided cottage to the Toreyevs, as well as what he had saved over his long and quiet life – eight hundred roubles. However, he was leaving them on condition that Aunt Agasha would be buried properly when she died.

'Just look how things turned out. Now, that's something to think about' was what they would say afterwards round about the well. 'She didn't think of herself, she returned what she'd found, eighty roubles, and that's a bit more than eight copecks. And because of that she got eight hundred. Now, that's something to think about.'

From the very first day, straight after Ivan Dmitrievich's funeral, the Toreyevs took Aunt Agasha under their wing. That is why it was none other than Shura Toreyeva who came to invite us to the meal. We set off.

Not only was the whole house tipped at a slant from the outside: the earth foundations, the windows, the roof, the chimney, even the little bench in front of the house; but inside, too, it turned out that all its doorways and even the smallest plank was at a tilt. Squeezing through the crooked outer door, we passed through a small, crooked porch into a crooked corridor and next found ourselves in a still more crooked little corridor and only then, bending down low, did we step into the room.

However strange it may seem, this tiny room in a cottage where everything was crooked turned out to be straight and even. Two tables had been set up to form a letter T, although they were not touching. When we arrived, seven of the village men were sitting at the top table which formed the cross of the T. So I had to take the eighth place, and soon after me the chairman of the collective farm arrived.

At the table which ran down the room, nearer to the door, sat the women. People moved up at both tables, clattering with their stools and chairs and we sat ourselves down.

The only reason why you sometimes do not want to be a guest in one or another of the village houses is vodka. Paying your respects is fine, having a heart to heart talk is fine, but then you remember. . . . For some reason it is not the thing to drink out of small glasses. You have just about taken your place when an octagonal tumbler filled to the brim is put in front of you. You cannot not visit people. Straight away they would say that the Muscovite thinks too much of himself, considers it below him to be with us, simple village labourers. But to drink up a tumblerful (and not only one, that goes without saying) is also of course quite impossible without risk of dying either right there at the table or back home in bed.

Apart from that, I discovered that in his will Ivan Dmitrievich had asked the old woman to collect the farm-workers together for a banquet in his memory and get them so drunk that 'they would have to be taken under the arm and led away'.

The following food had been put out on the table: herring in oil with onion, brawn, chopped egg in sour cream, open jars of tuna, various tinned products in tomato, biscuits and honey. No memorial dinner is complete without honey.

'Well then, men, now it looks as though everyone is here. Let's drink to his memory . . .'

'Now don't clink your glasses, men. It's not done at this sort of dinner.'

If someone had been listening to what was happening, without seeing anything, then from that cry alone, of 'Don't clink your glasses, men, it's not done', he could have accurately counted how many times the heavy octagonal tumblers were raised from the table.

I do not know whether there is much in the custom of not clinking glasses, but all at once everyone went somehow quiet, they all suddenly understood the importance of what was happening. Without clinking glasses they drank up and had a bite to eat.

'But just think how he died' came a voice from the women's table. Evidently they were telling the newcomer the exact details of how Ivan Dmitrievich had actually died. 'My head, he says, is splitting. I say to him, lie down for a bit, Vanya. Lie down and it will pass off. There and then he obediently lay down. Then he gave such a shout – "Old woman!" I went up to him, his eyes were open but he was already gone.'

'What a death, eh? A death like that's worth more than money.'

'It is, my dear, it is.'

'If only God would send me a death like that.'

'Oh, I know, my dear, I know.'

At our table the conversation was threading its way.

'No, it wasn't his.'

'My friend, it doesn't take notice of turns. Sometimes you'll get a young man, looks all right and so on, and before you know it he's gone. But an old man could still be alive.'

'It's well known a creaky tree stands longer.'

'It is. Nothing touches it, it just creaks away.'

'Now take, say, that neighbour of yours. Is he an alcoholic? Sure he is . . .'

'Well, let's drink, men. No clinking, no clinking, it's not done.'

'That's what I'm saying. Is your neighbour as alcoholic? Sure he is . . .'

'What is there to say? He's suffered hell from bouts of drinking all his life.'

'And how old is he?'

'Eighty-two.'

'There you are!'

'Hold it. Hold it, men. I want to ask you, is it harmful to drink wine?'

This contribution to the conversation was made by Nikolay, a farm-worker from Ostanino, known as Redface. All his life he's kept bees. And since there are few beehives in our area now and honey is expensive, he of course relies heavily on his wits. He expresses himself soberly, without hurrying, and does not simply chatter to no purpose, as will become clear shortly. His face really was red all his life – bright red, like a tomato. You can still see the redness through the tanned yellowing of old age. Now he walks bent and complains all the time that the hill he has to climb on the way to our village is getting longer and steeper.

'No, I'm asking you, is it harmful to drink wine?'

'It's a question of how you take it and how much you drink.'

'No, all the same, it's harmful to drink a lot?'

'Well, yes.'

'Is it harmful to drink eau-de-Cologne?'

'Really! What good will eau-de-Cologne do you?'

'Is it harmful to drink methylated spirits?'

Everyone began to guess what Nikolay Mikhaylovich was getting at, but they did not want to interrupt such an orderly scheme of questions.

'And is it dangerous to drink wood polish?'

'What is there to say? You know what polish is.'

'The ancients used to say *memento mori*. That is, remember death,' the chairman of the collective farm suddenly burst out, a man new to us who had been to the Agricultural Institute in Ivanovo.

'Well now, men, let's drink, only no clinking.'

'Would we clink glasses? It's not done.'

'So polish, too, is harmful to drink?'

'I should say so.'

'And is it harmful to drink powder?'

'Powder?!'

'It's easy, you add water and strain it.'

'So everything is harmful?' And Nikolay Redface eyed us all with the look of a victor, triumphant. 'So you wouldn't live long?'

'How could you possibly, after drinking powder?'

'True, true,' Nikolay Mikhaylovich was stretching out his triumph. 'Then what about Makushkin?'

We were floored, pulverized, annihilated. Makushkin from the neighbouring village really had gone about all his life with a small bottle in his pocket, containing some rubbish or other, from which he drank from time to time. He would have a gulp every half-hour. Methylated spirits he looked upon as something special. Makushkin lived to be over eighty.

'There! It took a long time to get him, but it did. Well now, Nikolay Mikhaylovich, we know you've stored up a lot of money. But I dare say there's no gold, is there?'

'Bring your hat and I'll fill it.'

'Men, who can explain to me what gold is needed for, even by the State, and what's in it and what's it all about?'

'What do you mean, you funny man? Gold, I think . . .'

'That's what I'm asking about. What's in it, what's it for, what do you do with it? We farm-workers, for example, don't have any but we're still alive just the same.'

'The ancients said: *homo homini lupus est.* That is, man is wolf to man. But in our case that can't be said,' said the chairman of the collective farm sharply.

All eyes turned on me in the hope that this Muscovite would make everything clear, but the deputy chairman of the farm, Alexander Pavlovich, took the role upon himself: 'Think about it. We buy things from the Americans, they buy things from us. You can even do it without money. They give us a machine, we give them wood or vodka . . .'

'Do they really not have their own vodka?'

'It's not a patch on ours.'

'Well then, men, let's drink. Only don't clink glasses, no clinking, it's not done.'

'But then it sometimes happens that we buy a hundred roubles' worth of goods from them, and they buy fifteen roubles' worth from us. It doesn't balance. So we settle the difference in gold.'

'Oh. . . . What complications. But is it true, men, that the year before last we poured out a ton of gold for grain?'

'You're making it up.'

'It can't be true.'

'And I heard a hundred tons.'

'A hundred – makes no difference.'

'And how is it then that Russia should be buying grain?'

'You're the one to ask about that. You're a farm-worker, you produce it.'

'How come they have grain to spare? Does it mean the people have less?'

'They had a good harvest.'

'Well then, men, let's drink to his memory. He was a darned good mate. Only no clinking, no clinking.'

'God grant him peace.'

Nikolay Redface once again took over the conversation: 'Now, you tell me. . . . If people start to get at you, do you get upset?'

'What else? You can make anyone angry. Makes no difference what sort of a cow she is, she'll still get you with her horn if you make her angry.'

'Right. And what sort of a man was Ivan Mitrich?'

'Well . . .''

'If you ooffend him' – I must point out that this 'ooffend' is very characteristic of our Vladimir manner of speaking an unstressed 'o' at the beginning of a word is pronounced just like 'oo'; 'oobligatory', for instance – 'no, you ooffend him and ooffend him and he . . . doesn't get ooffended! That's the sort of person he was.'

Recollections about Ivan Dmitrievich began to come to light. I remembered the warm July nights of my student years when I would return to the village for the vacation. Every night at two o'clock Ivan Dmitrievich would knock at my window with his stick and in exactly the same unchanging tone of voice, drone out: 'Vova, get up.'

The evening before, I would ask him to wake me at that time to go fishing. You get up before dawn. The first light is just beginning to show. The dirt-track is dry, dusty, and on the grass to each side lie drops of dew, heavy like peas.

There is a particular pleasure in getting to the river before the light. You know for sure you have not missed anything and that everything which is going to happen is yet to come. If they are not biting, at any rate you will not start thinking that they were rising probably during the first minutes of the dawn. No, there they are, the first minutes of the dawn, where it is just beginning to brighten behind the hill. The quiet, dark water is still covered with wisps of white mist, the first dawn breeze has not yet come to ruffle the mist and wrinkle the clear mirror of the water.

To this day I seem to hear those drawling words: 'Vova, get up.' Now all that is far away and cannot be brought back, not because Ivan Dmitrievich is dead and no one now will shout 'Vova, get up!' in just the same way as the deceased would, but because, even if you did get up, you would not feel that youthful enthusiasm and trepidation or that wonderful joy at the sight of every dewdrop, of every little pink cloud or of the last blue-tinted star as it fades before your eyes. Have those words 'get up' really gone for good, along with everything that followed upon that kind-hearted summons before the dawn?

'Men, let me speak. I want to tell you about Ivan Mitrich!' shouted one of our fellow drinkers. By this time the tumblers had begun to take effect. It was difficult for any one man to attract the attention of the others. They were talking and listening all at once. However, they quietened down. 'Men, I want to tell you – oh, what a man he was! I was going back from the fair at Cherkutino, there still were fairs then, I look and there is Ivan Mitrich sitting on the grass. What a man he was – well, you know yourselves.'

'Certainly.'

'He never in all his life hurt a living thing, let alone a human being.'

'You want to know what sort of a man he was? You ooffend him, deliberately ooffend him . . .'

'Yes, as I was saying, he was sitting on the grass and he asked me to give him a lift home. He said he would give me a measure of oats if only I would take him back. All right. I brought him home, but whilst he was in the cart and I was driving, the drink got the better of him. Aunt Agasha ran straight out with a thick stick and didn't she give him . . .'

'Hold it, hold it. It's not right to talk like that. We haven't got together for that. Stop it.'

The orator became embarrassed, fell silent and sat down.

'The ancients said: *de mortuis aut bene aut nihil* – either speak well of the dead or say nothing at all.'

Then the farm-workers' foreman, Vasiliy Mikhaylovich, jumped up.

'Let me tell you about one occasion. I was going around the village to get people along to a meeting. Now at that meeting they wanted to dismiss me.' At this point the speaker's throat became choked with emotion at the memory and tears came to his eyes. 'And he said: "I'll come. Only let me speak on your behalf. . . ."' The glass started to tremble in the foreman's hand. 'Ah! That's the sort of man he was.'

'Don't clink glasses, men, it's not done.'

Suddenly our quiet, at any rate peaceable banquet was noisily interrupted by an indignant cry, backed up by a fist striking the table.

'What's this, then? The foreman speaks and it's the truth, but when I speak it isn't the truth?' Foam flew from the lips of the offended man. 'No, I told nothing but the truth both about the fair and the measure of oats. . . . I'll show who's telling the truth. . . . Oh, that's it, is it? If I speak it's "Sit down, that's untrue." If the foreman speaks, it's the truth? Let me through. I'll show who's telling the truth!'

Perhaps it would have ended in a brawl, because his efforts to stand up for his truth were enormous, beyond control. But because of the nature of the occasion, they somehow managed to settle down.

In order to calm things down they began a conversation concerning an event with which everyone was familiar except me. They all laughed as they recalled it, only I did not know what was coming. The chairman, sitting to my left, began to tell me 'You know the man. He's a good man.' He named a farm-worker from the next village. 'He and a friend had evidently been to the Broomstick Restaurant.'

All this was new to me, but I guessed immediately what the talk was going to be about and remembered what Gogol said: that if a Russian slaps a nickname on you, he will hit upon just the right one. True, here it was a question of finding such a name for a phenomenon rather than a person, but it is the same thing. Buying vodka in the shop, tipplers glance around, wondering if there might be a warm place to sit where they would have a glass, a table, somewhere to put out onions or a jar of preserves. I do not suppose that Verukha, a middle-aged woman living on her own, herself invited the first such people in. It seemed to happen spontaneously but at the same time inevitably. As soon as the machine operators, drivers, farm-workers feel like it, off they go with their drink to Verukha, where without fail they will find all they need. That is, relative warmth, a table, glasses, a hunk of bread, even forks, even water if they need some to drink afterwards. Not least important is an ability to talk on the part of the mistress of the house. There is none of that sugary 'Please come in, come along, my dear guests.' Things are less polished there, but simpler for that.

'What, are you round again? So you're here, too?' (That is to someone in particular.) 'Didn't your wife beat you enough with those sticks on Thursday? Once you get a skinful, you forget everything.'

After that kind of introduction the guests feel somehow more at ease. They joke, drink, even fight right there, and there under the bench they sleep it off if they have too much. After each of these set-tos the mistress of this peculiar sort of tavern is left with the empty bottles – her only form of profit. Now, it seems, they call this improvised tavern the Broomstick Restaurant.

So, then, the hero of the adventure which the chairman had begun to relate had been in the Broomstick Restaurant. On the way home to the village he decided to put on a show. He started to roll about in the snow and shout: 'Oh, heavens! Heavens!' They heard him in the village. His wife gathered the neighbours together, grabbed the sledge and ran to help. They saw that the man was gripping his stomach, that he could not walk or even stand. But the man was big and heavy and the sledge was small. At this point they laughed louder than ever round our table. It seems the big chap's shoulders could fit on the sledge, but they had to lift his long legs and carry them, one person for each leg. Together they carried him down the steep hill and then uphill. They had to cross a river. This caused a great deal of trouble. The trickster should have made a joke of it all in time, before they had taken so many pains. But he held out right to the house. He had spent the time composing a rhyme; and he performed his new work near the porch:

> About the field the blizzard rages,
> White the snow falls from the skies,
> Home they carried me together
> And I can't believe my eyes!

Everyone who had run to help him and rescue him was angry. One of them even spat on the sledge. The joker, as they say, had gone too far. I, too, blurted out, in spite of myself, that you cannot play with people's trust, that you cannot get lower than that. The chairman suddenly paused and began to sing the praises of the luckless practical joker. But there was no need; I know myself that he is a thoroughly good man. I have to say that the chairman did not find any ancient Roman proverb to fit the occasion.

Meanwhile passions were running high around the table. That moment was about to be upon us of which the deceased, Ivan Dmitrievich, had dreamt when he left the instructions concerning the banquet in his memory: it was time to take us all by the arm and lead us home.

Alexander Ivanovich (a person too complex to sum up in two words) stood up and managed to achieve silence.

'Comrades,' he said, rocking noticeably, 'what are we doing? We are making a lot of noise, laughing, you might say we're chortling away,

but why did we come here? I propose. . . . You women, this concerns
you, too . . . I propose that we all stand and pay our respects in silence.'

Village people are not accustomed to solemnity. Tears shone in
nearly every eye.

'That's it. We've paid our respects. And now I propose – the
chairman of the farm, his deputy, the foreman are all here – I propose
that here and now we resolve to put railings round Ivan Mitrich's
grave and install electric light in Aunt Agasha's house.'

'When the snow melts and it's dry, why not put up railings?'

'What about the light, men? We'll make it Sergey Toreyev's
responsibility. He can take it on, agree it with the electrician and see
that in the space of two days. . . .'

The seeker after truth, whom they had not allowed to speak a short
time earlier, immediately raised a dissonant voice: 'Ah! Light for him
after he'd dead, but why not earlier when he was alive?'

'Oh, be quiet. Ivan Mitrich himself didn't want electric light.'

'So, it's decided. In a period of two days . . .'

The foreman raised his hand: 'I have another proposal here. Since
we have with us here, well, someone in television and so on . . . let him
describe it all – a small piece, a little note, everything that went on
here. It went well. . . . We've honoured his memory. . . . All's just as it
should be. . . . And then he can send it to a magazine or a newspaper.'

'Two days would be too little. Let him have tomorrow to recover
from the drink.'

'Let him have a week even.'

'All right. I shan't forget. If you put in the lighting, I'll write about
it.'

As it turned out, it took exactly two days to install the light for Aunt
Agasha. There was nothing more for me to do than sit down at my desk
and open the inkpot. It is not my business to judge whether or not I
have carried out the commission well. I have tried to be conscientious.

A WINTER'S DAY

Have you ever once left your bed earlier than usual and met the very start of the day not at home, but somewhere near a river or in a forest? Then you well know the feeling of regret, of belated vexation over sleeping so feebly and irretrievably through all those previous mornings – and how many thousands of them there were! It means, in fact, that you slept through the best that life so simply and easily wanted to give you.

It is precisely this feeling of regret that I must record before anything else; but then there follow delight, a singing heart, a sense of lightness and joy that this particular morning has not, after all, been wasted.

The morning was a matt lilac in colour, as if the world were lit by unseen, well-camouflaged lamps with shades of lilac porcelain. The snow which stretched endlessly in all directions was lilac, the hoar-frost on the birches was lilac, the trunks of the birches were tinged with lilac, the clouds were lilac at the point where the sun would appear at any moment. I should not have been surprised if the sun's globe had risen lilac into the sky from behind the snows. But, as if impossibly, the sun rose bright red, like an old-fashioned five-copeck piece heated in a flame, and everything in the world turned pink and red: a switch had been thrown and another lamp turned on, only this one had a crimson shade.

It was near to twenty degrees below. Every deep breath produced a prickling sensation in the nose.

I do not know if this is true of others, but I sometimes fall into a sort of ecstasy when breathing and the delight in breathing is not enough but I want more, a kind of fuller contact with the surrounding world. Usually this kind of ecstatic mood comes over me on a warm summer's evening. But now on this frosty, increasingly colourful and bright morning, I sensed within myself that rare but nevertheless familiar feeling.

It would be interesting to know if HE also feels something special today, or is it all the same to him what the morning is like as long as he can eat all he wants and hide away in a secluded corner? Or perhaps he, too, can feel ecstasy over such an unusual morning. And does he have any presentiment of the inevitable thing that is in store for him, does he have a presentiment of his fate? And his fate – is us!

Only for a moment did it seem to me absurd to set out to kill on such a morning. Anyway, most likely the walk would bring nothing. Of the five of us not one was a decent hunter, we were really just local amateurs. We only went because, in the first place, we had long been meaning to; secondly, we had at last obtained a licence to kill one elk and, thirdly, we thought of hunting as simple and quick. We would spot him and fire at him just as if he were a cow, and that would be that. Ahead of us would be a tasty hot meal. We would drink together, talk, joke, laugh; in what better way could you spend your day off in a small provincial town?

I am not a hunter but a fisherman. How many times did they tell me that I would be a hunter after the first shot; how they would try to convince me that I was not a hunter simply because I did not know what hunting was! But, no, I say that you have to be born a hunter.

I have an excellent small-bore rifle, with which I can hit a Michaelmas daisy, a fir-cone, a small jug or a ten-copeck piece, and at such a distance where a hit depends on the marksman rather than the weapon. I have been out in the forest a few times with my gun (I like shooting very much), and have brought back for dinner perhaps some blackbirds grown fat on ashberries, or a wild pigeon, or a grey-hen. After each hunting expedition I studied my feelings as exactly as possible but, alas, I was not able to trace any zeal, enthusiasm or thrill in a heart, as I concluded, unsuited to hunting.

True, today my interest had been a little aroused. Perhaps this was helped by our particularly painstaking collective efforts and preparations. Those cartridges, the sharp hunting-knives; and also the unusual nature of the game – it was after all an elk, not a wild pigeon, a grouse or a blackbird!

Perhaps I should admit to you that I had never seen an elk roaming free as an animal in the wild and not a prisoner at the zoo. Actually I do not recall having seen one even in a zoo, where you pay more attention to tigers, snow leopards and hippopotamuses. You are too lazy to take the extra fifty steps to the elk compound. Now I was faced not only with seeing but with killing this beast, killing it in the forest in accordance with all the rules of hunting and with the rights of an armed man; and man is the master of the earth and lord of nature, or at least he considers himself so.

Although, if you think about it, why should not birds, for example, which of course outnumber people on this earth (a hundred billion of them), not consider that the planet Earth is meant mainly for them? Why should the insects (three hundred thousand species) – all those mosquitoes, ants, beetles and butterflies – not look upon themselves as the essential inhabitants of the planet, and on all the others as existing for their, the mosquitoes' and ants', convenience? And that is not all. Perhaps some deadly bacillus will finally win out against all other forms of life and remain to rule over the earth alone! True, then there would be nobody to admire a frosty winter's morning such as this, to admire the dawn-tinted snow or the sky when your head swims with the call of its boundless blue.

And so ahead of me walks an employee of the militia, Manechkin. At his side is the director of a small textile factory, Syromyatin. Behind them two more lords of nature hurry along together, puffing at cigarettes as they go, the director's driver, Bykov, and an accountant, Krasnov. I am a district employee. . . . Anyway, that is not important. They invited me and I came.

Gradually the road narrows, we stretch out into a thin line and in single file enter the frosted forest, where nothing moves or stirs. Our tactics for the hunt are simple and reliable. We have to walk through the forest until we come across fresh elk tracks left during the night. Then we will split up and go to left and right of the tracks in a pincer movement. If we meet up again on the elk track, it means the pincers have caught nothing and the animal has gone on farther. If, on the other hand, we come together in a place where there are no tracks and none of us has crossed any, then it means that HE is somewhere inside the circle. On a hunt we do not say 'elk' or 'animal', but only 'HE'. I think the same thing applies in other hunts for big game.

When we were absolutely sure that HE was close to us in the forest we would go to our places and one of us would frighten him so that he decided to move out of the circle. Our task was made easier by the fact that in our area the patches of woodland are small, like little islands in a white sea of snow. It would be easy both to trace where he entered the wood and to satisfy ourselves that he had not gone out again.

We followed the edge of the forest and soon actually came upon some tracks. Frequent deep pits, or rather holes, stretched across the field from an aspen wood to our small group of birches. The elk had made deep marks in the snow as he stepped along. The track was like a wide ploughed furrow.

'Perhaps it's yesterday's,' the accountant, Krasnov, suggested timidly. The walk had made him breathless, he was red in the face, fifty years old and evidently wanted everything to end there. We had had a walk, blown away the cobwebs – and that was fine.

'Yesterday's!' the director's driver sarcastically repeated after the accountant. 'A hunter must have a sharp eye. Look, he knocked a hazel bush. There is no frost on the bush. And when did the frost appear? Today. That means he passed not long ago, when the frost had already formed. He passed by and knocked it off the bush. That's why there's no frost on it. That's it for sure, men, what else? Perhaps he went by five minutes ago. I fancy there is still an aura around the bush – the crystal particles are still in the air.' Bykov, pleased with himself, was showing off his scientific jargon.

Manechkin was in charge. He briskly gave the orders: who was to circle the wood from the right and who from the left; he left me where we were in case HE decided to make off along his own tracks.

'Don't stand right on the tracks. After all, it's a wild animal, get behind a tree twenty yards off. You can fire from behind a tree.'

As I stood at my post, for the first quarter of an hour I thought it would have been better if the accountant had stayed there. He would have been glad of the rest. But I suppose that was the way fate wanted it. I could not contradict Manechkin; they would have thought I was afraid to stay on the tracks. And, generally speaking, out hunting, as in war, you do not contradict.

Then I began to recall a number of episodes when wounded elks had attacked people and, as they said, punched a hoof right through them. One person took such a blow on his skull that it flew off. An elk drove another hunter up a tree and held him there until the poor man froze to death, sitting motionless on the bare branches.

I had a look round and could not see a suitable tree nearby that I might climb up: all around were birches with smooth trunks and some hazel brushwood.

And then there was the time when an elk fell down quite still and the hunter went up to it to skin it and then the elk's hind leg, perhaps in the agony of death, kicked out at him. The hunter flew off ten yards; well, not the hunter any more but the hunter's corpse.

After that, like parts of a hazy, half-forgotten dream, I began to recall a number of scenes from a book I had read in early childhood. The book was about a proud, strong elk that always lived alone, like a hermit. And it told of his inaccessible island amidst the marshes to which he would retreat, and of how he once fought with a huge village bull and won; and how a hunter tried his hardest to track down and kill this extraordinary animal.

You could say the writer turned that elk into a personality, so that it stood out from the crowd, from all the other elks on earth. And so he became dear and close to me. Not only would I not kill him myself, but I would prevent others from hunting him if I could.

And the one who is about to come out of the forest straight at your gun?

That one I do not know. That one is one of the crowd. He is ordinary, nameless, uninteresting. A good number of them are killed every winter.

Then he came. First I heard the shake of a hazel bush, then steps in the snow, then a loud, rhythmic breathing, like automatic bellows. A pinkish vapour curled about the animal's face. The characteristic humped back of the male had touched an overhanging hazel bush and the pink vapour of his breath blended with the pink-tinged snow as it settled, itself as fine and light as vapour. A few large stars of snow glinted in the mist.

I noticed that I was holding my breath and that my legs seemed to be not mine but someone else's.

The fact that this was the first time I had seen a real adult elk close up, that for the first time I had to kill such a huge, living creature, that his movement through the frosty forest had been beautiful – all this made me lose three or four seconds fruitlessly. And so I raised my weapon clumsily and hurriedly; because of my ungainly winter clothes the butt of the rifle did not fit into my shoulder, did not sit comfortably, as I was used to when firing my own gun. The sights which I sought feverishly were also unlike what I was accustomed to: the rear sight was too shallow, open and wide and the front sight was too low and small.

A few seconds delay was enough for the elk to pass my line of fire and, catching his hindquarters on the front sight, I decided it was useless to shoot there, quickly aimed at his head and let fire at a place below the ear. The elk shook his head and even, I think, roared or bellowed, jumped and, without looking back (without looking back, damn it!), went on his way. Then I let fire once more from behind, aiming anywhere, whereupon the animal broke through into some low shrub over which I twice glimpsed his hump before he disappeared from view.

I must have been firing mechanically and thoughtlessly though, as I did not immediately rush along the tracks into the bushes, reloading my rifle on the way, but stood with my mouth open, with an unloaded rifle, reliving the fantastic vision I had experienced.

The lord of the forests had proudly and decorously (without looking back, damn it!) passed by in a pinkish mist and now there was nothing.

I should have felt no surprise if there had been no tracks left on the snow and the pinkish mist had turned out to be precisely that and nothing more. But the tracks did exist. And there was more: starting from the place where the animal had shaken his head, the snow was liberally sprinkled with scarlet and extremely bright blood. And starting where I had let fire a second time, the footprints on the right were also spattered with red. That was how it went on from that place, with blood in the tracks and roundish splashes at the sides like scattered cherries.

The other marksmen ran up and interpreted things in detail: he was wounded in the head and one right leg, probably the hind leg. We had to follow him, he would not go far.

At first we rushed off along the tracks almost at a run (the snow at that time was still not deep, especially on open ground). In this way we ran as far as some low bushes. We thought he was lying right there, that we would merely part the bushes and straight away we would see him. But we had to pass right through the bushes into open country once more. This was transversed by a bloody track which led off into a group of firs, grey with hoar-frost but, nevertheless, black looking after the birch grove.

'No, men, that won't do,' said Manechkin commandingly. He was no less out of breath than the rest of us. 'There's a long chase ahead. No hurrying.Now, fellow, we'll see which of us holds out the longest! He's bound to lie down somewhere. He can't do otherwise. I know this animal very well.'

There began the lengthiest and most boring part of our hunt. Our initial enthusiasm had gone. We began to notice a degree of tiredness, the first signs of which, of course, go away and are forgotten on a long trip.

If anyone had told us straight away that we should have to make our way through twenty-five kilometres of snowy whiteness, right until evening perhaps – who knows? – we should have jacked it all in (the accountant would have, anyway!), but we knew nothing except that we had to press on farther.

Manechkin, like a regular tracker, informed us: 'You see, he's scooped up a mouthful of snow as he passed. He's out of breath. And there's some pink foam from his lips. He's going to snuff it.'

'A real Dersu Uzala,' joked the director's well-read driver about Manechkin.

It is a good thing that they did not criticize my really very poor shots. Manechkin, who was walking ahead of us all, shouted out joyfully: 'Ah, here he . . . lay down. . . . All right. . . . We'll run him down!

Now, old fellow, it's all patience, a case of who can stand it the longest!'

The place where the animal had lain, pink with red patches, was under a big-branched fir. And here as he lay he had scooped up the snow with his lips and rested for a minute, perhaps five, who knows? Gradually, as I became more tired, I grew more and more sorry for the elk. He was so proud, so beautiful, so free – and in such a pitiful, hopeless and degraded state. Could he not turn about? Could he not hurl himself towards his enemies? Of course we should have finished him off for sure. We will probably get him anyway. It would have been better for him if he had been in a blinding, wild frenzy. But I suppose he was following some forest law of the elks. Perhaps it was one of the foremost laws of elk life. That law is wise. It tells him to keep going on and on.

I also understood the whole horror, the total terror of this slow, fateful chase. The winter's day is advancing steadily. The morning is long passed. A plain, greyish shroud is drawn across the sky. Soon, little by little, the light will begin to fail – the December day is short! By four in the afternoon the darkness of dusk falls. And we are still walking and walking. If we had run in a fit of enthusiasm we should have run out of breath long ago and ceased the chase. But we are not running. We are more cunning, more experienced, more malicious than the elk. We are not hurrying; sometimes we rest on tree stumps, brushing off their caps of snow, and have a smoke. The driver or perhaps Manechkin takes the opportunity to tell a funny story, after which the teller laughs loudly and the others say knowingly: 'Oh yes! These things happen! I wonder who turns out such good jokes!'

We do not hurry and that is the whole horror of it for the hunted animal. He has already lain down to rest three times and the distance between his stops is shorter each time. Is he, perhaps, hoping to play for time until nightfall? That would be wasted effort. Tomorrow we shall renew the chase from the point reached this evening and once more we shall have a whole winter's day at our disposal. Once again he will be forced on, shedding his blood. Anyway, most likely he will die during the night. No, why at night? The day alone will be long enough. We shall press on a little harder and catch up with him.

The elk lay down to rest for a fifth time some one and a half kilometres on from his fourth stop. Manechkin signalled us to go more carefully and in silence. The animal was near. He could hurl himself out of the bushes in mortal despair and do all the damage he wanted to at least one of his hateful two-legged enemies, split him apart as if with an iron plough.

And, true, the animal has begun to lie down every hundred yards. He gets to lie down just when he hears steps and voices. He has to stand up once more on his strangely weakened legs, which no longer seem to be his and, even at a crawl, even right down on his belly, move on, on, on.

'He's lying there!' our leader whispered to us, although we could see for ourselves – this was in a sparse pine forest – that he was lying keeled over on one side, his heavy neck bent round, and looking at us as we came towards him, even if we were afraid to get close.

'He's bleeding to death! Come on, men, fan out from tree to tree. We'll fire at forty paces if we can get that close.'

I wanted to look into his eyes. I wondered what I should see in them: endless tiredness and anguish, an imploring look or one of burning, deadly hatred along with pain and anger over his lost strength? However, the elk was looking not at me but at Manechkin. Perhaps he instinctively felt who was his chief enemy. Perhaps because Manechkin was about five steps nearer to him than the others. Going up to a distance of forty paces, or so it seemed, we began to fire pell-mell at the animal where it lay. After the first shot he started up, got on to his knees but crashed down once more, this time on to his other side, his face towards us.

From ten paces (mindful of those hunters' tales), we each took one more shot to make certain. The torture which for him had lasted a whole winter's day was over. Now nothing hurt him anywhere.

First of all we examined the earlier wounds, the result of my shots. One piece of lead had hit the base of an antler and from this there came the splashes, as large as ripe cherries. My second shot had splintered his hind leg. So he went for twenty-five kilometres on three legs. Is that likely? Can any living being endure a run like that? Evidently it is possible.

Manechkin and the director and the driver began to busy themselves with knives around the carcass. The accountant and I, being more tired than the others, sat down a little way off.

'We've got a good one here,' muttered the butchers. 'Not less than fifty kilos. And the head, look at the head on him – like your barn!'

'A head the size of a cart! It's a pity it's caked with blood.'

'It will wash off, no trouble!'

'You know what, men, there's no point in bothering with him now, you know.'

'Why not?'

'It's beginning to grow dark. We've come a long way and we're tired. I recognize the area. We're not far from Mitrofan's hut. So I suggest we cut out the liver and go to Mitrofan's place. In an hour, an hour and a half at the most, we'll be there in the warmth, sitting down to eat. We'll fry up the liver, and we won't be short of other things.'

'And where do we put the elk? Leave it for the wolves?'

'What wolves are there here? He'll keep until tomorrow. And tomorrow we'll find a horse and pick him up. Judge for yourselves. We can't carry off fifty kilos on our shoulders. Wolves or not, we've no choice in our situation. And the liver's fresh, the best food there is for a tired man.'

The forester Mitrofan's hut was oppressively hot. He had not yet gone to bed and was waxing a string with cobbler's wax, making it strong, black and shiny. At the arrival of guests he brushed off the bench some felt remnants, an awl, his cobbler's knife and some other things, into a plywood box. He pushed the box under the bench, followed by his low cobbler's stool – a tub with some raw leather stretched over it to sit on. He was visibly pleased to see guests; guests for him brought variety to his forest life, and besides, fresh elk liver was an excuse for a drink.

In the hearth of his Russian stove beneath the trivet there brightly burned a piece of birchwood and some resinous spruce kindling.

Cutting the liver into large, shapeless pieces, Mitrofan slapped it into a huge frying-pan. With each new piece there was the sound of crackling, hissing and sizzling. For a moment the smoke from the burning oil engulfed the pan. Mitrofan held back his head and turned his face aside, afraid of the acrid smoke and still more of the spluttering oil.

With what pleasure had we anticipated a thousand times, as we plodded on through the winter's day, this priceless moment when we should be warm, when we should no longer have to trek on across unknown country, when there would be a freshly cooked hot meal of elk liver on the table, something to drink and friendly, happy people at the table with their uncomplicated tales. After all, here both the surroundings and the way of life were themselves plain and uncomplicated.

Manechkin (in command to the last!) poured into our glasses some green, strange-smelling vodka, adding cordially: 'Arkhangelsky Suchok vodka, damn good stuff! All the frost and tiredness – that will all disappear. An exhilarating and successful hunt – and such a prey. Well done, my dear huntsmen! Let us drink, as they say, fresh from the kill!'

It is strange, but as he spoke I did not feel any exhilaration or sense of success, or the slightest feeling of satisfaction. The others also seemed to be completely indifferent. But that was to be understood: a terrible tiredness had got the better of us.

We were drinking on empty stomachs. Is it surprising that we pounced with animal greed on the hot, smoking food? We ate quickly, hurrying to fill our stomachs, helping the pieces in with our hands, almost jamming them into our mouths by force. If a piece was too hot, we rolled it about in our mouth from side to side, sucking the air backwards and forwards in our mouth in order to cool the unbearably hot chunk. And as always happens after a long time without food, we grew full unexpectedly quickly and joylessly.

To revive our appetites we drank another glass each. But the food was going down with increasing difficulty. Our eyes grew dim and misty, losing their human expressiveness and lustre. Our forks moved more and more slowly, our tongues became heavy – we seemed to be falling asleep at the table.

The factory director suddenly belched loudly and, his hand clasped to his mouth, ran to the door.

'He didn't chew it,' Manechkin explained to us. 'He swallowed it in chunks. And the drink could not have agreed with him. Arkhangelsky Suchok isn't so good.' And suddenly he started to go slightly pale, his attention taken by what was going on inside him; and, as if without thinking, he moved his chair back, clearing the way.

The driver was vomiting in his sleep, although without waking up, and we were unable to shake him out of it.

I, too, began to feel bad and I went out for some fresh air.

There was a starry, moonlit, fairy-tale silence in the outside world. The forest was sunk in moonlight, like weed in the crystal waters of an aquarium. On the porch of the hut fell the shadow of a huge mossy pine. Because I was myself in shadow, the universe seemed yet brighter and more blue. And because from time to time there came a cracking noise from the forest, the moonlit silence seemed yet more translucent.

I clasped one of the supports of the porch, put my hands round it, almost hung on to it and stood without noticing the cold. All the events of the day (apart from the first lilac-pink of the morning) began to seem sad and absurd to me. What was it all for? So that Manechkin and Bykov could end by gorging themselves on fresh liver.

But perhaps none of it had happened? Perhaps we had not tortured that huge, bleeding animal with the insufferable agony of the chase, had not shot at him point-blank with five deadly rifles? Perhaps he is standing there, hiding in the black shadows cast by the moon and listening to the rustling of the winter forest which we, humans, cannot distinguish. And his hump is silvery from the frost and a greenish, moonlit vapour curls about his face.

In the distance rose up a shrill, heart-rending, screeching howl. Evidently the hungry, yellow-toothed wolves were gathering for the feast.

THE GUESTS WERE ARRIVING
AT THE DACHA . . .[1]

We shall say straight away that this was a different dacha, these were
different guests and that it was a different time of day; and things were
different not simply because people came late in the evening on that
earlier occasion. . . . Anyway, we can read about it again:

> The room was filling with ladies and gentlemen who had arrived
> simultaneously from the theatre, where a new Italian opera was
> being performed. Each guest made his way through to the circular
> table where they were pouring out tea, hurriedly bowed to the
> hostess and disappeared in the crowd. Little by little order was
> established. The ladies occupied their places on the sofas. A circle of
> gentlemen gathered nearby. Games of whist were begun. Only a
> few young men remained on their feet and the general noise of
> conversation was replaced by the perusal of Parisian lithographs.

In our case it was not night at all but, on the contrary, not so long
after midday when the guests gradually began to gather at the dacha in
Michurinets. Some of them had come on the electric train and walked
up the green dacha-lined street, but the majority arrived in cars –
Zhigulis and Volgas.

Oleg Sergeevich Vetlugin, who had a quite responsible job in one of
the ministries (which one is not important, there are over a hundred of
them now), and his wife Tamara Vasilyevna, were celebrating their
Silver Wedding. They had waited a few weeks so as to combine the
festivities with Tamara Vasilyevna's birthday. Her age was not
mentioned, but somehow everyone simply knew that Tamarochka
Vetlugina had hit forty-seven.

Although Oleg Sergeevich worked in one specific department, he
was a man with wide interests and had, as you might put it, a
particular talent when it came to getting along with people. Amongst
his friends and acquaintances there were artists and scholars, military

[1] The opening words of an unfinished prose work by Pushkin.

people and sportsmen. That day even the managers of two large stores in the capital happened to be invited. Your obedient servant, the one now writing these lines, was also among the guests and also, by the way, came in his own car.

The guests were all married and arrived in couples: man, wife, man, wife. Whenever a new married couple appeared at the dacha gate, the exclamations, hugs and kisses would begin all over again. The guests, embarrassed, pretending to have their minds on other things, handed the hostess presents wrapped in paper and she, just as embarrassed and with an air of indifference, carried them away, without unwrapping them in front of everybody, and placed them together on a table in one of the rooms. They brought few flowers, which was understandable: why take flowers to a dacha where there are already plenty of flowers growing?

Two of the hostess's lady friends had arrived before the others and were at work, along with some female relatives, in the kitchen, whilst the guests, who immediately separated off upon arrival (the women to the women, the men to the men), were wandering in groups about the plot and smoking as they waited to be called to the table. Many of them were well known to each other but had not met since the last such occasion for a feast.

Of course, if the same kind of gathering were happening somewhere abroad, everyone would immediately have a glass in his hand with whisky and ice in it, or gin and tonic or some such aperitif; but, thank God, that has not yet caught on with us, and, God willing, it will not do so. What a way to carry on: you drink without eating anything before you sit down at the table, and when you do sit down (which is the right time for a proper drink), they will not give you anything good and strong, only light dry wine. I can see neither logic nor charm in that. No, we must use all our strength to protect our Russian way of eating and drinking from foreign influence. You sit squarely down at the table and load your plate with all sorts of tasty things perfected by your grandfathers and great-grandfathers over the course of centuries. Small salted, pickled or chopped mushrooms, brawn with horse-radish, salted tomatoes, pickled white cabbage, jellied meats with horse-radish, herring with home-made mustard sauce, pork fat (with mustard), well-boiled potatoes, two or three kinds of salad (dressed preferably with soured cream rather than mayonnaise), then come as much red and black caviare as you can afford (or, more exactly, as much as you can get), some nice salmon with lemon, cured fillet of sturgeon, smoked sturgeon or simply boiled sturgeon, again with horse-radish, cod livers (which should be mixed with finely chopped onion), soused apples, small rice and egg pasties, fresh little cucumbers, slightly salted cucumbers, tomatoes and various sorts of greenery.

It is not hard to see that I have not listed even half the possible good things which may embellish a Russian table. Well, let us add ham, or cold boiled pork, boiled tongue, crabmeat, prunes stuffed with nuts, black and greeen olives, cold roasted leg of mutton, pickled wild onions, pickled or stuffed peppers, *satsivi* (Georgian dishes are in vogue at the moment), garden radishes, black radishes, marinated summer squashes, salted water-melons, tripe with mustard, sprats and sardines, smoked sausage, naturally – well, there is plenty of it, as I say, I have not listed even half. And then, when it is all set out on the table, you place some of this and that on your plate, and that is when you should raise the goblet to your lips, and not with some sort of crushed ice in it, but ordinary clear vodka, or, even better, wine which you have made yourself from, say, horse-radish. Or caraway. Or blackcurrant leaves. Or aspen bark. . . . No, God keep us from losing our own ways of doing things and from going over to those absurd aperitifs. . . . And even then the hostess will give notice (so that the guests leave a little room) that there will be borsch or that there is a leg of pork roasting in the oven.

Finally the order was given and, although not really all at the same time (when there are many people, they always string themselves out), the guests made their way to the table and began to sit down. There is no longer any need to describe the table, because everything listed a few lines back was on it; and, in addition, there were jugs of home-made kvass and bottles of brandy and mineral water, soft drinks and dry wines.

It was immediately apparent that only married couples had gathered here for the Vetlugins' family celebration. The eldest were approaching sixty and the youngest, the hosts' son and his young wife, both with blue eyes, fair hair and good looks, were no more than twenty-five, a fact which, by the way, had not prevented them from having a second baby. At this moment the baby – eight-month-old Nastenka – was asleep in one of the upper rooms of the dacha. The young couple were called, as if deliberately, Vanya and Masha, or, to put it another way, Ivan-and-Marya.*

People were sitting in pairs even at the table. Perhaps no one had thought how to seat the guests, or perhaps it is an ingrained habit with

* 'Ivan-and-Marya' is the Russian name for the plant *Melanpyrum nemorosum* (cow-wheat). – D.M.

us, but it so happened that each husband ended up sitting next to his own wife, whom he was going to have to look after the whole time. The only advantage to be gained from this was that you would not have to try very hard, you could forget to do it, get talking, and she would serve herself.

. . . Perhaps because of my age or because I have stored up such a quantity of impressions over many years which have, in the well-known manner, suddenly acquired quality through quantity, but I could name a few, let us say, aspects of our national life which have become not only annoying to me but, to put it bluntly, even quite intolerable. Well, you tolerate them of course, for how can you escape them? But tolerating them is becoming more and more unbearable and arduous.

Without straying from the subject too far, let us look at two annoying habits that have relevance to the banquet at which we happened to be present.

I remember a fellow villager, Vasiliy Mikhaylovich Zhiryakov, coming up to me in Alepino and saying: 'I have been meaning to ask you about this for ages, 'lekseich. . . . I have a relative in Moscow who I was staying with and we had an argument. I simply couldn't believe something he said, so I thought I would ask you some time, 'lekseich.'

'What was it, then?'

'My relative works abroad in our embassy. The town has a funny name, it's hard to say, but that's not important. Well, he says. . . . No, it can't be true. . . . Nothing will make me believe it.'

'What does he say, then?'

'He says that abroad. . . . No, I got into an argument over it then, and I'll say now that it can't be true. . . . But you can decide it, you're my only hope.'

'Well, what is it he says about life abroad?'

'He says that abroad. . . .' Vasiliy Mikhaylovich was about to balk at it again, but managed to pluck up courage and blurt out: '. . . that abroad they don't wash their vodka down with anything! Can it be true?'

So this is the point. Throughout the length and breadth of our country, women, young and old, and, even more surprisingly, men, have got into the habit of downing something with their vodka. Nowadays you see the same thing everywhere: a man (or woman) with a glass of vodka in one hand and a tumbler or cup full of some soft drink, usually fruit flavoured, in the other. Sugared water, in other words! The idea is, then, that you must gulp down some scented sweet drink after your vodka. But how, after this scented sweet stuff, are you going to eat herring or anything else with seasoning and taste? Why mix and mingle a superb glass of vodka and equally superb Russian-style savoury dish with this sweet and scented rubbish? Since the time of our great-grandfathers and way before them it has been understood that a glass of vodka requires a salted mushroom, a few spring onions dipped in salt, or brawn with horse-radish. Or you can take a small slice of brown bread, spread butter on it, place a spicy sprat (or two) on it, and half a hard-boiled egg on top of the sprat. . . . Why on earth, I ask you, drink lemonade between the vodka and such a 'piece of stuffing', as people in the know call it? Ugh!

I think the initial impetus for this habit must have come from the doorways where drunks gather in threes and hurriedly splash round the vodka. In those circumstances, of course, the easiest (and cheapest) thing to do is follow up with lemonade. But at the table there are plenty of titbits. . . . You must agree that there is something tasteless, unbeautiful, banal and, if you like, plebeian in the sight of a man or women holding a glass of vodka in one hand and a tumbler of lemonade in the other. Ughhhh!

The other thing is the speeches we make during meals.

I remember the Silver Wedding of my Bulgarian friend, Dimitriy Metodiev, and his wife (a Moscow girl) Natasha. About a hundred people were invited. One speaker congratulated the 'newly-weds' on behalf of the friends and acquaintances present, and Dimitriy himself thanked them for coming. Otherwise it was eat, dear guests, drink, sing (if you like), chat away with each other over the meal, peaceably and wisely (as far as possible), but do not force yourselves on people at the table, do not torture them with your long, not always interesting speeches.

It's no good, though! Some will even take offence and say they were passed over and not given the chance to make a speech, whilst others will feel offended because nobody made a speech about them.

I am not against speeches at banquets altogether, that would be another extreme. I remember what a remarkable speech Iuriy Lvovich Prokushev delivered at Vasiliy Fedorov's sixtieth birthday party. He talked about Russian writers and poets. He spoke wonderfully and touched everyone present; but, you know, I studied at a technical college, my original profession was technician-toolmaker and I know what timekeeping is. Well, I once surreptitiously kept time at an ordinary, run-of-the-mill dinner of the sort we have these days, at which about forty people were present, and of the hundred and fifty minutes (two and a half hours) that the dinner lasted, we spent one hundred and seventeen holding a wineglass in our hands, and only thirty-three, on and off, eating, drinking and chatting with our fellow guests. It is as if we are afraid to leave people to themselves during a meal, as if we are afraid they will be bored, that they will not be able to occupy themselves without some authority to organize and direct them.

The following law exists: if seven people or less are sitting at the table, then it will be united in a single conversation. If, on the other hand, there are more than seven present, not to mention twenty or thirty, they will split up into groups of three or four, each with its own topic of conversation. In order, then, to give each speaker in turn a chance to say his piece, the person in charge has to interrupt a few such conversations around the table. But what if the talk is interesting? For the first few speeches the flock of diners is more or less obedient to its leader, but afterwards, when the drink begins to do its work, it is not so easy to quieten people down. The speaker makes his speech, but they carry on talking to each other and even laughing. Sometimes you have to call for silence by tapping with a knife against a bottle, goblet or decanter, and sometimes you have to give a shout. Somehow or other, thank heavens, the noise will diminish and die away. But the drink has a disorganizing effect, not only on the masses, but on the oratorical capabilities of the performers. The speeches become more and more empty, long and tedious. Suddenly, right in the middle of the speech, noise, chatter and sometimes even giggling spring up again. Those at the head of the table realize by this time that the speeches should be brought to a halt, but it cannot be done, not everyone has said what he has to say, not everyone has been toasted. It is frightful.

Whether because at some time or another I had explained all these notions to Oleg Sergeevich, today's host, and he had taken my ideas seriously, or simply because it happened that way, but our banquet did not abound with long and frequent speeches. What is more, the people did not split into little groups, even though there were over twenty of us gathered there. I, with my pathological fear of toasts, got in first with a story, which was listened to right through, then a few jokes with a similar theme were told, and after that the general chain of conversation began to unwind. Well, we drank of course to the hosts – it was their day – and shouted 'bitter' at them,* and then we drank separately to the hostess and after that to the youngest present, the

* Guests at a wedding in Russia shout 'It's bitter' after tasting a drink, inviting the newly-weds to sweeten it with a kiss. – D.M.

blue-eyed Ivan-and-Marya, and to their daughter Nastenka, who was asleep somewhere in an upper room. But for the most part people simply talked and laughed instead of making speeches with a glass in their hand.

The conversation turned (as is natural at a Silver Wedding) to the way marriages and families instantaneously form and just as instantaneously disintegrate: seventy divorces to every hundred marriages over the last two years. That is a lot.

'It's because we do not think much of marriage,' one man argued. 'So, you get married, but does that mean everything's over, then? Look, I was walking past a cinema not long ago. It was eight in the evening. The film was going to start in five minutes and it was one I had wanted to see for a long time. There were still some tickets. Why shouldn't I watch it?'

'And what would you have said to your wife? Where were you? she'd say. At the cinema? Why did you go without me? A likely story!'

'Yes, but why shouldn't a grown man be his own master and go to the cinema? A man might want to go to the cinema by himself, sit in the foyer, gaze about and eat ice-cream. Independently like that, on his own. Why is he deprived of the right to do the simplest human things?'

'What did Tolstoy say about marriage? It's as if a man who had been striding out freely through the fields were to go and tie one leg to a woman.'

'Come on, now. . . . You wouldn't get very far without women. You would be lying about in the ditches.' (That is the women speaking, of course.)

'They would become savages, all of them.'

'Or take something else.' The men were not going to give in. 'Let's say there's a wedding and dancing. Before, it used to be looked upon as wrong to dance with your own wife at a ball, you know, and, really, to think of engaging your own wife for a mazurka. . . . It would have been impossible. Nowadays, though, all a wife does is watch her husband to see he doesn't go and dance with someone else. So he dances with another woman once, then two or three times, and she starts to glower and go stony-faced and at the first opportunity tugs at his sleeve and hisses: "We're going home right now." And you can be sure that on the way home he'll get what's coming to him . . .'

'But I think women these days have got so much initiative and independence. Look what is happening. Men, many of them, are giving up smoking, whereas women all smoke, even young girls. If you go to a concert-hall or theatre, to a literary evening or even a church, for God's sake, the majority are women. I mean the vast majority, eighty per cent or more of those present. And what do they do, especially if they are research workers or have a doctorate? They have a child and live by themselves, without a husband. And it's not always because they've been left. They do the leaving. Why, they say, do I need him? He'd only be sitting staring at the television or playing chess with a friend . . .'

'I remember a funny thing. . . .'

(I hope there is no need for me each time to describe the appearance and behaviour of the people taking part in this conversation, or to mention their names and what they do. It is not individual characters but the drift of the conversation, and even then in the most general terms, which forms the subject at present.) So, then, one of our company wanted to tell a funny story.

'An old acquaintance of mine rang me once. We used to work together. She's on the technical side, and a Doctor of Science, by the way. Zinaida Vitoldovna. She's over forty. She lives with her grown-up daughter in a good flat with two rooms in a fine old building within the B. Ring Road. Her daugher is at the University. Those two women were just like friends. Well, Zinaida Vitoldovna rang me as an old friend and asked me to come straight round. She needed my advice. So off I went. When I got to her apartment I found the corridor full of suitcases. About twelve of them. Some leather, some metal, with straps and buckles. In a word, foreign suitcases. Some of them were just like chests. "Zinaida Vitoldovna, what's this you've got, where's it all come from?" "That's the point. I don't know what to do. What do you think?"

'It seems that this is what happened. Two years earlier Zinaida Vitoldovna had been at someone's house and met a man there in the diplomatic service. So, he took her home and, well, he must have spent the night. And in three days he had to go off to some distant country somewhere in Africa. The letters and telephone calls went on for two years. And then, when his period of service in this distant place came to an end, he went straight from the airport to Zinaida Viltoldovna's, together with all his African suitcases.'

' "And where is he now?" I asked.

' "He's working in that Trade Delegation of his."

' "But what's the problem? You obviously wanted him to come here to you."

' "In a way, of course. A woman needs someone to lean on, to feel she is being looked after. She's like a vine. She needs a support, someone to cling to."

' "So what's the matter? When did he appear?"

' "Yesterday evening. We had dinner, of course, and . . . everything was fine."

' "So what's up, then?"

' "You see, I got up this morning and went to the bathroom, and it was locked. From inside. I couldn't get into my own bathroom! This really hit me. I was stunned. So my Ninochka was also going to go to the bathroom and find it locked, was she? And it's always going to be like that, is it? From now on are we going to have an odd, irrelevant, extra person hanging around our flat? What for?"

' "So throw him out, along with his cases."

' "I don't know. . . . I'm a woman on my own. . . . I need the support."

'In the evening she rang and said that the suitcases were no longer in the corridor. So that's what happened.'

'Women's liberation! But women, in liberating themselves, obviously do not know that they are their own worst enemies. A woman's strength is not in her mathematical abilities or trade-union activity. Her strength is in her femininity, and only that. Does trade-union – or any other such – activity help her show her femininity? I rather think the opposite. But the part women have played in social life, military exploits, art, now, that's a question that has not been sufficiently studied, or even begun to be studied. What about the role of women in the appearance in the world of Dante's *Divine Comedy*, *The Sistine Madonna*, *War and Peace*, the 'Moonlight' Sonata, and Beethoven's Sixth Symphony. No research has been done and no discoveries have been made in that area. Countess Walewska did not have to be a politician to get Napoleon to create the Grand Duchy of Warsaw, she simply had to be Countess Walewska. And now they've arrived at total equality. And what happens? Our houses are no longer homes and there are more divorces than marriages.'

'Well, I think casual sex is to blame for it all. A murky wave of it has engulfed the entire world. Matter of factness in such matters has exceeded all bounds.'

'So, you tell me, why has nature herself created special conditions for man in this respect?'

'What special conditions?'

'In nature a few days a year are set aside for animals, birds and fish to make love. Only we enjoy the special privilege of embracing daily, all the year round, over the whole course of our lives. Why's that? If we had only a few days a year for it, all these problems would disappear immediately, along with the infidelity, family dramas, suffering and murders caused by love and jealousy – and the suicides. Nobody has yet gathered even elementary statistics on this using of a confidential questionnaire. Out of every thousand families, how many are there in which, after three years, neither the man nor the woman has been unfaithful? What about seven years? Or fifteen? It would be useful to know.'

'Does science exist or not? Is there or is there not such a thing as science?'

'Yes, it exists, so what do you want it to tell you?'

'Let them decide once and for all what a human being is, and then they should work out the laws, the moral as well as the juridical ones, on that basis. The whole of the animal world – and man is also an animal to a certain extent – may be divided into two categories, the monogamous and the polygamous. . . .'

Whilst this conversation was going on nobody noticed that Masha had been upstairs and brought down enchanting little black-eyed Nastenka. Yes, her eyes were just like little blackcurrants! And her cheeks were pink and chubby. She was happy and wide awake now. As Masha held the tiny baby in her arms there was something Madonna-like in her (as in every beautiful young mother), and her husband, who was also young and handsome, looked on calmly, confidently and happily. This joyful young family did not take part in the conversation-cum-argument, yet simply through their blessed and wonderful existence, through their presence alone, they began unwittingly (as I noticed) to influence the conversation, even if it did continue along the old path for a time as if by inertia.

'. . . Yes, that's it, two categories, monogamous and polygamous, mono and poly. A wolf chooses himself a she-wolf, and then they live together. It would not enter the wolf's head to look round at other females, and she is just the same. They are just not programmed to be unfaithful partners. Nature herself attended to that. On the other hand, a stallion keeps a whole herd of mares. The male and female swan live together as a couple. Why, there is even a legend which says that if you kill one, the other hurls itself down to earth from the sky. But with partridges there is one cock for a whole big flock. So this is what I want to know – is man monogamous or polygamous? Religious and moral principles and laws, the moral code, that's all fine, but what has nature programmed man for, monogamy or polygamy? Let science clear that up once and for all and then you can compile your juridical laws on the basis of the laws of nature. Infidelity in marriage has existed

in all ages and with all peoples. "Caesar's wife is beyond suspicion."
Fine. But the fact that such a sentiment was necessary shows that there
was the question of suspicion. And we are not talking of any wives of
Caesar's, either, when it comes to deceiving husbands. Napoleon
found out that Josephine was being unfaithful to him in Paris whilst he
was with his army in Egypt. Unfaithful to Napoleon! Muslims are
people, too, but polygamy is the norm with them.

The ancient kings of the East had a multitude of wives, and with the
princes of Kiev before the acceptance of Christianity it was the same.
It's possible that morality and the moral code are intended to retrain
people, like parents retrain a left-handed child. But, you know, you are
born left-handed. It isn't the hand that matters, but the motor centres
of the brain. When you retrain a child, you have to destroy the already
existent chain of control to the hand and create a new one. And that
costs the body quite a lot. But you can still recognize a left-handed
person quite easily, even if he has been retrained. You have to watch
him jump over a ditch. If he jumps left foot first, then he was born left-
handed. You see, he's been retrained, but he's still naturally left-
handed deep in his brain.'

Of course all these discussions were sprinkled with jokes and
laughter. One man with a rich imagination even put forward this
really fantastic project (in fun): 'If I had my way,' he said, 'I would
introduce the following system in the country. I would make it
obligatory to hand over the sixteen-year-old lads as husbands to the
thirty-year-old women, thus placing them, so to speak, in their wise
and experienced hands, and when these husbands got to be forty or
even approaching fifty, I would further make it obligatory for them all
to marry the fifteen- and sixteen-year-old girls.' This project was met
with laughter all round.

But there were also zealous defenders of the family as a division or
unit of the State, who set about proving the rather obvious truth that
with the weakening of the family as such, society as a whole is
undermined and weakened, and the State itself is likewise undermined.
If each separate brick is weak and no good, then that would affect, you
would suppose, the soundness of the whole building.

'All your "monos" and "polys" are pure fantasy!' one woman
argued. 'It's all because of this looseness everywhere. Infidelity is due to
loose morals and nothing else. "I'll do what I want," they say.
Everything is permitted. The French are right when they say that it's
easier not to be unfaithful to a woman at all than to be unfaithful just
once. So, then, find a way of avoiding that first time. Here, look at these

two good-looking young people, in love with each other, a wonderful couple. Well, why, I ask you, should they be unfaithful to each other? What for? They should realize what they've got. And we women all have the same thing to offer. . . . We only seem different. No, don't talk to me about inborn tendencies. As far as I'm concerned, it's nothing but looseness and irresponsibility. Let's drink rather to this young family and their Nastenka. May God help them to be just as happy, close and beautiful in the future!'

I, like everyone else, also admired this young couple and their healthy, chubby little Nastenka, who was still pink from sleep. But there was a growing sense of uneasiness in my mind. It was as if I had to remember something urgently, like trying to recapture part of a dream. You try to grasp it by holding fast to the final image and working back along the chain, but the chain slips away, the image disintegrates, you will never see it again and so you will not remember the rest of the sequence. Yet you sometimes have a different feeling, the feeling that you are sure to remember what you are looking for. It is not so far beneath the surface. You will remember it now, in a second, just one final effort; or, better, find a distraction, talk and think of something else and then in a while what you are looking for will surface from the depths of your memory of its own accord, bright and new, like a transfer, freshly done and still wet.

And when it actually did surface, it shook me. The thing is that in a novel I wrote some time ago, when I came to introduce and describe the character of the heroine, I gave her a Georgian grandmother. At the time, I wrote, really without thinking, the following sentence (which I had to put right later on): 'And so, this fair-haired, blue-eyed couple suddenly had Engelsina, with her black eyes and eyebrows which met at the bridge of her nose.' Well, I wrote it and thought no more of it. What can you not write in a novel? Nevertheless, I very soon received a number of letters from geneticists. Our readers are very attentive and strict. For example, when this sentence slipped into a newspaper article, 'The tiger started to sweat with rage', the editorial office was bombarded with letters from veterinary surgeons and zoologists. It seems that tigers have no sweat-glands and so it could not have begun sweating. And it was the same in my case – the geneticists corrected me unanimously: 'Two blue-eyed parents could not have had a black-eyed girl. That is out.' I had to put the phrase right in the novel – five seconds' work.

I remembered all this and began clutching at straws. After all, a baby's eyes can still change colour up to six months, perhaps not all was lost. I nonchalantly asked the young mother how old Nastenka was.

'Oh, we're already eight months old,' answered her mother joyfully. 'We are already growing up, soon we will be walking, and then talking.'

And she played and fussed with Nastenka, showing her off to us, and Nastenka looked at us with as yet not very comprehending, but for all that extremely black little eyes.

Then Masha caught my glance. I did not intend my look to be searching, or knowing, penetrating or revealing, I simply looked at her a little more attentively, and a little longer, than I should; but still she felt something and understood, and in an instant she lowered her shining blue eyes, as if putting out some enchanted fairy lights.

A LITTLE GIRL
BY THE EDGE OF THE SEA

People ask for advice when they are in two minds. Some decision has not yet been taken. One course of action is still open, but then so is another. The chain of life, of events, facts and fates, beginning at the moment the decision is made, will be knitted and woven together either in one direction or another. Tell me, how can one avoid hesitating at such a point?

Say you advise your friend, Sergey, not to marry a girl, Tanya. He takes your advice and does not marry her. What in fact has happened? Well, taking upon yourself a responsibility so amazing that it might be better to call it irresponsibility, you have moved levers and changed some very important points, and now a number of trains will rush off in space and time along tracks different from those they would have rushed along were it not for your advice – about which, possibly, you will not remember upon waking the next day.

But the trains are people's fate: the fate of Sergey himself; the fate of poor Tanya, though, perhaps, she is not so poor; the fate of Sergey and Tanya's children, but not now, you see, of the children they would have had together! They should have had Svetochka, Irochka and Andryushka, who in time would have become a popular singer, a teacher and a technician repairing television sets. But now Tanya will not have any children at all and Sergey will have Tanechka and Slavik. Tanechka will somehow find her way into the Forestry Institute and Slavik will be called up into the army. Their unit will be stationed in the Ukraine. He will marry a local girl and settle in Vinnitsa. He will find a job driving a tractor on a State farm and at home will raise piglets and pumpkins in the vegetable garden.

And that is what you did with your advice!

And do we after all know what sort of children would have been born to Svetochka, Irochka and Andryushka, and what sort of children will be born to Tanechka and Slavik, and what they will get up to whilst they live on this earth?

When I gave a piece of advice some time ago I did not stop to think about the importance of what was happening. And I was busy with the most prosaic of things: I was sitting at a table eating a Southern dish made from sweet peppers, vegetable marrow, tomatoes, green beans and onions.

I first got to know the house about twelve years ago (my God, how time flies!), and completely by chance. I was walking along the street on a hot day by the sea-shore, looking for a room. In the middle of September the seaside becomes noticeably less crowded and vacant rooms crop up on every side, but it is always more difficult to choose one from many than simply to find one.

A most attractively shaded small yard and little white house, visible in the depths of the greenery, made me stop. I opened the gate and went along the straight path, and as I did so bunches of black grapes, dusty with white pollen, hung over me and seemed constantly to ask me to place my ample palms beneath them and receive a heavy, cool bunch.

I was shown a room that looked out upon an old, knotty persimmon, wild and dotted with yellowish fruit as tiny as cherries, and upon some bamboo-like stalks of maize, amid whose yellow colour could be seen the bright blue of the nearby sea. In the room were a single bed, a table and a cupboard for clothes – that is to say, everything I needed.

The lady of the house also undertook to feed me. I came to the table three times a day and I soon got to know the whole family.

The head of the family, Mikhail, worked in a fish-processing factory. He used to return home after six in the evening smelling of salted fish.

The mistress of the house, Katya, worked only on the plot of ground at home. The land needed to be cared for and the children, too.

A special time began in autumn. They put the leeks into bottles, then sealed them with wax and wire and buried them in the ground. They made spicy sauces. They boiled, pickled, salted, dried and cured. They pressed grapes. The scent of wine hung over the village.

The family was Russian but they did all the things the local people did; that is, whatever was decided by the climate, the land, the fruits of every kind which ripened on the land and by the customs of the people who cultivated it.

Mikhail was about forty-five, Katya seemed about ten years younger, but it is possible that the difference between their ages was not so large.

My landlords' eldest son was fourteen. He was in his eighth year at school. Lyudochka, their daughter, had just entered her sixth.

As often happens, the following year we exchanged letters and I went directly to my kind hosts. And since then I have arranged to visit their clean little house every autumn. You put out your things, your papers are on the table, you look out of the window and see the blue of the sea amid the stalks of maize, and in your soul you feel cosy and quiet, easy and happy. Does a man really need such a great amount?

So, then, I was sitting at the table eating the Southern dish prepared from sweet peppers, marrow, tomatoes, green beans and onions and drinking with the food some young, aromatic 'Isabella'. Katya was sitting opposite me cleaning some garlic for salting. Victor came into the room, took his underwater gun and flippers and went off to the sea. No one knew where Lyuda was. Mikhail had not yet returned from work.

My conversation with Katya concerned the most normal, everyday things, I cannot even remember what we were talking about at the time, and it is not important anyway; although, perhaps, it would not be a bad thing to recall exactly how our trivial conversation arrived at that unexpected point when Katya, a little embarrassed and blushing, began to confide in me.

'No, Misha and I are definitely decided. We can say that Victor is now standing on his own feet. Lyudochka, too, is a big girl. Can we really start all over again? That seems all right only to others, or to people who have had to live without children. They are unhappy and I can understand that. And then what they say is right: "It's bitter without children, but twice as much with." Thank God, we've brought up two. We've done our duty before nature.'

She mentioned nature and duty somewhat mischievously, with a twinkle in her eye, but in everything else she was serious, even very serious.

'Now we are as free as birds, our hands are untied. If we want, we can go on living here, or we can move to Russia, nearer to where we were born. And anyhow. . . . Does anyone really know what I went through when Lyudochka had double pneumonia when she was two? And what it was like for me to carry her about on my shoulder for nights on end – for a whole year?'

'Why did you have to carry her?'

'She was howling. She was quiet during the day, but as soon as it was time for us to go to bed the concert began. She howled and howled. Whilst you carried her on your shoulder, she would keep quiet. But as soon as you put her down, more howling. I was like a shadow. And giving birth is not exactly a piece of cake. We forget. Women are probably meant to forget like that. It's really a terrible torture. You know we shout and squeal like piglets having their throats cut. Oh no, when you remember that. . . . Brrr! And I'm older than I was. And Misha, as you know . . . likes a drink. There are lots of ways it could affect the child. I'd give birth to a baby with three lips or something. When are you leaving, on the twentieth? Well, then, I'll see you off and on the twenty-third I'll go along. It will be a Thursday, a good day for it.'

What on earth came over me? I myself understood that these two people, who with the passing of time had experienced youth, love, marriage, nest-building, the birth of children, had no need now of a new little wailer. And even if they did need one, well – lord! – neither Victor nor Lyudochka were going to drag their feet. They would not know what was happening before there they would be – grandchildren! The woman's nimble fingers cleaned the garlic. The heads of garlic cracked and fell into pieces with a light rustle. The white and lilac husks were left on one side and there was a great number of them compared with the firm, shiny cloves in the dish, containing that extremely powerful and complex extract invented by nature, which in human usage we call garlic.

Katya's fingers deftly cleaned the garlic. I was looking hard at them and it was that movement of her fingers, their scarcely perceptible look of agitation, which made me realize that, whilst Katya and Mikhail may have reached a decision, nevertheless now, this very moment, Katya was constantly waiting for my word, my advice, my approval of their action.

I remember clearly what I wanted to say: 'You have made the right decision. Of course, you will have to undergo an operation. These days, I should think, nobody dies of it. Have a rest, take things easy. Soon there will be grandchildren. And did you know that people love their grandchildren more than their own children?' At this point I might have developed some theory concerning degrees of biological kinship amongst close generations and subsequent ones, but instead of these thoughts I unexpectedly and artlessly inquired: 'But aren't you sorry?'

The fingers shook and dropped the clove of garlic they were cleaning. Katya raised her head and looked at me in surprise.

I had not realized that at that instant, in fact, a human life depended upon me: was he to be born or not born, to be or not to be? Lofty matters were foreign to me at that moment, I wanted to approve the family's decision, but instead I blurted out my absurd and ill-timed, 'But aren't you sorry?'

'If everyone were sorry . . .' Katya began but did not finish the sentence.

Someone continued to speak for me, following his own line of argument: 'To an extent that feeling is familiar to me. I am a poet, but I am forced to deal in prose.'

'But you write verse as well.'

'From time to time. But if I didn't spend time on prose, I should have written much more verse by now. I am short by a few hundred poems. It comes down to the fact that the prose suffocated them and they never saw the light of day.'

'But aren't you sorry?' Katya asked, her smile touched with bitterness.

'Not so much sorry,' I answered seriously, 'but sometimes I feel like knowing what sort of poems they would have been, their themes, how good or bad they would have been and, believe me, sometimes you feel depressed. The irreversibility of what has happened is frightening, the fact that I shall never know now what choked and perished in me under the heavy flagstones of accursed prose.'

After a moment's silence I dealt a blow – to use a sporting term, below the belt: 'And don't women think of the children they never gave birth to, then? It's probably not your first unborn child. Tell me, did you never want to peep just with one eye at the children you poisoned?'

Katya went white, her lips trembled. 'Why do you say things like that?'

'Forgive me. I was being rather blunt, of course. Usually women don't regret it. Only one particular woman is regretting it and suffering agonies and that's only because her small daughter died and because the daughter had a dream.'

'What sort of dream?' Katya was on her guard. 'And how could the little girl have a dream if she was dead?'

'Before her death. The little girl was dying and knew that she was dying. And the mother knew it. And, well, on the day of her death, in the morning, the little girl said: "Poor Mamma, you will be left on your own. I dreamt last night that you were standing in a clearing with lots of children around you. Three girls and four boys. Only they were all terrible and pitiful. One had a head like a bottle, another had three legs. One of the girls had tiny paws instead of arms, like the little wings of a plucked chicken. It was a frightful, really frightful dream. And you put your arms round them all and cried. And then I think I ran up to them and they let me play with them." The woman hardly listened to all this, her head was full of other things. But then, a month later, the woman, who spent all her time thinking about and recalling every detail of the poor child's last day and every word she had spoken, suddenly went cold on account of a certain coincidence. She remembered that she had had precisely seven abortions in her life. And there had been seven children in the dying girl's dream. So, you know, she nearly went crazy. I think she was even treated for it.'

'You are telling me horrible things. I didn't know you were so malicious. . . .'

Then Lyudochka ran in. Our conversation was cut short and we did not return to it. A few days later I went back to Moscow and then was unlucky for a number of summers which passed by without the Southern sun, the warm sea, the room that looked out on the old knotty persimmon and the maize which rustled loudly during those hours when bright, white fluffy clouds appeared against the rich, resounding blue of the sky.

Septembers and Octobers passed, just as beautiful, with the fallen leaves in the birch groves, the striped saffron caps of mushrooms amongst young pines, with crystal-clear frosts in the mornings or black, inclement nights in which there is just as much mood and feeling as on a clear morning or under a midday sun.

But my body grew tired with longing for the salty, iodine smell of the breeze, for the warm though no longer scorching shingle and for that inexplicable velvet caress which seawater alone can give.

I could no longer wait. I dropped everything unnecessary (my main work I always take with me) and set off, rushed off to the sea. After such a long interval I approached the group of houses near the fish-processing works like a homesick man coming to his native village. At the familiar garden gate I sat down on my case, savouring in advance the waving hands and shouts that would be bound to accompany such a sudden meeting. A smile was already playing on my face, and however much I tried to rid myself of it, it became only wider and brighter – or so I should describe someone else's smile; of my own I had better say that it became increasingly stupid-looking.

It was increasingly stupid-looking for the further reason that no one was coming to meet me along the little path from the small white house to the garden gate beneath the bunches of black grapes, still hanging down in just the same way from the vines which were twisted and turned to form an arch.

I left my suitcase in the street, went towards the house and discovered a little girl whom I did not know, playing with pebbles from the beach.

The little girl stopped playing and looked up at me with – well, how did they put it in old-fashioned sentimental novels? – cornflower-blue eyes. Or eyes like forget-me-nots? Some children have such dark-blue, bright eyes! Moreover, there was no childish naïveté in the girl's eyes, none of that – how shall I put it? – pale-blue colour that goes with cherubs or, perhaps, little angels. On the contrary, her eyes were full of seriousness and even some severity.

I had to fix my attention on those eyes for as long as possible, as if grasping at a straw. What else could I do? For in the same moment I also saw that the little girl was strikingly, hopelessly ugly. There was something old-womanish in her face, something that reminded me of a wrinkled baked apple or pitiful monkey. But the main thing, and this struck me like a bullet, was that the girl had a cleft harelip. Hoping frankly for a miracle – as if I had fallen out of an aeroplane and hoped to live (such cases after all have been known) – I asked: 'Who are you?'

'Mironova,' the little girl answered clearly.

'What do you mean, "Mironova"? I know all the Mironovs.'

'I am a Mironov. It's not my fault.'

My God! But of course it's not your fault! The thought crossed my mind in a blinding flash. It's mine, my fault all the way! I had launched myself then into all that rubbish, touched a sore spot, and here is the result! I had given my so-called advice, dissuaded, convinced. . . . Little girl, my dear, do you know that if it were not for me, you might not have been here? . . .

I looked at her as if she were a miracle. Her ugliness seemed less apparent and took second place now. Those arms, legs, that little upturned nose, the freckles on her nose and those eyes, like apertures for looking into a vessel in which an even, dark-blue flame is burning. A magic flame. The flame of love, purity, acceptance of the world. The flame of the soul. And now all this exists, moves, answers questions, furrows its brow, smiles. And all this might not have been; was not going to be. But then where would it have been? Where would it have gone? Absurdly, there surfaced in my memory the words of some Indian sage (Gandhi?), which I had not consciously tried to remember but which I had evidently picked up at some time: 'In this world it is a rare thing to manage to be born a human being.'

'What is your first name, then, little girl?'

'Annushka.'

'And where's Mummy?'

'She's gone to the bazaar. Who are you?'

'My name is Uncle Petya. I used to live in your house in that room over there.'

'And now my bed is there.'

'That's good. Only may I take my suitcase in? I shall wait for your mummy.'

'Do you want me to show you my secrets?'

'If you're not afraid of showing them . . .'

'I am not afraid of you,' Annushka answered sharply and led me round the corner of the house. We came to a small, flat area covered with sand. Annushka's tools were lying about there: little scoops, spades and moulds. 'Now you will see my secrets. They are very beautiful. Watch.'

In one place Annushka began to scoop up the sand, which formed quite a thick layer there. I expected her at any moment to pull out of the sand a toy or something else she had hidden. Or perhaps she had something buried there – a bird, for example. This made what I saw all the more surprising. I did not even grasp straight away what it was or how it had been done. But Annushka had not deceived me: it was beautiful. It is strange that we did not know about this in our childhood and that I had never met it before. Could Annushka herself have thought of it?

The secret was that, some distance down in the sand, some flowers had been stored away, just the heads of the flowers without stalks or leaves. These flowers were placed tightly together, one touching the other, weighted down with a piece of glass about the size of a saucer and then covered with a layer of sand. When Annushka scooped the sand away the flowers, pressed even and flat under the glass, presented to your eye a bright, attractive-looking sight, like something valuable suddenly discovered in the earth.

'What a secret!' I could not help saying.

'It's beautiful, isn't it?'

'Very beautiful! Show me more if there are any.'

Annushka led me round the area of sand from one spot to another, looking intently at each for some time as if seeing through the ground, then she would begin to dig up her next little miracle. The flowers were of different types. And they flashed and shone even more brightly and unexpectedly when Annushka dug down to a 'secret' for me, not in the sandy part but in ordinary brown earth, near the cucumber patch. In one place multicoloured pebbles from the beach had been placed under the glass, and that had also turned out to be novel and beautiful, although it did not equal the flowers.

'They're nice pebbles, aren't they?'

'Yes.'

'Let's go to the sea. I'll collect some like these for you. I know where the most beautiful pebbles are.'

'Why not, let's go. I'll have a swim after my journey. It's been so many years since I had a dip in the blue sea.'

'How many years?'

'You had still not appeared on the earth.'

'But the earth existed?'

'Yes, it did.'

'And the sea existed, and Mummy?'

'Yes. Just you were missing. Amazing.'

'Amazing,' Annushka agreed, and we set off for the sea. I stretched out on the shingle, delighted by the warmth that was radiating from the stones. Flinging out my arms, I bathed in the golden, cloudless sky.

I had only to lift my head a little and I could see on the line between land and sea, right at the water's edge, to give it its proper name, a small girl in white cotton pants with large red spots. The little girl would run back after a wave which seemed to recede especially for her, grasp the pebbles she needed from under the wave and rush back, because the wave would begin its return motion. And that is how they were playing – the little girl and the sea.

The girl was small and the sea was big. And one could enlarge endlessly on what surrounded the little girl, because the country is bigger than the sea, the ocean is bigger than the country, the earth is bigger than the ocean, the sky is bigger than the earth and bigger than the sky is. . . . But, however far and wide our imagination might rush, like a noiseless explosion, the little girl still remained the same and became no smaller. The little girl is one thing and the universe is another. Perhaps they are both like grains of sand; perhaps they are both boundless; and perhaps, even, they are equal.

Meanwhile I thought: I persuaded her against it, came out with advice, and I glanced all the while at the little girl. And what will happen to her in the future? It would be possible, of course, starting from the present moment, to develop one or two story-lines in the twinkling of an eye and, filled out to form a novel (or long story), those story-lines would be convincing and plausible.

Oh, there are millions of themes and variants which it would be useless to reduce to two or three deliberately rough-hewn literary patterns.

That is the point. We, our lives, are like pebbles on that sea-shore. We are all similar, but you will not find two the same. And although all the pebbles taken together make a mass of shingle which, measured in tons, can be scooped up in the bucket of an excavator for various building needs, nevertheless every pebble is a thing in itself: this one has yellow veins, this one has pink dots, this one is as black as agate (and of course sometimes it is agate), this one is as white as sugar, that one as transparent as glass.

And so there are millions of themes and variations that do not lend themselves to imaginary interpretation, but there are also many traditional ones that do, including Ulanova, Tarasova, Goar Gasparyan; or, in a different area, Kosmodemyanskaya and Tereshkova; or you can continue and include Esenin's mother and Archpriest Avvakum's friend and fellow in his spiritual struggle; or, again, the simplest thing of all: a house and a husband who works at the fish-processing plant. A bazaar. Vegetable marrows and tomatoes, the laundry, cooking, ironing, sweeping, lodgers from Moscow, two children who are over school age.

At this point it became clear to me what it was that I had felt during all that time, during that hour or so, something which had been vaguely but persistently disturbing me. I realized that I was afraid of facing Katya.

Did she not feel reproach in her heart when she looked at her sleeping non-beauty, her unsuccessful one, her ugly one, did she not shed a tear over her, either secretly or openly? Of course she would not show it, but she would receive me coolly, coldly. Would she let me stay in the house? The room is occupied by Annushka, it would be very easy to refuse. If it is going to be the cold shoulder, I could leave by myself without waiting for the refusal. So I must remove the suitcases as soon as possible, before she comes, and move off to another street, to the other end of the village, to another town. And so what – after all, I am an independent human being!

The little girl and the sea continued to play.

'Well, will you come with me? You're not afraid here by the sea? You won't drown?'

'I'll go with you. Something has kept Mummy at the bazaar.'

'And . . . your mummy, does she love you?'

'I haven't asked. Are there actually some mummies who don't love their children?'

To leave without showing myself would after all be ridiculous. At the same time I did not unpack my suitcase for the moment. I lay down on the little bed on top of the coarse woollen blanket and a light, nodding drowsiness came over me. I think I even fell asleep. At any rate I did not notice whether much time had passed before I heard in the garden that familiar voice, the same as ever.

'My little sunshine, my little swallow! You've had a long wait. I dropped in on Nadya Kavun and got chatting. Oh, you lovely thing! How have you managed here without me? But why are your pants damp? What did you do, go swimming? On your own?'

'I am not on my own. A man has come.'

'What sort of man?'

'An old friend, from before I was born.'

'But where is he?'

'Asleep in my room.'

'Oh lord! Do you know who that is, most probably? Let's change as quickly as possible so that he can see how beautiful you are. We can't have you looking such a dirty scamp with him here. And I had to be out! Come on, you can put on your nice white dress, red sandals and do your bow. Oh me! You see, you could say that he is your godfather or another father. And you were such a dirty scamp when he came. That's no good.'

Could it be my age, I wonder. After the simplest words, or a song, or a scene in a documentary film, I can feel the tears coming; but, apart from that, I was stung with shame that fifteen minutes earlier I had thought so badly of Katya and, along with her, of all humanity's mothers.